The Heart of FALCON RIDGE

by
D.L. Roan
Copyright 2015

Description

Three hearts beat as one, for one; always.

Claira Robbins technically didn't exist until two weeks before she began teaching at Grassland Academy. Her new identity may have given her the credentials she needed for the job, but it hasn't helped one whit to soothe her frayed nerves caused by years on the run. It also didn't come with instructions on how to handle three ravenous cowboy brothers intent on seducing her.

Six years after losing their wife, the McLendon brothers are focused on running their family ranch, Falcon Ridge, and raising their rambunctious twin boys. They've never believed they could find another woman with which to share their hearts and family.

When Matt and his twin, Mason, meet their sons' classy new teacher, hope and love aren't the only things that spring back to life. Matt is convinced she was Heaven sent to heal their family. Mason hopes he's right, but knows they have a bigger problem than convincing Claira to take a chance on their unconventional family; a much bigger, surly, older brother kind of problem.

After their wife died, Grey McLendon planned to live the rest of his life comfortably numb from the neck down, even if it killed him...and it just might if he can't reconcile his guilt and desire for Claira before her treacherous past catches up with her.

Never Miss a New Release

Direct from my insider's Writer's Cave Club, read free novellas, exclusive excerpts, exciting character updates, behind the scenes editorials and more when you sign-up for my no-spam newsletter at www.dlroan.com

More Books by D.L. Roan

The McLendon Family Saga

The Heart of Falcon Ridge
A McLendon Christmas
Rock Star Cowboys

Survivors' Justice Series

Surviving Redemption
One Defining Second

Standalones

Blindfold Fantasy: A Novel Ménage

ISBN-13: 978-1519765376

Published by D.L. Roan. First print edition, December 2015
Originally published as Second Chances, February 2013

www.dlroan.com

Editing/Proofreading by: Read by Rose
Cover Design by JAB Designs
Interior eBook Design by D.L. Roan.

Dedication

To all my fans and friends who've supported me throughout my writing career and cherish my characters as deeply as I do. To the fabulous Indie Author community, whose invaluable advice and support has propelled me to become a better writer and tell the tales that are forever etched into my heart. To my husband and family. Thank you.

Chapter One

Claira Robbins closed her eyes and drew in a calming breath, running a sweaty palm over a non-existent wrinkle in her prim skirt. Though it wasn't her first time substituting as a first grade teacher, it was her first day at Grasslands Academy, and the official start of her new life. She was nervous, but determined. She was safe; hidden in a quiet, small Montana town, her past well behind her.

I'm safe here. She repeated the mantra silently, willing herself to believe it.

In the past, she'd fallen in love with each and every one of the children she'd helped. This time would be no different. Remembering the ones she'd left behind, the ones she would never see grow into their exuberant personalities, her next breath came out a little shaky.

This job was a temporary one, and only a few weeks remained until the end of the school year at that. Even so, she clung desperately to the hope that she would soon find a more permanent position; a way to rebuild her life doing what she loved. She had to.

Her heart leapt at the sound of the first screech of laughter that filled the hall. Unable to contain her smile, she sprang from the chair at her desk and hurried to her classroom door to greet the children as they began to trickle down the hall. One by one, she took the time to greet each child with a brisk handshake, asking their names and introducing herself. She knew it was silly, and resonated *'newbie'*, but she couldn't help herself. It had been so long since she'd been able to embrace the kind of love only a child could give.

Ignoring a few condescending smirks from the other teachers as they passed by on their way to their own respective classrooms, Claira welcomed her last student and closed the classroom door.

Once they were settled into their seats, she took one last breath and began her day with a fun round-robin game her mentor had taught her to help learn the children's names. She was immediately taken with the sandy haired, twin boys. Connor and Carson McLendon—Con and Car—they'd not-so-shyly corrected her. Promptly assuming the teacher's helper roles, they both jumped at the chance to help her arrange the little desks into a circle for the next game.

One shy girl refused to speak at all, relying on her friend to share her name. Claira made a mental note to ask the school counselor if there was anything she should know about little Meg that could help her overcome the girl's crippling shyness. She may only be a temp, but it would be nice to put her *almost* degree in child psychology to good use.

It took more than half the day, but when Robbie Nichols stood, green paint covering all but the whites of his eyes as he strained his little biceps in a Hulk pose, she knew she'd found her class clown.

Claira didn't think twice before she grabbed a nearby cup of green paint, scooped out a big glob and smeared it over her cheeks, striking a strongman pose that mimicked Robbie's as she released her own thunderous roar.

The room fell deafeningly silent. Someone behind her cleared their throat. Sweat broke out between her shoulder blades and her stomach plummeted. *This is not happening.*

Following the stares of her students over her shoulder, she turned to see Mr. Dawes, the school principal, standing in the open doorway. Beside him stood the most intimidating, heart-stutteringly handsome man she'd ever seen.

Taking in the crisp black suit Mr. Calendar Model wore like a suit of armor—and he was positively sexy enough to get a whole calendar to himself—a surge of embarrassing self-awareness danced over her skin.

Her gaze snapped back to the principal as he cleared his throat with another grunt of disapproval. How oddly frail and frumpy the scholarly man looked standing next to the green-eyed god beside him.

"Miss Robbins?" Principal Dawes dipped his head and peered over the rim of his wire-framed glasses.

Good grief. Her boss, her new and very uptight boss, was standing in her classroom with Mr. January as she posed as the new runway model for green finger paint. She chewed on her bottom lip to keep from groaning aloud at the embarrassing timing of their visit. *Way to make a first impression.*

She was never going to get that full time position. By the haughty look on his face, and the straining smirk on Mr. January's lips, she would be lucky if she wasn't tossed out on her rear before the final bell rang.

She recognized the disapproving, small-minded expressions on their faces. She'd seen it countless times before on her own father's face. These people assumed themselves better than her as well. Mr. Tall, Dark and Brooding had masked his amusement and now glared at her with unmistakable disdain. They may be small-minded, but she wouldn't let them make her feel small. She still had to play nice, though, if she had any hope of salvaging this job.

"We were just wrapping up our arts and crafts hour, Principal Dawes." She crafted her tone to mirror their haughty demeanor and swiped her hand over her skirt, smearing a big, green handprint down the front of the beige cotton material. *Brilliant!*

Completing a mental eye roll, she jerked her hand away and gestured toward the little hulk impersonator. "Robbie has quite the imagination and acting talent for such a young—"

"Miss Robbins!" Principal Dawes closed his eyes, peeled off his glasses and pinched the bridge of his nose, holding up his other hand to stop her interpretation of the seemingly offensive scene. His shoulders drooped in exasperation as he released a frustrated breath, propping his bifocals back onto his overly prominent nose. "Mr. McLendon is here to collect the twins, Miss Robbins."

She turned to see Connor and Carson, noticing the somber expressions on their faces as they quietly packed their things into their desks and made their way to the door. Mr. McLendon knelt onto his haunches and whispered something to them.

They certainly didn't seem happy to see him. Taking one of their little backpacks, Mr. McLendon shot the principal a searing glance and ushered the boys down the hall and out of sight.

Nope. There was no way was she going to see a full week's paycheck, much less the few weeks that were left of the school year while Mrs. Wittington finished out her maternity leave. She wondered what atrocity the temp before her had committed to be fired within her first week. Whatever it was, she'd clearly exceeded it.

"Get the rest of the children cleaned up before the other parents arrive," the principal snapped as he stared over the rim of his glasses. He took one more inspecting glance around the room then left without another word, the door clicking closed behind him.

Claira released a breath she hadn't realize she'd been holding and rested her hands on her hips, green paint and all.

"Dat's Beaker Dolls." A quirky voice pulled her attention away from the dread that began building in her chest. "He's got a big nose." Claira turned to find Robbie holding his green finger in front of his nose, arched in a perfect imitation of Principal Dawes' big snout.

At the small sink in the back of the classroom, she snatched up a stack of paper towels and walked back over to Robbie. She couldn't help but giggle, at both Robbie and herself. Imitation was the finest form of flattery, but she didn't think Principal Dawes would appreciate the likeness. And judging by the glare he'd given her, neither would Mr. McLendon; not that there was anything about him that could be mocked.

The enthusiasm with which she'd started her day had been sucked into the vortex of doom that was her life. Everything had been so much more difficult, more terrifying than they'd told her it would be.

She continued wiping away the goopy, green paint until Robbie's face beamed, and then moved on to the next student, all the while missing her little helpers, Con and Car. She thought of Mr. McLendon and the intense flutter in her stomach returned. How abruptly his expression had turned, his cool, green eyes so full of mischief one second, then cold as ice the next as he took in the sight of her. Yeah, she should undoubtedly pack up her things before she left for the night, save Principal Dawes the time of firing her.

She didn't need the money. She needed to teach; needed the children. She'd sacrificed everything for this new life. She had to make Mr. Dawes understand that art was a way to connect to her students; to get them to open up and be themselves.

The sun had set and the parking lot was empty when she gave up trying to outwait her boss and decided to call it a day. She'd been sure he would come back to her classroom and give her the bad news before he left for the day.

As the hours ticked by, Principal Dawes never showed and she began to think that maybe she was in the clear. She noticed the little piece of paper taped to her locker as she walked into the teacher's lounge to get her things. Each teacher was assigned one classroom, but as a temp she wasn't allowed to make any changes to the room or store her things in the desk. She ripped off the note and leaned against the bank of lockers as she read the edict.

Miss Robbins, please meet me in my office at half past seven tomorrow morning. There are a few things I would like to discuss with you.

Principal Dawes.

Half past seven. "Who talks like that?" She snorted as she opened the locker, threw the crumpled note into the bottom and grabbed her lunch sack and a few notebooks. If he did fire her, at least she wouldn't have to listen to his pretentious drivel any longer. She didn't like snobby, sneaky people and something about the man set off her well-tuned creep-o-meter.

Fifteen minutes later Claira pulled into the short driveway in front of her little rental. Nestled in Grassland's historic district, it wasn't much. Two bedrooms, one she used as her office, and a small communal bathroom. The kitchen had been what sold her. She loved to cook and try new recipes as a way to relax. The spacious floor plan and marble counter tops would be perfect for the fudge she loved to make.

She took notice that her porch light was still on, sighing in relief. She'd rigged a little warning to let her know if someone had entered the house while she was away; a lightweight thread looped over the inside light switch that was hooked over a thumbtack on the bottom edge of the door. If the door was opened without removing the looped end from the tack, the tension on the line would flip the switch and she'd know before she pulled into her drive if someone had been inside.

Of course, that didn't account for blown bulbs or if the intruder saw the half-baked setup and flipped the light back on. It was silly, really, but her thought at the time was that it was something she could see from her car, giving her a better chance to escape. She shrugged. Silly or not, it always helped slow her heart rate to see the light shining when she arrived home. It was a shot in the dark, but if her past ever caught up to her, she'd need as much advanced warning as she could get.

"All's safe." She gathered her purse and slid from the car, stepping over the line of pebbles on the front step. Arranged in a familiar pattern only she would recognize hadn't been disturbed, they gave her a second layer of security.

She climbed the bare, concrete steps to her front door. Stretching up on her tip toes, she removed the broken toothpick from the top of the door jamb and the paperclip from the bottom. If someone found the first, they may not look for the second. Everything in layers. Plan A had a plan B; B had a C, and so on. She unhooked the delicate thread from the thumbtack at the bottom of the door, unlocked the two deadbolts and rushed inside, throwing both locks back into place before she entered the security code to reset the alarm.

I need to get a dog. A big dog. She'd convinced the landlord to let her have one, with a sizeable deposit of course, but she hadn't had time to find one. She'd only arrived in town a week ago. Between finding a place to rent, finding a job and putting all the other security measures in place so that she could at least *try* to sleep at night, she'd scarcely had time to get groceries.

Like it or not, paranoid was her new reality. They'd told her he would never find her, but she knew better. She tried to believe in them, in their ability to keep her safe. She had to do her part of course, most of which consisted of keeping her secrets just that; secrets. Somewhere deep down, she knew he wouldn't give up until he found her.

She tucked her keys into her purse and carried them to the bedroom with her, flipping on each light as she went. She still couldn't walk into a dark room and she always kept her purse and keys within arm's reach in case she had to leave in a rush.

After rechecking all the window locks, preparing a quick salad for dinner and taking a long shower, she pulled back the covers and laid her head on her new pillow. The bed felt cold, strange. The whole house felt wrong. She missed Daniel.

Deputy Marshal Daniel Gregory had been quiet and aloof for the first month of her father's trial—which took three years longer to conclude than they had promised—but before long he became almost like a father to her. More than her real father had been, anyway. He always made her a cup of hot tea before bed and then sat and talked with her. She'd felt...safe. The long months he was assigned to her had been the only time in the last few years she'd been able to truly sleep.

He'd also taught her how to become invisible. *No social media, use disposable phones, keep your head down, and don't make eye contact if you don't have to.* That had been the easy part. She'd had enough practice being invisible around her father and his men. It was the constant running and endless state of panic those first days in hiding that had nearly broken her. Not to mention the bullets. Things only got worse from there.

Once her father's trial was over, Daniel helped her build a new life, or the start of one. With his help she'd been able to salvage a little of her old life, but she knew she would never be the same inside.

Gabriella no longer existed and *Claira* was supposed to be invisible. She didn't want to be invisible any longer. She wanted to be real, to feel and breathe and love. That's how she felt when she was with her students. Only then did she matter. Only then could she make a difference.

Realizing her need and love for children, Daniel had made sure her new background included something in the childcare profession. He couldn't obtain a counterfeit degree in psychology, and with her new identity she'd lost the credits she'd earned toward her real one, but being a teacher was better than nothing. He'd even set up her interview at Grassland Academy for her.

I miss him.

Fighting the urge to pick up her cellphone and call him, she reached up and flipped off the bedside lamp. It took a few moments before her eyes adjusted to the soft light coming from under the closed bathroom door. No, she wouldn't call him. He'd done so much for her already and it was time she learned to survive on her own. Alone. She'd never felt more alone.

The second her eyes closed, she saw Mr. McLendon's cool, green eyes staring back at her.

Chapter Two

Grey mumbled a string of curses he hoped his sons couldn't hear, reaching down to adjust the hard-on in his pants. Despite being repulsed by his carnal attraction to his sons' newest substitute teacher, he still couldn't get the image of the woman out of his head; thick, brown curls that hung loose around her angelic face, flirting with her eyelashes. His fingers curled into a fist at the memory, longing to reach up and brush them away from her eyes. And those big doe eyes, like dark chocolate so rich and warm, seemed to see straight through to his very soul.

When he'd locked gazes with Miss Robbins he'd been besieged with feelings he hadn't felt in years, and never so strong; protectiveness, possessiveness, pure and undiluted lust. *What the hell?*

In direct conflict with his agitation, he chuckled at the memory of her mortified expression when she'd turned and seen them standing in the doorway, along with that ridiculous green paint on her face. He wondered what she'd been thinking at that moment.

He'd wanted to strangle the principal of that stuffy school for being so condescending to her. Then strangle her for making him care!

He'd never liked Preston Dawes, even when he was a scrawny, twig-dick, big-nosed, ass kisser in high school. The only reasons he and his brothers enrolled the twins in that uppity school was because their late Aunt Dunny had helped found it, and that's what their mother would have wanted.

The McLendon family had been an intrinsic fixture in Grassland since before Montana had joined the Union. They weren't Silicon Valley rich but, as one of the two founding families, they held the lion's share of land in the territory. That didn't make them much in the world, but when they spoke, the people of Grassland listened, and damn if he hadn't wanted to snap his fingers and have that prick fired.

Aunt Dunny, rest her soul, would roll over in her grave if she knew that sniveling bigot had been elected to take over as principal of her beloved school, even if only for the last half of the school year. He hated that his kids were around the pretentious asshole at all. If he'd had his way, the boys would be homeschooled, but their schedules wouldn't allow for it. Ranching meant long, hard days and all hands on deck. Still, he would be reconsidering their choices before the next school year started if Dawes was still there.

Wonder what the delightful Miss Robbins thinks of the little weasel.

Grey snorted at the thought, and then stiffened in his seat, gripping the steering wheel a little tighter as he released another disgusted grumble.

What did it matter what she thought? He had no business thinking about her, period. He glanced at his boys in the rear view mirror as he pulled out of the pediatrician's parking lot onto Main Street. God, with every passing day they looked more like Sarah.

Following the country road that stretched out before him, he tried again to remember their mother's eyes. They were blue, he knew, but the image that came to mind was nothing but a faint whisper, a feeling more than a memory. He'd already lost her sweet scent, and now he couldn't remember her eyes!

He pounded his fist against the steering wheel when the memory refused to surface. She'd been gone only six years and he'd already begun to forget her.

"You okay, daddy?" Con asked as he handed Car his lollypop the nurse had given them for good behavior at the doctor's office.

Grey glanced back at the twins again and saw his own eyes staring back at him. Although they favored his brothers with their sandy brown hair and freckles, he could see himself in their bright green eyes. Only if he looked closely could he see the thin, dark-blue ring around the outside that held their mother's azure depths.

"Yeah, I'm okay, boys. Just forgot to pick up the medicine we're going to need for the puppies." Grey hated lying to his boys. He hated it almost enough to forgive them their disobedience of the day before and lift the grounding that was to begin as soon as they pulled into their driveway. Almost.

"Think Bernie will really have the puppies this week?" Car asked, straining against his safety belt to look through the windshield.

"That's what Doc Fisher says." Grey smirked and shook his head. Three mares about to foal, twelve-hundred head of cattle to rotate into the back pasture, a set of twins that can't hold still for three seconds—he knew because he'd timed it—and now a half dozen or more puppies.

He could have shot Mason for not having that cur beast of a mutt spayed after he'd talked Grey into keeping her. She was a good herder, though, and great with the twins, so Grey agreed to keep her on. In truth he couldn't wait to see the boys' faces when they saw their first litter of puppies being born. He'd never let Mason know that, though.

"Daddy, can you park at the barn when we get home? I wanna' go check on her." Con sat up and looked out the side window as he pulled into their long gravel drive.

"No sirs. You're grounded. Remember?" Grey cringed as he heard his poppa Jake's voice in his head. "No barn, no puppies and no television."

"Aww man!" Car bounced his head against the back of his booster seat in protest.

"You should have thought about that before you two climbed up that old dead tree after we told you not to."

He needed to remind Matt about cutting that thing down. With the livestock convention in Billings and getting the feed barn rebuilt after a freak fire had all but destroyed it, there hadn't been time.

"But what if she has the puppies before we're done being grounded? Can we still see 'em?" Con asked.

"We'll see how well you behave and talk about it if it happens. You're only grounded until Saturday. She might hold out until then."

"We're never gonna' be done with being grounded," Car pouted. "Saturday is for-e-ver!"

Grey smirked as he pulled up and parked his truck near the front of their farmhouse. Yeah, he remembered the feeling. He and his younger twin brothers, Mason and Matt, spent what felt like for-e-ver being grounded, too, when they were that age.

He helped the boys down from the truck, hiding a smirk as they stomped up the porch stairs and through the front door. He was expecting to hear the screen door slam, but Con turned as it was closing and gently latched it, his bottom lip still stuck out in a pout.

"What's got them all in a snit?" Matt asked, lowering the stack of two-by-fours from his shoulder and loading them into the back of Grey's truck.

"Grounded," Grey reminded him.

~*~*~*~*~

Short, sweet and to the point. That was Grey. Lately he'd been just plain grumpy. Matt wondered what or who was stuck up his ass today. "What'd they do this time?"

"You should know, you were there plucking them out of that tree with me," Grey grumbled.

Yeah, he did know, but he didn't think it merited grounding. Car was curious and rambunctious. Connor was a little quieter, slower and tended to follow Car's lead like a horse on a bit. That *bit* tended to land them both into a heap of trouble, but nothing worse than they ever did as kids.

"Give em' a break, bro. They were just bein' boys." Matt slapped Grey on the back and bounded up the front steps ahead of him. "We've gotten into worse scrapes than those two could ever think up. Remember the time we tried to carry that bee hive down to the lake to drown em'? We were younger than they are now. I thought mom would never stop cryin', and the dads—"

"Exactly!" Grey shot back without missing a beat or a step as he continued on into the house. "One or all of us could have died from anaphylactic shock if we'd been allergic. Those dead branches could go at any time and those boys could break their neck. When are you going to start acting like an adult and take on some of the responsibility around here? We need to cut that damn tree down for good."

Unoffended, Matt reached into the fridge and grabbed two beers, shoving one at his older brother. "Coulda—shoulda—woulda," he said. "If we lived like that, countin' all the ways things can go wrong, we'd never get anything done. We lived through it."

Matt studied Grey as he sipped his beer. They were talking about more than just bees and dead trees and his big brother knew it. Since Sarah's death, Grey had all but given up on living any kind of normal life. He'd shut himself away, keeping them and their boys at arm's length. Oh, Grey loved those boys. Matt had no doubts about that, but they could all see the way he lived in a virtual cage, afraid if he let life in or attempted to live outside the bars, he would lose it all.

They all loved and missed Sarah. She would have never wanted to see Grey this way. Hell, she's the one who taught them that to have fun, you had to get a little messy. *'Life is messy. If it isn't, then you're not doing it right'.*

"It doesn't matter," Grey said. "They don't listen, they don't get to play."

"They're *six*, Grey. Six! I know you didn't listen to a damn thing our parents said when you were six."

"And I spent almost that whole year in my room, grounded from anything but homework and chores." Grey took another pull from his beer and leaned against the kitchen cabinet. "Where's Mason?"

"Out stackin' the last of the hay from the east pasture," Matt said. "He should be finished up in about an hour. We *were* goin' to make a run down to the creek with the boys, but I guess that's out of the question now, since that's too close to havin' *fun*." He was pushing Grey's buttons, but someone had to.

"You'd be right." Grey gulped down the rest of his beer and set it down with a thud onto the counter before he turned down the hall toward his bedroom. "What time's dinner?"

Matt studied Grey's back as he disappeared down the hall, wondering how far he should push the issue. "*Six,*" he said and chucked his own empty bottle into the kitchen trash. "Betty Crocker couldn't make it so I'm stuck peelin' potatoes again!" he shouted in the general direction Grey had fled. "First I gotta' get that lumber out to the feed shed and covered up before it rains."

He shook his head as he headed back toward the front door, resisting the urge to slam it on the way out. He was going to get through to that man if it was the last thing he did. *Who does he* think *is going to cook the damn dinner?* Grey hadn't touched a pot or pan in six damn years.

With a frustrated sigh, Matt stormed out the front door, walked around to the side of the house and looked up at the twins' window. It'd been a long time, but he bet he could still scale a drain pipe.

He tossed his Stetson onto a nearby tree stump, spit into his palms and rubbed them together. Within seconds he was tapping on the twins' window, pushing his finger to his lips when they screeched with laughter at his sudden appearance.

"Shh. Don't want ya' gettin' into any more trouble today." He loved his boys. He knew Grey was right about holding them accountable for their actions. Probably wasn't the best idea showing them how to climb out of their second story window, but Grey was being *adult* enough for all of them. He wanted to go swimming with his boys.

Chapter Three

"I'll see you all tomorrow." Claira dismissed her class as the clock ticked one minute past three. Her little chat with Principal Dawes that morning had gone exactly as she'd expected, except he hadn't fired her.

This is a private academy, Miss Robbins. We expect a higher level of participation from our students, Miss Robbins. We don't tolerate diversity as other schools might, Miss Robbins. Structure is of the utmost importance, Miss Robbins. I want you to succeed here, Miss Robbins, so please don't hesitate to come see me should you have any questions about appropriate curriculum.

She'd kind of liked her new name. Now, she'd be happy if she never heard it again, ever.

She was still a little shell shocked that she hadn't been fired. She'd tossed and turned all night, which was nothing new. Stress from the thought of losing her job had made sleep elusive, but once she finally did nod off, her dreams had been haunted by a pair of sexy green eyes. The more she thought about Mr. McLendon's reaction, the more she was sure that she would be jobless as of seven thirty-one that morning.

At one point she'd convinced herself that she'd seen passion in his gaze, even if only for a breath of a second. Those desires were wholly foreign to her, having spent her life keeping everyone at arm's length where they belonged. But oh, how it would feel to have those big, strong arms wrapped around her, keeping her safe. *It can't happen silly girl. Give it up.*

She'd never allowed herself a passionate connection to anyone or anything other than her job. She wasn't a virgin, *barely*. She'd had her first and only sexual experience during her freshman year of college with a guy she'd known since third grade. They were both virgins and the whole experience had been awkward and somewhat painful, at best. Soon afterwards he disappeared; literally. The State police combed the surrounding counties for weeks, but found nothing.

Claira knew. Like everyone else she'd ever loved or cared for, he'd been '*dealt with*'. Since then, she'd bottled her desires and kept all her hopes and dreams of having a family of her own to herself. Until recently, she'd all but forgotten she'd even had desires or dreams.

"Daddy Matt!" Car yelled out as he ran from his cubby with his shoes in his hands and leapt into the outstretched arms of the most handsome man she'd seen since…yesterday. *Dear God! What did they put in the water in this town?*

He was almost the same height as Mr. McLendon, with the same broad shoulders and defined muscular build, but that's where the similarities ended. Where Mr. McLendon was dark and brooding, with raven hair, this new Adonis had sandy-brown hair that looked as though it had been kissed by the sun and licked by the wind.

His thin, plaid button-up strained against his biceps as he lifted Carson into his arms. She followed the line of buttons up to an open V of his collar. Her throat closed around the knot that rapidly constricted her airway as she noticed the deep-tanned skin that peeked out from under that V. Her gaze, which seemed to have developed a will of its own, traveled up his thick, corded neck. His sharp jawline and narrow, straight nose accentuated his round and playful eyes which were the color of a hot blue flame. She tried to swallow again, but her tongue was glued to the roof of her mouth.

~*~*~*~*~

"Hey, Car-Car! What happened to your shoes there, buddy?" Matt sat Carson down and looked up to locate Connor when his gaze locked onto the image of an angel. Every ounce of blood in his body pooled in his groin and the hair on the back of his neck prickled against his skin. *Who is that?*

"That's Miss Robbins," Connor said as he hopped across the room on one foot, his finger stuck in the back of his shoe as he as he tried to pull it onto his foot. "She's our new teacher while Mrs. Wittington is out with her new baby."

He looked at Con and then back to the angel. *Did I ask that out loud?*

16

"Yes," the woman answered in a shy whisper.

Matt's head whipped around. "Yes what?" He had a feeling the room was going to start spinning at any moment.

She giggled again, her gaze darting away from him as her cheeks turned a pretty rosy pink. "Yes," she said again and paced to the blackboard, picking up the eraser. "You asked that out loud."

Matt shook his head. What was happening to him? Ordinarily he didn't have a problem talking with women. He and Mason, and well, Grey too for that matter, hadn't exactly joined the priesthood since Sarah had passed away, but he'd never been so taken by a woman that he lost the capacity to hold a coherent thought to himself.

"Sorry," he said as he walked over and leaned against the blackboard. "I'm Matt McLendon." He held out his hand, hoping like hell she'd take it. He needed to touch her.

Her arm froze above her head and he fought like hell not to glance down at her boobs. She finally turned to face him, placing the eraser in his outstretched hand. Tiny. Her hand was small.

"Gab—," she stammered and cleared her throat. "Claira Robbins."

"Claira." Matt rolled the name around on his tongue, surprised that it didn't twist his gut, being so close to 'Sarah'. "What a pretty name," he said.

He took the eraser, dropped it onto her desk and then took her hand in his. Heat weaved its way through his arm and flowed straight to his groin. "My sons neglected to tell me they had a new teacher."

Claira's brows furrowed for a second before a shy smile peeked through her questioning gaze.

"Oh." She giggled. "I'm sorry. I met a Mr. McLendon yesterday and I thought he was—"

"Grey," Matt interrupted with a grin and a nod. *God she's beautiful.* She was so…small. Not chubby, yet not skinny. She was curvy and delicate; almost fragile. Her skin was like a flawless silk. Her starched, white blouse formed to her curves, tucking smoothly into the tiny little waistband of her long brown skirt. He'd bet he could wrap her up twice in just one arm. The faintest hint of her lacy bra showed through her shirt and his fingers itched to reach up and trace along the swell of her breasts. She was elegant. She was…she was…*perfect*.

"Grey?" she asked.

"Huh?" Matt fought to lift his gaze back to her eyes, only to lose the battle as they caught on the sight of her plump bottom lip as she worried it between her teeth. His gut twisted and he stifled a groan, his cock screaming for release.

"Grey?" Claira repeated.

"My brother," Matt blinked to clear his head. He couldn't think for shit with her standing in front of him. "He picked the boys up yesterday." At least he thought that sounded right. Right now he felt lucky to remember his own damn name.

"Oh, your brother," Claira sighed.

"What are you doing for dinner tonight?" Matt asked before he could stop himself. *Smooth*, he thought. This woman was different. *She probably eats ten syllable words for dinner.*

Her gaze shot to the twins who were attached to either of Matt's legs and had latched onto every word of their conversation. "I'm sorry, Mr. McLendon."

"Matt," he hastily corrected her; proud that he actually *had* remembered his name.

She nodded, glancing back at Con and Car before fixing her gaze on the wall behind him. He could see her internal struggle with her reply. At last, she looked him in the eyes and shook her head. "Matt, I'm sorry. I don't date my students' parents."

Of course she didn't, but that didn't deter him. "I make a mean lasagna. And the boys would love the company." So would he and Mason. *Mason.* God, if she stirred Mason's libido into the same frenzy… Could it be possible? *Could she be the one?*

"The one what?" Claira asked, her brows furrowing again, creating the most adorable worry line above the bridge of her nose.

"What?" Had he said that out loud, too? For Christ sake. He needed to get out of there and talk to Mason before he screwed this up even more than he already had.

"The one and only woman who could refuse my lasagna," he quickly covered. "They always told me that I'd be rejected one day. I mean, that my lasagna would. I mean…" Matt felt his throat close up and sweet *Jesus*, it was getting hot in there.

"I guess it's just us tonight, boys." He grabbed Con and Car's hands and made his way to the door. He paused and turned to drink up one last sight of her. Before he blurted out another of his wayward thoughts, he gave her a flirty wink and a smile. "I won't give up." He studied the small dimples at the corners of her mouth. "Have a good evening, Miss Claira." With those brilliant words he was gone.

Claira sunk down into the cold, metal chair behind her desk. *What just happened?* Her blood raced, her lungs pumped like pistons to deliver oxygen to her brain. The manliest *male* she'd ever met just asked her to dinner and she'd turned him down! Was she insane?

"No." She shook her head. She'd done the right thing. She wouldn't bring her troubles to them. Those boys didn't deserve that. Neither did their father. No one did.

She hoped he was wrong about not giving up. She wasn't sure if she was hormonally capable of resisting him again.

Chapter Four

Mason had spent the entire day working with a three-year-old gelding; a beautiful paint that kept bucking his rider. The best horse breeder and trainer for three hundred miles, he'd been hired to work out the kinks.

He'd always had a way with animals in general. At times he'd swear he could hear a horse's thoughts; feel what they felt. People were a little different, but he always seemed to see through things well enough to make a difference.

Within a couple of hours he'd figured out the problem. The horse had a simple case of ticklish flanks. Too much pressure or a quick heel to his side would set him to bucking. He'd put money on his suspicion that the owner was the one with the bad habits. Owning a horse and knowing how to ride one were two different balls of wax.

Even though this particular job had been an easy fix, after a few hours of watching and working with the paint, the last two of which he'd spent listening to Matt drone on and on about one Miss Claira Robbins, Mason was hot, sweaty and his dick was hard enough to hammer horseshoe nails.

Hell, the damn thing didn't even so much as twitch for two years after they lost Sarah. He knew, though reluctantly, they had all slaked their needs on a one night stand or two at some time or another since then.

He wasn't entirely resigned to a solitary life and had grown accustomed to the occasional fuck with friendly benefits, but he'd never allowed himself to hope they could ever have again what they once had with Sarah. He knew for a fact that Grey had given up on that possibility all together.

What if Matt was right? Was it possible to love someone like that again? For them *all* to love her as they'd loved Sarah? He'd often wondered what would happen if one of his brothers found someone else. Would they move on, go their separate ways? What would happen to the twins? How would they share them?

He'd never settle for splitting them up or living without them. That was the main reason he'd never allowed himself to entertain the idea of finding someone else to share his life with. His boys were enough. But, what if? Could this Claira woman be the one to heal their family?

"Okay, I'll go." Mason hung the lead on the tack hook next to the paint's stall and turned back to fetch the water pail. "But I'm telling you right now, Grey will never go for it. And if I don't see what all the hoop-la is about then you're on your own. By that I mean you can fuck her, flirt with her, hell, you can pick daisies with her for all I care. Just get her out of your system before you go and do something that we'll all regret."

"Don't talk about her like that, man. She's different. You'll see. She's better'n that."

Mason was stunned at the protectiveness Matt was already exhibiting over this woman.

"I need you to convince her to come to dinner," Matt continued. "I know once you and Grey see her you'll both feel it, too."

Mason hung the pail of water in the stall and dumped a bucket of feed into the trough. "Do you really think it's possible? I mean, you don't feel guilty or anything?"

Matt shook his head with confidence. "Sarah's gone. I hate it and I miss her like crazy sometimes, but she would want us to be happy again, Mace. I don't think any of us could ever be happy in a relationship on our own. Our home is here, with each other, like mom and the dads. It wouldn't be fair to the twins or whoever was left behind."

Mason nodded his agreement. At least he knew he and his twin were on the same page. A fluttery and almost nauseating feeling in his gut told him his life was about to change. He only hoped it was for the better. There was a sneaky notion that it could go either way. "If I agree to do this, you're doing the cooking."

Matt rolled his eyes and slapped Mason on the shoulder. "So what else is new?"

As they were walking out of the barn, Matt noticed a trickle of dark fluid running out from under one of the empty stalls. He stopped and flipped the latch on the stall door, pulling it open to peer inside. "Jesus!"

"What the hell?" Mason pushed him out of the way and knelt beside a bleeding and laboring Bernie. "Call Doc Fisher!" He winced at the amount of blood the dog had lost. Two small pups were rooting blindly in the dirt, but something was wrong. She couldn't have lost all that blood from birthing two puppies.

Matt pulled out his cellphone, called the vet and then knelt beside Mason. "Fisher is on his way. What the hell happened to her?"

Mason cautiously inspected the mutt's neck and pulled back a bloody hand. "She's been cut up by something." He brushed the sweat from his brow with his elbow and, with a gentle touch, continued to probe the area. "It's a clean cut. Looks like a stab wound. Grab that lamp in the tack room and get me some water and clean towels."

"What the fuck? Who would do something like that to Bernie?" Matt raced to the tack room and back to Mason and Bernie with the supplies.

"I'm afraid to guess, but I have to tell you. Tom Grunion was pissed as hell when I out bid him on that stallion last month."

The Grunion and McLendon families had feuded over land, horses and women since they first settled in the Montana Territory back when the Salish Indians still occupied most of the land. Their sordid and volatile history seemed to settle a little as the generations passed, considering some of the bloody stories told by their grandfathers, but there was obviously still plenty of bad blood between them.

"He knows we don't need the stallion for our stock, but I couldn't stand the thought of such a beautiful animal going to an abusive son of a bitch like him. Rumor has it, he's been making some threats and Grey caught one of his hands poking around one of the barns last week."

"In our barn?"

"Yeah," Mason winced as Bernie whimpered. "Gave him a song and dance about looking for work. Grey recognized him from Grunion's place. He got the feeling he was snooping for something."

Matt watched as Mason tried to clean the wound. There was so much blood. "I can see him gettin' all surly, but this? God, Mace how did she get locked up in here?"

"I have no idea." Mason dipped his hand in the water and brought it to Bernie's mouth, careful to only drip a little on her tongue. "There ya go, girl."

He picked up one of the pups and noticed it wasn't breathing. Placing it between his palms, he rubbed the pup between them, trying to massage him to life. "Come on, little one. You can do it. Breathe for me." He dipped his head, covering the pups nose and mouth with his own and blew in a short breath. After a few more rubs, the pup screeched out a cry. "There ya go lil' bit. You're a fighter aren't you?" He handed the pup off to Matt and turned his attention back to Bernie.

Matt kept rubbing, keeping the puppy stimulated, awake and breathing. "I'll tell you one thing. If Doc Fisher confirms Bernie's been purposefully cut up, Grunion's goin' to pay for this."

He heard the anger in his twin's voice. Matt felt violated and so did he. No one came onto his land and hurt one of their own, not even a dog, but he had to keep Matt calm before he lost his cool and went off half-cocked.

"Don't go borrowing trouble, bro. Even if she makes it, there's no way of telling who did this. We'll have to keep an eye out for trouble is all."

Bernie's breathing picked up to a heavy pant as another contraction hit her. If he found even one shred of evidence that Tom Grunion was behind this, he wouldn't have a problem breaking that no-good bastard's nose himself.

~*~*~*~*~

Four more puppies and twenty-four hours later, Mason was standing in the middle of their kitchen staring at his dumbstruck twin.

"She's really going to be here tomorrow night?" Matt asked. No matter how many times Mason told him, Matt still couldn't believe it.

Mason nodded, grinning like an idiot.

"Tomorrow? Friday night. You sure?" Matt was acting like an untried fifteen-year-old nervous about his first date.

24

He'd done it. Claira was coming to dinner, and if Matt had his way she'd never leave. He knew it was crazy. He didn't know the first thing about her, but after meeting her, he'd begun to think his brother might be right.

"Yup." Mason nodded again. Since he'd left the school, he'd been incapable of more than one syllable words. The moment he'd laid eyes on Miss Claira standing by the swing set on the playground he'd lost all his blood and more than half of his brain cells to the demands of his cock.

Damn, she'd been like a goddess beckoning him to her. A brisk wind had blown in the night before and teased her shoulder-length curls as they billowed around her heart-shaped face, reflecting the sun like a bronzed halo. A sudden gust caught her flowing skirt and pressed it against her shapely legs, leaving nothing to his imagination. He'd counted it as a minor miracle that he hadn't come in his jeans. The thought of those legs wrapped around his hips as he plunged balls deep. Mmm—he bit his lip to keep from groaning aloud at the memory.

Beautiful didn't come close to describing her, but it was more than that. Something inside him had shifted. He was drawn to her in an instinctual way he'd never experienced before.

There was also something about the way she looked at him, the way she struggled to meet his gaze. He couldn't quite put a name to it, but it was more than simple shyness and he felt an undeniable impulse to rid her of that haunted look; protect her from whatever was chasing her.

"It's amazing, isn't it?" Matt said. "I mean, the dads always said they knew, that *we'd* know, when we found the right woman for us. It was different with Sarah, I know, but Claira's different. It feels…right."

Mason smiled. "Yeah, it's different, but she's suffering, Matt. We need to be careful with her."

"What do you mean, sufferin'?"

"I can't put my finger on it, but she's running from something. We need to make sure she doesn't take off and run from us. This will be a lot for her to take in."

Mason knew a skittish filly when he saw one. The best thing to do was to remain still and let her come to them, but damn if he thought he could wait for that. He hoped they were right because, no matter how Claira reacted, they had a bigger problem to worry about; a much bigger, surly, older brother kind of problem.

He studied the lovesick look on his twin's face. Being a twin definitely had its advantages. He could read Matt like a book because he was thinking and feeling the exact same things.

Mason crossed his ankles and braced his palms atop the counter behind him. Matt brought a hand to the back of his neck and tried to work out some of the tension that came with the new direction their thoughts had taken. They had to talk about it.

Mason finally bit the bullet and brought the subject to life. "He's held on to his grief for so long it will be like taking a bone away from a bulldog with our bare hands."

"Grey's not grievin'. He's just stuck." Matt believed Grey had accepted Sarah's death, but couldn't get past the feeling that he was breaking his promise to her by moving on with his life.

Mason shook his head and snatched up the dishtowel from the table. "It's still not going to be easy."

Matt clapped his brother on the shoulder and looked him in the eyes. "Let's just get her here and let the rest happen like I know it will. I trust my gut, our gut, on this." He gave Mason a playful shove. "If we're right, Grey won't know what hit him."

Mason shrugged and moved to the sink. "You cooked. I'll clean up." He waved Matt off and plunged his hands into the suds. "Go help Grey get the boys ready for bed."

Matt gathered up the remaining dirty dishes and stacked them next to the sink. "No, bro. We're a team." He paused before turning back to the sink. "How'd ya do it? Get her here, I mean?"

Mason chuckled. "She's not here yet, bro, but I asked her to tutor Connor."

"That's brilliant!"

Con had been struggling, falling behind in his class. The school counselor had talked to them on more than one occasion about maybe holding him back a year. The last thing they wanted to do was split the boys up.

"I'm telling ya. This is it. I can feel it."
Mason sure as hell hoped Matt was right.

D.L. Roan

Chapter Five

"What a day," Claira said with sigh. The trouble had started at daybreak when her water heater decided to take the day off. After shivering her way through a cold shower, she found herself in the kitchen staring at a coffee maker that refused to spit out the nectar of life she needed so desperately after another night of bone-jarring nightmares.

In that quiet moment, while she was straining to hear any sound of life from the coffee gods, her phone rang, the shrill tone like a bolt of lightning to her decaffeinated system. When she'd answered there was only silence.

She managed to ignore the first two calls, but after the sixth hang-up she began to get a queasy feeling in the pit of her stomach. She'd shoved the familiar paranoia away, managing to get through lunch, but by the end of the day the uneasy feeling began gnawing at her nerves. Everything was quiet when she'd arrived home. All of her security measures were intact and there was no sign of trouble.

As she checked the last window lock, a strange but welcome fury began to set in, stiffening her spine. She was being ridiculous. She had a new life, darn it all to hell and back. She was safe and time that she began to believe it. She couldn't let a few prank calls twist her into knots again. Resolved, she decided she would go to the McLendon's ranch, enjoy a nice dinner and put a stop to the incessant fear that had taken so much from her.

A picture of Mason's gentle eyes and Matt's playful smile flashed before her. *Twins*. Of all the beautiful people in the world, God had made two of *them*. At least now she had two pairs of blue eyes to go with the green ones that haunted her dreams.

An hour later, Claira sat in her car, idling at the stop sign at the end of town. If she went straight, the road would lead her to Falcon Ridge. She tapped her finger on the steering wheel as she studied the road ahead.

She should have never agreed to Mason's request. Standing in the playground, staring into Mason's bright blue eyes, she'd wanted him. That was it; plain and simple want. She wanted his lips on her, his strong arms folded around her.

She'd never allowed herself to want those things in the past, knowing it would only end in disaster. But things had changed and she couldn't seem to help herself when she was around a McLendon. She was equally attracted to both Mason and Matt. And God help her, Grey, too. What did that say about her? *I'm in way over my head, that's what it says.*

She should turn around, go back home. She could call and tell them something came up, that she couldn't make it; a headache, car trouble, an alien invasion. Anything would be better than the alternative. She shook her head. Who was she kidding? She could think of nothing she'd ever wanted more than the alternative.

How could she have let herself give in to them? After being besieged by McLendon charm and overabundant testosterone for three straight days, how could she not have? It was ridiculous, really. She couldn't have a relationship with any of them, let alone twins. That was it. They were twins, so of course she'd be attracted to both on a physical level. That was all it was, a mere physical attraction. Her hormones were on overdrive. She could control that. *Right?*

She propped her elbow onto the top of the doorframe and shoved her hand through her hair. It didn't matter. She was going there to talk about tutoring Connor, period. If she happened to have something good to eat and stimulating conversation with two devastatingly sexy men, then so be it.

When the bullets start flying and they're all dead I'll wake up in a pool of sweat and realize it was all another torturous nightmare.

She couldn't do it. The risk was too high. She wasn't ready for this kind of social experimentation.

The sound of a car horn behind her jolted her from her thoughts. Her reflexes had her stepping on the gas, propelling her through the intersection and down the long, winding road to Falcon Ridge. *So much for going back home.*

The wind had picked up throughout the day. When she parked next to the silver pickup truck in front of the charming, two-story farmhouse and opened her door, a strong gust pulled it from her grip and sent it crashing against the side of the big truck.

"Shoot!" She jumped out of the car and pulled the door closed, wincing when she noticed the foot-long crease in the truck's door. *Could this day get any worse?* She knew she should have stayed home. For a moment she thought about sliding back into her car and sneaking back down the drive before they knew she was there. Of course, then she'd have to call and tell them what happened. She was being a coward, but she didn't care. She was reaching for the door handle when she heard a door slam behind her.

"Leavin' the scene of an accident is a crime, ya know."

Claira flinched at the sound of Matt's voice and took a step back from the truck. "I…I'm sorry. The wind…it just…"

~*~*~*~*~

Matt saw the panic in her eyes and he could have kicked himself into Sunday for being so careless. He had her in his arms before he knew it. "It's okay, darlin'. It's just a dent." He pressed a gentle kiss to the top of her silky hair. God, she smelled good, like vanilla and spring, and woman. *Our woman.* He felt her tense and forced himself to release her.

She broke the connection and looked down at the damage she'd done, running a trembling finger over the crease. "I'll pay for it. What…whatever it costs."

"Claira." Matt pulled her hand away from the damage, lacing their fingers together. He couldn't *not* touch her. He wanted to touch every inch of her. "It's not the only dent that old truck has, and it won't be the last. Hell, the first thing I did when I bought the thing was take a hammer to the bumper." He pulled her to the front of the truck and pointed out a small dent in the shiny chrome. "See? I did that right after I bought it. That way I don't have to worry about when that first dent is gonna' happen and it lets the truck know it belongs to me. Sort of like a brand."

Claira looked up at him and she couldn't help but laugh. She'd never heard anything more ridiculous. "Do you do that with everything you own?"

"What? Hit it with a hammer?" Claira giggled again and the melodic sound shot straight to his cock. If she kept that up, he'd hike up that little skirt of hers and take her right there against the grille of his truck.

God, it was going to be torture, but he had to take it slow. Mason was right. She was as skittish as a newborn colt, but man was he ever going to enjoy seeing her fall for them. She would, he knew. He just had to be patient.

"No," she said on another giggle. "Do you brand everything?"

A haughty smile played on his lips at the thought of leaving his mark on her. "Oh, yeah." He took in a deep breath, inhaling her scent as the wind whipped around them. '*Slow*' had just become his most despised, four letter word in the English language. "Come on, dinner is almost ready."

Chapter Six

Claira glanced back at the truck, then down to their joined hands as Matt pulled her toward the front steps. When he'd reached out and drew her into his arms, she'd been stunned. The raw desire she saw in his eyes reached out and grabbed her, stirring something inside her that longed for more. It had been so long since she'd been held by someone.

She knew she should release his hand, but as they approached the front door his grip had tightened. She liked the fluttery feeling it brought to her stomach. She liked him. He was funny and that simple connection had helped her forget herself for a moment.

Matt held the door open and she stepped inside. The aroma of fresh basil and other Italian spices tempted her lack-luster appetite. She looked back at Matt and found him watching her. "I told you I make good lasagna," he said. Her hand still in his, he led her through the narrow entryway, deeper into the hall.

The house was older, but with the soft colors and comfortable spaces, it felt like a home. Not just a house filled with random people. There was a history here and she could feel a warmth she'd never felt before surrounding her like a thick handmade quilt.

The first room they passed was a large sitting area with a cozy, brick fireplace, pictures and knickknacks lining the hearth. Next was a smaller room with another small fireplace and a large desk that sat in front of a bay window. It would be a nice room to hold her tutoring sessions with Connor. She found the typical kitchen table sessions far too distracting when the family was at home. Of course she was used to her visits being more of an emotional or behavioral nature than arithmetic, but she would adjust.

"Mason?" Matt called out as they rounded a corner into the kitchen, but it was empty. "Oh, good. He remembered to take the bread out of the oven before it burned." Matt released her hand and pulled out a seat at the small island bar that separated the kitchen from a common living area. "Have a seat and I'll get you somethin' to drink. Wine or beer?"

Matt stretched up to retrieve something from a tall cupboard, the muscles in his back and broad shoulders flexing against the tight material of his white tee-shirt as it strained against his flesh. She was going to need a fifth of tequila to get through this.

"Um, wine would be nice."

Matt pulled a bottle from the fridge and uncorked it. "Where is Mason?" she asked as she glanced around the charming little kitchen. From what she'd seen so far, it was the only room in the house that had a woman's touch.

"I was just washing up." Mason's smooth voice fluttered over her skin like the wings of a butterfly.

Claira turned in her seat to see Mason leaning against the doorframe, his long, lean legs crossed at his ankles, his thumbs tucked into the front pockets of his faded blue jeans. His eyes were as warm as she remembered and she fought the urge to walk up and snuggle into his arms.

"Hi," was the only reply she could manage.

"Hi." He smiled and pushed away from the doorway. Claira's insides melted as he brushed his knuckles over her cheek. "I'm glad you came."

Heat rose in her cheeks to meet his touch. She looked away and caught Matt watching them. She'd expected to see jealousy, or shock, but instead she saw an answering passion in his eyes. What was he thinking?

"You look beautiful." Mason said as he withdrew is hand and crossed the small space to stand next to Matt, who grinned and nodded in agreement.

Claira felt the room shrink. She clasped her purse in her lap and tried to keep from pressing her thighs together. With both of them standing side by side in such a small space, the testosterone level became like a life force all to itself.

She couldn't help but stare. The similarities were overwhelming, but now she could also see their differences. Matt was a little more tan and thicker in the chest. Mason's hair was longer but had more sun streaked highlights than Matt's. They were both lean in the hips and as far as she could guess were a little over six feet tall. She realized she was staring and dropped her gaze to the wine glass she found herself gripping as firmly as a drowning victim would a life preserver.

"Sorry, you probably get that a lot." She shook her head then took a long sip from her glass, resisting the urge to gulp it down. "I didn't mean to…it was rude of me to stare." She felt herself blush again and stared back into her glass.

"Hey, don't be sorry." Matt chuckled as he turned to the stove and removed a covered dish from the oven. "And you're right, we do get our fair share of attention because of the twin thing. It's not all that bad." He wiggled his eyebrows, making her giggle again, disarming her with his effortless charm.

"Yeah, being identical twins has its definite advantages," Mason said as he whipped around with a stack of plates in his hand. He placed the plates on the bar, and she immediately noticed the missing place settings.

"Speaking of twins, where are Con and Car?" She knew it was going to be a struggle keeping her haywire hormones in check, even with the rambunctious boys to keep them distracted. How was she going to get through a whole dinner with just the three of them? She was *so* going to need another glass of wine.

"They spent the afternoon with our parents," Matt said as he sat the hot, aromatic dish on the island counter and he and Mason took a seat on either side of her. "They live on the south side of the ranch, about a half mile further down the driveway. They should be dropping them off in a couple of hours."

"We thought it would give us a chance to talk," Mason added. "You know, about Con and the problems he's been having in school. Come up with a plan."

Claira released an unsteady breath as Matt dished out a healthy portion of lasagna onto her plate. That made sense, she guessed. As she reached to pick up her fork, her purse began to slip and she drew it back onto her lap.

"Here, I'll set it on the table in the entryway for you." Mason reached out for it, but years of habit made her pull away and clasp it to her chest.

"No, that's ok. I'll just keep it here with me, next to my chair." Reluctantly, she let it drop to the floor.

Mason drew his hand back and gave her a quizzical stare. "We won't go snooping through it until you're out of the room, I promise."

Oh God. They must think I'm an escaped mental patient. She could hear the Rain Man's voice in her head. *Wapner at seven.*

"It's not that. It's just," How did she explain that she was so used to picking up in the middle of the night, or any time really, and running for her life.

Once, when she'd been in a hotel gym in Los Angeles, the Marshals had come to get her and she hadn't had time to go to her room to pack any of her things. She'd lost her phone, her identification, her money; everything. It took them weeks to replace it all, but she never saw the pictures of her mother and brother again. That was all she'd had left of them.

"It's okay." Matt shrugged and shared a look with Mason that she didn't understand. "We get it. Women and their purses are like men and their p—"

"Matthew!" Mason coughed into his hand.

"What?" Matt paused, his fork perched at his lips, and grinned. "I was going to say men and their pick-up trucks. What did you think I was going to say?"

Again, Claira couldn't contain the laugh that bubbled out. The whole evening was like that. Easy. Any time she began to feel uncomfortable, Mason would say something soothing or Matt would make her laugh. As the time went by, she found herself so at ease with them and their bantering, she'd hardly touched her second glass of wine.

They talked about everything under the sun, except tutoring Connor. She tried to feel uncomfortable about that but couldn't.

She'd learned that Mason bred horses and was a talented trainer. Matt ran the day to day operations of the ranch, from managing the herds and the ranch hands to mending fences. Their older brother, Grey, with the haunting green eyes, had both agricultural and finance degrees and managed the business end of their three-way partnership. They all lived there. Together.

When they asked her questions about herself, she tried to follow Daniel's advice and stick to the truth as much as possible. She hated lying to them. It was difficult at times not to let anything slip that could reveal her old identity.

She'd almost told them where she was born, but managed to change it from Maryland to Maine at the last minute. Daniel had told her it would get easier, that over time she would almost believe the made-up version of herself to be the truth. She knew it was only a matter of conditioning, but she also knew she'd never truly forget.

By the time Mason filled his glass with the last of the wine, she'd learned everything there was to know about raising horses, herding cattle and mowing hay fields. The one thing they hadn't discussed was Con and Car's mother. She felt the need to know warring against her common sense. If they wanted her to know, they would tell her, right?

"The twins' mother? Is she still…in the picture?" she asked, her rampant curiosity getting the better of her.

Mason and Matt shared another one of their knowing glances. Mason cleared his throat before he spoke. "Sarah," he paused and glanced up at Matt again. Matt inclined his head in a slight nod and returned his attention back to Claira. "Our wife passed away giving birth to the twins."

Claira's heart dropped. She didn't know how it felt to lose a spouse, but she understood the pain of loss. *Wait.* "What?" *Did he say our wife?*

A small grin that blended into a grimace pulled at the corner of Matt's lips. "You caught that, huh?"

Mason turned in his chair and met her confused gaze. "Sarah was our wife; Con and Car's mother."

She must have heard that wrong. *Twice.* "As in, you were both married to her…at some point?"

"At the same point," Mason clarified. He tried to smile, but he knew it looked the same on him as it did Matt; painful. He found it more difficult than he expected to talk about Sarah with another woman. The desire he felt for Claira mixed with the sense of loss he sometimes still felt for Sarah, and the combination made his chest ache a little.

"But… isn't that… illegal?" Claira asked, her head swirling with so many questions she'd blurted out the first one that sounded coherent in her head. She considered herself open-minded about the different types of relationships, but two men married to the same woman, at the same time? Was there even a name for that?

"Technically, on paper, she was married to only one of us, but in our hearts we all belonged to her." Matt said, his voice weakening to a near whisper. He reached out and took one of Claira's hands in his as Mason took the other. They laced their fingers with hers and the raw emotion she saw in their eyes broke her heart and set her on fire all at the same time.

She found it hard to breathe. Her heart raced, her spine turned to jelly. What were they doing to her? She pulled her hands from theirs and took a sobering breath. She couldn't think with both of them touching her that way; looking at her with such intensity.

When she was within sight of either of them she was overwhelmed with emotions she'd never experienced before. She was good at working with children, but she was a walking wreck when it came to her body's reactions to these men.

"Claira? Are you ok?" Mason asked, his thumb stroking gentle circles on the back of her arm where she rested it on the counter.

"I'm fine. I just…" She blinked and gave her head a quick shake to clear the lust infused fog from her brain, struggling to find the right words to explain what they were doing to her. Should she explain? She was probably just being overly sensitive to such familiar displays of affection from men she hardly knew, but it felt like the butterflies in her stomach had gone on a bender at an all-night keg party.

"You disapprove," Matt said, the playfulness in his eyes replaced with a frigid coldness.

"Oh. God no!" She glanced at Mason and found the same trepidation in his expression. "It's surprising, is all. I've never heard of the type of relationship you described."

Matt studied her as she spoke. She glanced up to see suspicion in his eyes that hadn't been there before and she wondered what she'd done to cause it. "I'm sorry if I gave you that impression. I didn't mean to imply that I thought there was anything wrong."

Mason's lips curved into a soft smile and he reached for her hand again. "While it's a familiar way of life for us, it's not a common situation. We've all had to deal with those who were less…accepting. We wanted you to know."

They thought she was judging them? "Mason, I'm no one to judge how anyone else should live their life. I—I'll be honest," she paused and fiddled with the napkin in her lap, her inner psychologist doing backflips at the thought of delving into this one. "That is…I don't want to seem nosy, but truthfully, I'm fascinated. I have about a hundred questions I'd love to ask you both about how a family dynamic like that works, but no one's opinion matters as long as it does."

Beside her, Matt released a relieved breath and took her other hand back into his own. "I'm sorry, Claira. When I saw your reaction I thought you were one of those people."

"No! That's not what I have a problem with. I mean…" She lowered her gaze back down to her hands in theirs. Her stomach fluttered and her nipples pebbled beneath her shirt. Mason caressed gentle circles in her palm with his thumb, sending a throbbing tingle shuddering through her pelvis. She closed her eyes as she tried to remember what she was saying. *Oh, yeah. That I can't think when they touch me like this.*

"Oh," Matt chuckled. Her eyes flashed open to see a haughty grin plastered across his face. *Oh my Lord, what have I gotten myself into?*

Chapter Seven

Please, please, please let me not have said that out loud!

With one of his hands coupled with hers, Mason's other arm came to rest on the back of her chair. He rubbed small circles at the base of her neck, fiddling idly with the strands of her hair. The muscles in Claira's shoulders relaxed, only to tense up again as Matt leaned toward her.

Her eyes fluttered closed and she could feel his hot breath brush across her lips. Mason's fingers slid up her neck, caressing and massaging as they progressed to the base of her skull, sending a rush of chills down her arms and a flood of heat between her thighs, causing her lungs to short circuit and refuse to release her last breath.

"I have that same problem when I'm with you." Matt's voice vibrated over her skin. His lips feathered over hers so softly it tickled, teasing her with tiny nips and caressing glances.

Claira swallowed as she fought against the need to lick her lips. The dire need to breathe began to burn in her chest and, God help her, she wanted to kiss him.

"Wha—what problem is that?" she finally asked, breathing the question out with a long sigh, her lungs clawing at the inside of her chest for her next breath.

She could feel Matt's grin against her lips. His breaths came in short, rapid puffs as the tip of his tongue traced her bottom lip with flirty touches. "I can't seem to keep my thoughts inside my head either when I'm around you."

His hand came to rest on her cheek, the sudden touch startling her into a gasp. Matt captured the sound and took her mouth with his own, ever so tenderly prodding her to open to him.

Claira released a whimpering sigh when his hot tongue slid past her lips and caressed the tip of her own. A fire ignited in her womb, sending tendrils of heat snaking up to her breasts and down between

41

her thighs as he deepened the kiss, twirling his tongue leisurely against hers and then retreating to nip at her bottom lip again.

Her body softened against him. She moaned into his mouth, surrendering to another invasion, this time meeting his demand with her own. It had been three years; three long years since she'd been kissed. And never like this. The way Matt was kissing her, possessing and teasing her, it was as if she were the most cherished person on Earth.

"That's it, sweetheart. Taste him. You're so beautiful."

Mason hadn't wanted to say anything, for fear of startling her out of the moment, but he couldn't contain the rush of admiration and lust that accosted his senses. She was glorious, like an angel. She was so sensuous and responsive. The way she leaned into Matt's embrace and her little moans of desire were killing him.

His heart pounded a rapid beat inside his chest in a vain attempt to circulate the blood that had vacated its chambers and flooded to his groin, creating the hardest erection he'd ever had in his life. He couldn't wait until it was his lips that tasted her. He didn't want to scare her off by pushing her too far their first night but, God help him, he didn't think he could wait until the next time he saw her.

Claira wasn't sure if it was the sound of Mason's voice or the car door slamming in the distance that pulled her out of a near meltdown and back to the harsh reality of her life. She flinched away from Matt, sobering with regret when she glanced at Mason. How could she have kissed his brother while Mason watched?

She opened her mouth to apologize but Mason cupped her face in his hands and dropped an innocent kiss to the tip of her nose. "Don't panic, sweetheart. It's just our parents and the boys. They'll be glad to see you."

Just their parents? Just their boys? *Someone, please dig a deep-deep hole and bury me.* What had she been thinking, coming here? Kissing them? Well, technically she'd only kissed Matt, but even that was just…wonderful. No. No. No-no-no. It was wrong. She shouldn't be kissing anyone.

She bolted from the chair and ran her trembling hands down the front of her skirt to smooth out the wrinkles. She checked all the buttons on her blouse and then ran her fingertip over her lips. With any luck, most of her lipstick had been wiped away with her napkin during dinner. Her gaze darted to Matt's lips. Oh, thank God it wasn't smeared all over his face. She was a teacher. Their children's teacher. Their parents' grandsons' teacher. This was so not good. Not professional in the least.

She grabbed up her purse and ran a hand over her hair. When she noticed Matt and Mason slouched comfortably in their chairs, both sporting a mischievous smirk, she felt a spark of anger flash through her.

"You're laughing at me." She pulled her purse strap over her shoulder and crossed her arms over her chest. "You think this is funny? Oh my God, you do!" When their smirks turned to full-on grins and Matt chuckled, she turned on her heels and marched toward the door.

"Darlin', don't be angry!" Matt shot up from his chair and took off after her. He reached her in three strides and wrapped his arm around her shoulders, pulling her to a stop. "We couldn't resist, darlin'. You are so damn cute when you're all flustered."

"Don't you darlin' me. You…you set all this up. You never intended to talk about tutoring Con, did you? You—you what? You expected me to come here and—and…" God she didn't even know what she thought they wanted from her.

"We expected—no, we hoped, you would have dinner with us and we'd get to know each other better." Mason stepped around Matt and cradled her neck in his hands, tilting her head back to look at him, "That's all, sweetheart. We do want you to help Con. We'd like for you to meet our parents, but we didn't expect what happened in there tonight. Hoped, maybe. Prayed? Yeah, a lot, but not expected."

Claira looked at Mason and her whole world was reduced to just them. She wanted to believe him. She did believe him. She didn't know why, but she hated being angry with him. Matt, she could be mad at Matt. For whatever reason, Matt pushed her buttons; all of her buttons, including the ones that made her want to rip off her clothes. Mason was a gentle soul, gentle with her. She wanted to trust him.

She released a sigh and found herself snuggling into Mason's chest when he wrapped her in his soothing embrace. "I believe you.

It's just…I've had a trying day and I'm a little overwhelmed by all of this."

"Aw, Claira, darlin'. We didn't mean to upset you." Matt stepped up and ran his hand along her arm in such a gentle caress that she reached out for more when he pulled away. Darn, she wanted to be mad at him. "Let us get the boys settled into bed then we'll sit on the porch for a little bit, have some coffee. We want to hear about your bad day. Maybe we can help you forget about it, or at least feel better about it. Our folks won't stay long. I promise."

Claira would bet they could make her forget. All it would take is two seconds of another one of Matt's kisses to send her straight to Amnesiaville. That was part of the problem. She couldn't afford to forget herself. She didn't know if he was out there, watching her, but she did know the consequences for anyone she might let get that close.

Before she could tell them she was leaving, the front door swung open and two Tasmanian whirlwinds rushed inside. Claira wrenched herself from Mason's arms.

"Daddy Mason! Daddy Matt! Papa Jake and Papa Nate want to see the puppies. Can we go show em'?" Car shrieked as he ran up to Mason, unfazed by the presence of their teacher standing in the hallway with their dads. "I know we're still grounded until tomorrow, but they haven't seen em' yet and we want Papa Jake to help us pick out the one we're gonna' keep."

"Whoa there, sport. Aren't you two going to say hello to your teacher?" Matt playfully scolded as he scooped Con into his arms.

Con smiled at her, Car sparing her the briefest of glances before he greeted her. "Hi, Miss Robbins." Before Claira could respond, he looked back up at Matt and held his hands out in a show of impatience. "Now can we go show the Papas the puppies?"

Matt let Con slide to the floor. "Make it quick. You're still grounded for tonight so that means lights out by eight."

"Come on, Con! I bet they pick the white one." Car pulled Con back through the front door, the screen door slamming behind him.

Claira was stunned on so many levels. She'd been worried about the twins seeing her with their fathers. They obviously couldn't have cared less.

The biggest thing she was still trying to process was the 'Papas', plural. Did that mean their dad and Sarah's dad? Or were they saying they, too, had more than one father like the twins. And how did that work, really? How did they know which one of them was their biological father?

Her first question was answered when the screen door opened again and a petite, dark-haired woman was ushered in by the tallest man she'd ever seen. He held two bags in his long arms and reached for one of the trays in the woman's hand.

"Don't just stand there, boys. Help your mom get this stuff to the kitchen," the man ordered.

Matt and Mason jumped to their mother's side and began taking the load from her arms. "Hey, Mom. You didn't have to go to all this trouble. You know we can cook for ourselves these days." They each laid a kiss on her cheek.

Once her hands were free, their mother reached up and patted them both on the cheek. "It's never any trouble taking care of my boys."

Matt and Mason walked back toward the kitchen with their goodies, leaving Claira alone in the hallway with their parents. She stood unnoticed and watched as their mother turned and removed her sweater.

"Most of it is leftovers from the Ladies Auxiliary luncheon this afternoon," their mother shouted down the hall as she searched through her purse for something and then hefted the designer bag to the top of the growing pile in her husband's arms. "I think Mrs. Porter made an extra apple pie just so I'd take it home to you boys. I had room in the oven for an extra pan of chops when I made dinner tonight. It doesn't take a rocket scientist to know those boys can eat you out of house and home. Never hurts to have…Oh!"

Claira felt like an intruder as the older woman froze in mid-turn and looked at her with a wide eyed expression. She made her way to Claira with her arms outstretched in a warm greeting.

"Good Lord, boys. You didn't say you had company." She pulled Claira into a friendly hug. "I'm Hazel McLendon and I apologize for the lack of manners my boys are showin' tonight. But," she shrugged, "you do the best you can while you have them and then their fathers go and mess it all up." She turned a slanted gaze back to the man at the door. "Josiah McLendon, did you know about this?"

Josiah's sheepish grin said he did.

"I'd extend a hand," Josiah lifted the bags in his arms, which were now weighted down with all of the other things Mrs. McLendon had piled on top of them, "but I drew the short stick and got to play pack mule."

Claira suppressed a giggle when Mrs. McLendon rolled her eyes and swatted his backside, prodding him toward the kitchen. "Nice to finally meet you, Claira," he mumbled as he marched obediently down the hall.

"You know her name?" Mrs. McLendon shouted after him. "You did know about this!"

Well, shit. Joe bit his lip to keep from cursing aloud. When Matt called and told him about Claira, and asked them to take the boys for the afternoon, he and the other dads had made up some crock about them not having time to get to town for supplies and groceries. He didn't know what their sons were up to and hadn't wanted Hazel to go nosing around. Joe made a mental note to tell his brothers that one of them was sleepin' on the couch tonight. It sure as hell wasn't gonna be him.

Hazel shook her head and grabbed up Claira's hand with a chuckle. "It's not every day they get one over on me, but when they do…"

Claira liked the woman on the spot, but she still felt out of place. She had no experience with a family dynamic like theirs. "I'm sorry if I'm intruding. I drove out to speak to Matt and Mason about tutoring Con. I guess dinner ran a little later than they planned."

"No need to apologize, honey. It's been a long time since my boys entertained anyone of the female persuasion in this house. And don't you worry, as soon as I get the food put away, and my men gathered up, we'll be heading out and you can carry on with your dinner."

Her men?

"Oh, that's ok. We were pretty much finished up anyway, Mrs. McLendon." Claira lied. They hadn't even discussed Con at all. Of course she had no problem feeling guilty about that now.

"Call me Hazel, dear," the other woman insisted as she pulled Claira toward the kitchen.

She could hear voices as they approached the kitchen, but a sudden silence filled the room when they entered. The men shared glances with their father and then their mother. Josiah cleared his throat and smiled at his wife. "Am I released from duty, Mrs. McLendon?"

Hazel reached up on her tiptoes and kissed Josiah's chin. "Yes, dear. I'll only be a minute. Go pry your brothers from the twins so our boys can get them ready for bed."

"Yes, ma'am." Josiah turned and gave Claira a fatherly squeeze. "Don't let our boys cause you any trouble, missy. If they do, you give me a call and I'll straighten them out for you." Claira chuckled and nodded her agreement as another deep voice called out from the hallway.

"Mom! Poppa Joe! Did you guys buy a go-kart? What is that thing parked next to Matt's truck and how did that big dent get—?"

Grey froze in the doorway as he took in the scene in his kitchen. His brothers, who were both sporting shit-eating grins, were leaning against the sink behind their mom, who still wore the look of sympathy she'd had for him since Sarah passed away. His dad had his arm wrapped around the one and only star of his recent and unwanted wet dreams.

The delectable Miss Robbins was standing in his kitchen. In Sarah's kitchen. His cock sprang from half mast, where it had pretty much stayed since the last time he saw her, to a full blown hard-on right there in front of his mom. *Ho-ly hell.*

Chapter Eight

Guilt slammed into Grey's chest, squeezing the blood from his heart. What the hell was she doing in Sarah's kitchen? And why the fuck was his dick inflating like a damn parade float on speed?

"What's wrong, Grey, honey? You eat something for lunch that didn't agree with you?" His mom discarded the pie she was putting away in the fridge and reached up to place a hand on his forehead like he was still a two year old. Grey jerked away from his mother's ministrations and glanced at his brothers, and then back to Claira.

"Yeah, bro. You look like you've been suckin' on a sack full of lemons all day," Matt taunted him with a knowing smirk.

"Daddy Grey is home!" Two small but loud voices called from the hall. The twins slammed into Grey's legs with unabashed excitement. "Daddy Grey! Daddy Grey! Papa Jake says he likes the gray puppy, but...but Papa Nate says we should pick the white one." Car pulled at Grey's pant leg and reached up to tug at his hand. "I want you to help us decide, daddy."

"I like the black one." Con sniffled and wiped at his runny nose with the back of his shirt sleeve.

"Here, Con." Hazel ripped a paper towel from the roll on the counter. "Blow," she ordered and Con complied without complaint. She dabbed at his face and then tossed the towel into the trash. "What did the pediatrician say about his allergies, Grey?"

Grey stared at Claira. He couldn't look away. He'd spent the last three days trying to work her out of his system and now she'd invaded his home, his only safe place.

"Grey?" Hazel prodded. "Con's allergies?"

Grey snapped his focus to his mom and scrubbed a heavy hand over his face. "They're running tests, Ma. Doc Jessop said we should keep him out of the barn during haying season." He looked down at his sniffling son. "Which, other than being grounded, is another good reason for both of them to stay out of the barn." He ruffled Car's hair and gave them a both a pat on their rumps. "Go brush your teeth and get ready for a bath. Then it's bed time for both of you."

"But, daaaad! I'm not sick!" Car whined.

"I've had enough of your arguing, boy! Do what you're told! Now, or you can kiss your puppies goodbye!" Grey snapped back. The boys' excitement withered and they sulked their way up the stairs without any further arguments.

Grey's burning glance shot to Mason and Matt, daring them to challenge him, then back to Claira again. She felt it hit her square in the stomach like an invisible force. The tension in the room was thick enough to stir with a wooden spoon.

She found herself pinned by Grey's icy, green stare. Besides her embarrassment over their first meeting, she also began to feel like Alice in Wonderland; specifically the part where she would drink the potion and shrink to the size of a thumbtack. Or was that when she ate the cookie? Either way, Grey's intense stare had reduced her to the size of a bug and he was looming over her with his big foot poised above her head, about to crush her to smithereens. The expression on his face told her that was exactly what he thought of her; a parasite that had invaded his home.

And clearly, he'd also been married to Sarah. Matt's words came back to her with a haunting rush of clarity. *'In our hearts we all belonged to her.'* Even though she didn't understand Grey's surliness toward her, she couldn't help but think what an incredibly blessed woman Sarah had been. And what an idiot she'd been to think she had any business here.

"Grey," Mason cleared his throat. "This is Con and Car's new teacher, Claira Robbins. She's going to be tutoring Con a couple nights a week during the summer break."

Grey nodded and snapped his sharp stare back to her. His nostrils flared as his breaths deepened. Something shifted in his expression but Claira couldn't quite make out what had changed. "We've met." He said in a clipped tone.

Claira cleared her throat and pushed her purse strap higher onto her shoulder. "I should be going." She glanced at Josiah, and then Matt and Mason who stepped to either side of her.

"No, honey, you finish up with the boys here." Hazel patted her arm and winked at her. What that was about she wasn't exactly certain, but she was sure that she couldn't stay there under the torturous stare that Grey seemed determined to wield, like a sword to her soul.

"But—"

"But nothin'," Joe insisted. "I parked the truck behind your car anyway, so you can't leave until we do. Tiny little thing that it is, I damn near ran over that contraption before I figured out what it was. Don't see you makin' it up this driveway in that thing come winter. You might ought to be thinkin' about tradin' it in for an adult version before the snow sets in. Maybe somethin' with four-wheel drive and a motor, instead of a hamster."

"Josiah! Stop teasing the poor girl!" Hazel slapped his arm and pushed him past Grey, out of the kitchen and down the hallway.

"I'm just sayin'!" Joe went on as he made his way down the hall. "Hamsters tend to freeze up around here about mid-November. It wouldn't do anyone any good if she got stranded out in the middle of a storm because her hamster died of hypothermia."

Shaking their heads, Matt and Mason took Claira's hands and pulled her past a fuming Grey to follow their parents to the door. Claira felt the heat rolling off Grey as she ducked past him in retreat without looking back. "Goodnight, Ma, Papa Joe. Thanks for the leftovers." Mason helped Hazel slip on her sweater and she leaned in to give him a peck on his cheek.

"It was nice to meet you, Mrs. McLendon, Mr. McLendon." Claira allowed herself to hug the woman back when she'd pulled her into her arms with an unexpected strength.

Hazel gripped her shoulders in her hands and leaned back to look at her. "Now I'm only going to say this one more time, then I'm going to have to unleash Joe on you again. It's just Hazel. You make a young woman feel old when you start in with that *Mrs.* business."

Claira laughed and gave her a shy nod. "Sorry. I'll remember that."

"You do that, honey." She patted Claira's arm and then swatted Matt and Mason on their backsides as she tipped her head toward the kitchen. "Don't be too hard on your brother, boys. I imagine he's had a rough time of it today and he'll need some time to sort it all out."

Matt nodded, but he had every intention of giving Grey exactly what he needed; an all-out, old fashioned ass whipping. It had been years since they'd gone at it, but that dry spell was one he would damn well be putting an end to. Being a giant fuckwad to Claira was bad enough, but he'd be damned if he was going to let him use their boys as a whipping post for his unresolved emotional problems.

Seeing her opportunity to escape, Claira ducked out the door behind Hazel. Matt and Mason followed her out onto the porch and captured her hands, putting a halt to her determined strides toward the steps. She tugged against them, but they tightened their grip, tugging her back to them as they leaned against the wooden railing that surrounded the porch.

"Wait," Mason said as he pulled her against him and snuggled her to his chest. "Sorry, sweetheart. That kind of got a little out of hand in there."

A little? Since their kiss—which was how she'd come to think of it, as if she'd kissed them both—her head hadn't stopped spinning and her stomach was in knots. All she wanted to do was go home, hope that her water heater had had second thoughts and was willing to play nice, and take a hot shower. Then crawl into bed and bawl her eyes out.

"Hey," Matt said as he cupped her cheek in his palm. "What's that look for, darlin'? What's wrong?"

Where did she begin?

"Don't close down on us, darlin'." Matt pleaded.

Claira released a frustrated sigh and rubbed her aching temples. The psychologist in her wanted to list, catalog and self-analyze all of the feelings that were eating away at her. A few off the top of her head made their way to a mental checklist; overwhelmed, scared, excited, aroused and sad. The one that she scrawled in big, bold letters at the top was *tired.* Going with that one was unquestionably her safest option.

"I'm just really tired. I need a long, hot shower and some time alone to think, but even that won't be possible tonight." She tried to keep the whine out of her voice but failed.

Mason placed a soothing kiss to her forehead then turned her until her back was to him. He gripped the top of her shoulders and began a smooth, slow massage of her tense muscles. "Why's that, sweetheart? It sounds like a good plan to me if you're that tired. Besides, it's Friday. You don't have class tomorrow. Get all warm and toasty, snuggle into bed and sleep in tomorrow."

The things Mason was doing to her shoulders felt so good that she had to focus all her inner strength into breathing and keeping her knees locked so she didn't melt into a gooey mess at their feet.

~*~*~*~*~

"That's just it," Claira sighed.

Standing in front of her, Matt knew Mason had found a weakness when her head fell forward and she relaxed against his chest. "What's it, darlin'?"

"My water heater," She answered in almost a slur.

Matt groaned to himself. He could imagine her husky voice, in that lazy tone, moaning his name as he licked the evidence of her climax from her pussy, her slick channel milking his tongue as she fell from the orgasm he'd given her.

"What's wrong with it?" Mason asked, snapping Matt from his entranced state.

"Mmm," She moaned as Mason found a particularly tender spot. "It's broken. I have to call the landlord tomorrow. It will probably take him a few days to get it fixed so I won't be...ahh...taking any hot showers for a while."

"Who's your landlord?" Matt asked, reaching down to adjust his raging hard-on while she wasn't looking. Much more of this and he'd need a cold shower, not that the last three he'd taken had helped any.

"Uh...Dillon, I think. Drummond? Frank Somethingorother." She hissed as Mason found another tender spot.

"Frank Dryson?" Matt asked. "You rented his place over on Harvest Lane?"

"That's it." She nodded. "You know him?"

"He's our cousin." Mason chuckled. "We did the remodeling work on the kitchen for him."

"So you're the ones I have to thank for that."

"You like it?" Matt asked, sliding his hand up between Mason's to caress the back of her neck as his brother continued to massage her shoulders. He loved the silky feeling of her soft, curly hair. They weren't the frizzy, kinky type of curls that women paid to get with those perms. Hers were fat, soft curls that fell around her face and flirted with her shoulders.

"Do I like what?" She slurred again, and slumped further against Mason, trapping Matt's hand against his brother's chest.

Mason chuckled this time, moving his hands from her shoulders and wrapping his arms around her waist, holding her up as she relaxed against him. Matt watched her relax in his brother's arms.

"It's my favorite room," she finally said. "I'll have to make you some fudge one day. The counters are perfect for it."

Call him a sexist pig if it fit, but Matt pictured Claira, bare feet and all, bending over to peer into their oven, the smell of something delicious filling the air as he and his brothers came in from a hard day on the ranch; her hair mussed around her face and her cheeks flushed from the heat rolling from the oven.

His chest ached as his picture of Claira mingled with memories of Sarah, but it wasn't the painful squeeze he'd expected. It was a fullness the likes of which he'd never felt. Not even when his boys were born.

It wasn't just Claira. It was the hope that she brought to them. He'd never let himself believe they would ever find what they had with Sarah, but now… And he could see the same thoughts mirrored in his twin's expression.

Grinning a stupid-silly grin, Mason pushed away from the railing and took Claira's hand, pulling her toward the end of the porch. "Come on, I have something I want to show you." Claira looked back at Matt, but he stayed where he was, waving them on.

Matt knew where Mason was taking her. Mason always got that look in his eye when he was thinking about some animal or another, especially horses and puppies. He'd let them have a few moments to themselves. As much as it pained him to let her go, to not touch her, he knew from experience the importance of them spending some alone time with Claira.

Even though they would be sharing equally in her life and love, they needed to build their own relationships with her too. "You guys go ahead." He waved them off. "I'll help Grey get the boys settled into bed and meet you there in a few."

No matter how hard he tried, he couldn't take his eyes off them until the darkness swallowed their silhouettes and then moments later a soft glow of light filled the barn. He'd bet his last buck that Mason was trying to figure out how to talk her up the ladder to the hay loft. He chuckled as he reached for the door handle and pushed his way inside. The sooner he kicked Grey's ass and got the boys in bed, the sooner he could join them.

Chapter Nine

Self-loathing wasn't something Grey was unfamiliar with, at least not lately. He needed his ass kicked for the way he'd spoken to his boys downstairs. Hell, he'd kick his own ass if he could, but that wouldn't erase the picture of Car and Con looking back at him as they climbed the stairs, expressions of disappointment and rejection smothering their innocence.

An apology wouldn't fix it. Not this time. His behavior toward his sons, toward everyone, had been inexcusable, and not just since he'd met Claira. Even though she'd thrown a wrench in his plans to live comfortably numb from his neck down for the rest of his life, Grey knew that he'd been acting like a prick for months.

He knew it, but he couldn't seem to stop himself. When he'd begun to notice the things he was unable to recollect about Sarah, bitterness and guilt devoured him. The more the bitterness ate at him, the more he'd pulled away from his family, afraid they would see him for the failure he was. The more he pulled away, the more they seemed to go on without him, without her. As he watched them all go about their lives the more bitter he became. It was like watching a train wreck with no power to stop it or to even look away.

Meeting Claira seemed to ignite something inside him that intensified the bitterness. Witnessing his brother's reactions to her, feeling his own body's betrayal, made him realize he no longer had a choice. His family, even his own damn body was moving on whether he wanted to or not. Having his choices taken from him made his blood boil. He was always in control, goddammit. Why couldn't he control this? Why couldn't he fix it?

"Is daddy Matt coming to read to us tonight?" Con's small, innocent voice pierced his heart, snapping him from his silent rage. "Or is that part of our punishment, too?"

Grey's heart broke. It was all he could do to hold in the sob that filled his chest. He'd been so caught up in his own misery that he hadn't said a single word to either of his sons as they bathed and he got them ready for bed. He was such an ass. He fell to his knees and pulled Con out of his bed into his arms, reaching out to grasp Car's little arm.

Car flinched away from him and sat on the edge of the bed, refusing to look at him. Oh God. What had he done? "Car, come here, son."

"No!" Jumping from the bed, Car ran past him. Grey looked back to see Matt holding Car's trembling little body in his arms, his face buried in the crook of Matt's neck.

Grey's gaze connected with Matt's. The unspoken anger that radiated from his brother and the scared expression on his son's face would have brought him to his knees if he hadn't already been there.

Without a word, Matt turned with Car in his arms and walked to his bedroom down the hall, the door clicking closed behind him.

"I'm sorry, daddy." Con sniffled. His arms snaked around Grey's neck. "We didn't mean to make you mad at us again. We don't need daddy Matt to read to us."

"Oh, Con." Grey hugged his son to his chest and fell back to the floor with him in his arms "Don't say that. You didn't make me mad, son. Daddy Matt can read to you any time you want him to. I'm the one who should say I'm sorry. I shouldn't have yelled at you and your brother."

"But we shouldn't have gone with the Papas to the barn to see the puppies. I wouldn't have gotten sick with my nose and then you wouldn't have needed to yell at us."

"No, Con." Grey sat up and stood Con on his feet. When his son wouldn't meet his gaze, he hooked a finger under his chin and lifted his little face. When he saw his bottom lip trembling with the effort to hold back his tears, it was more than he could bear.

He stood and picked Con up, setting him on the bed next to him. God, how did his fathers do it? He'd never seen them cry, not once, and he was one breath away from bawling like a baby in front of his six year old. He had to fix this; had to fix himself.

With an effort he thought was beyond him, Grey took a deep breath and cleared the lump in his throat. He could do this. If he didn't get this right he would lose any respect his sons had for him, if he hadn't already lost Car's. That, above all else, was intolerable.

"No, you weren't supposed to be in the barn. But, son, I had no right to speak to you and your brother that way." He paused and draped his arm around Con's little shoulders. "I know I haven't been easy on you boys lately, and…and…" God, how did you say you were a dickhead asshole in first grader language? He swiped his hand through his hair and took another deep breath, reminding himself that he could do this.

"You haven't done anything wrong, Con. I couldn't ask for two better sons than you and Car. And I want you to know that I would never, *ever,* get mad at you for being sick. Understand?"

Con nodded and wiped at his eyes as Grey fought against his own tears again. "You'll still be grounded when you do things me and your dads tell you not to," he continued on to keep the lump in his throat from choking him. "But I'll never dismiss you or talk to you again the way I did tonight. Okay?"

Con nodded again and Grey pulled him onto his lap. "I love you. Don't ever doubt that." He gave Con a tight hug and held him out so that he could look into his eyes. "Am I forgiven?"

"Sure, daddy, but, tomorrow can you talk Car into picking the black puppy? I really like him, but he won't even think about it."

Grey laughed and lifted Con from his lap, settling him under the covers. For life to be that simple again. "I'm not sure if I can talk Car into anything tonight, buddy, but I'll give it a shot in the morning." He wasn't sure how to fix this brokenness inside him, but he had to do something. He needed his sons.

"Night daddy. I love you," Con said with a yawn.

Grey leaned down and ruffled his hair. "Good night, buddy. I love you, too."

He turned out the small Scooby Doo lamp beside his bed and walked to the door, pausing to glance back at Con before he eased the closed the door behind him.

When he stepped out onto the porch, in desperate need of some fresh air, Grey noticed the light that flooded the barn. He peered down the driveway and saw exactly what he expected. She was still there. Mason must have taken her out to the barn to see the puppies. No way in hell could he deal with seeing her again, but he couldn't make his feet move to retreat back into the house. Instead, he found himself crossing the field between the barn and the house, keeping to the shadows.

He felt ridiculous sneaking around in the darkness on his own property. He told himself he wasn't spying on his brother, just waiting for her to leave so that he was sure he didn't interrupt them. That was it. He was doing Mason a favor by hiding in his own fucking tractor. He climbed up into the cab of the nearby combine, concealed in the darkness, where he waited for Claira to leave.

He wasn't dumb to his brothers' plans, nor could he blame them. She was beautiful. He'd felt the same attraction to her the first time he'd seen her. The feminine sway of her hips when she walked, the small dip at the base of her spine, and her plump little ass that made him want to sink more than his teeth into her. He was an ass man, through and through, and what he'd seen of it, her ass was flawless. Sarah's ass had been flawless, too.

Grey cursed and banged his head against the tractor's steering wheel. When he thought about Sarah and Claira in the same moment, his chest felt like it would burst open and spew out what was left of his heart. That was one big problem he didn't know how to fix. How could he ever let go of Sarah enough to be with a woman that compelled him and his brothers the way Claira did? How could he possibly forget her more than he already had, and still be able to breathe?

No other woman had made his body want to try until he saw Claira standing in the middle of her classroom covered in green paint. What was it about her that called to him? Grey didn't know the answer. All he knew was that he wasn't prepared to deal with any of it.

His breath stilled when the barn door opened and the light spilled out into the yard. It was a good thing Mason had closed it behind him or Grey's hiding spot would have been exposed. She was snuggled against Mason as they strolled through the darkness. His gaze was drawn to the gentle sway in her hips as they walked toward her car. *Jesus*, could he get any harder?

Once they were out of sight, Grey climbed down from the tractor, groaning against the pain in his groin as he slipped unseen into the barn. Even over the aroma of hay and horseflesh, he could still smell her. The light fruity scent had driven him fucking mad when they'd all been crammed into the kitchen together. Now, he could detect the faint spice of her arousal mingled with that fruity concoction. At least he imagined he could. Had Mason tasted her? He would know for sure when Mason returned.

~*~*~*~*~

The last person Mason expected to see when he stepped back into the barn was Grey. The smile on his face fell and he steeled himself against the urge to punch him straight in the gut. All that would accomplish would be to push him further away from them.

He could see the war Grey was fighting with himself, felt it even, but like a stubborn thoroughbred, he would have to let Grey make the first move toward trusting in himself, and them. The old saying *you can lead a horse to water* came to mind. Grey was his own man. He was a control freak. Mason knew that asking for help was going to be damn near impossible for Grey. He also knew it was inevitable and he was determined to be there for his brother when that time came.

Instead of challenging him, he simply nodded and walked to one of the far stalls in the back of the barn. He picked up a curry comb and began grooming one of his prize brood mares, Darza. When Grey leaned his arms over the stall door, Mason held his tongue and ignored him. Long moments passed. Only the rhythmic sounds of the horse's breaths and the wisp of the brush could be heard.

"She's breathtaking," Grey said, breaking the silence between them.

"That she is," Mason agreed without missing a stroke of the mare's illustrious, chestnut coat.

Mason watched his brother out of the corner of his eye. After another silent moment, Grey coughed to clear his throat. "I wasn't talking about the horse."

Mason moved the brush from the horse's neck and ran it along the length of her side. "I know," was all he said, again without looking up at Grey.

"I've been a prick," Grey added after another awkward moment of silence.

Mason paused, considering his reply before he moved to the horse's hindquarters. "I know that too," he firmly replied.

Grey shook his head and leaned back to look down at his boots. He swiped at the hay poking out from under the stall door with the toe of his boot, wondering what in the hell he was doing out there. "Is there anything you *don't* know, smart ass?"

Mason ignored his brother's taunt and walked around to the far side of the stall where he began the grooming routine on Darza's other side. He wasn't going to be lured into a fight with Grey, but he wasn't going to let him get by with an easy out.

"Yeah," he said and rested his arms across Darza's rump. He looked at Grey. "I don't know *why* you're being a world class prick. Care to enlighten me, or do you plan on taking your show on the road?"

"You threatening to kick me out?" Grey didn't take to threats too well. It chafed his ass to have to take one from his little brother. It made his gut churn to think he'd pushed this thing so far that his brothers were actually considering it. They would hate him if they knew the truth.

"Nope." Mason leaned into the mare and began stroking her coat again. "Just figured you were so damn unhappy here, you'd be leaving. I'd like the chance to prepare our boys, is all. Before we come home and find a note that you'd up and left us."

Chapter Ten

"I'd never leave them," he choked out. "I could never live without our sons, without our family or the ranch. You know that! How could you even think I could walk away from them?"

"You haven't been here for months, Grey. I figured all that was left was the packing." Mason walked over and tossed the comb into the tack box. He pushed past Grey and headed toward the stack of fresh hay on the far side of the barn.

"I've been here every goddamn day!" Grey pushed the statement through his clenched teeth.

After pulling off a fresh slice of hay from an open bale, Mason turned around and stopped dead in his tracks. The look on Grey's face was staggering, all the pain and the guilt. *Guilt over what?*

"What the fuck happened, Grey?" Mason dropped the hay to the floor and stomped toward his brother, shoving him up against the stall. Darza gave them a startled snort when Grey crashed against the latched door. "What could you have possibly done that has you so eaten up inside you can't even stand the sight of your own sons?" He pushed Grey again when he didn't answer. "Answer me!!"

"That's not true!" Grey bit out and pushed away from the stall. "I love those boys! I'd never hurt them like that!"

"Then start acting like it, you stupid fuck! We only get one shot at this and I'll be dammed if I'm going to let you screw it up!" Mason hadn't wanted to say so much, but now that he'd opened his mouth, it was like trying to stop a stampede with a traffic whistle. "You think they can't see what's going on with you? That they can't feel it? You've got your head so far up your own ass they can't help but taste the shit you're spewing all over them every time you open your mouth."

Mason paced in front of Grey. He'd never been so worked up. Grey flinched when Mason stopped a breath away from him and glared at him, anger seething from every pore. "Answer my question!" Mason demanded, standing toe to toe with him.

"What question?"

"What—the—fuck—have—you—done?" Mason inched closer, waiting for Grey to either take the first swing or answer his question. When Grey didn't speak, Mason fisted his hands into his shirt collar and pinned him against the stall. "What are you so guilty of that has you scared shitless?"

Before Grey could answer, Matt slammed open the barn door and threw off his Stetson. Mason released Grey and pushed him away. Without a word, Matt stormed down the aisle between the stalls and punched Grey in the face with enough force that Grey's feet left the ground before he landed flat on his back two stalls down.

"If I ever see that look on either of my sons' faces again, I'll kick you off this ranch myself. I don't care if you are my fucking brother." Matt leaned over Grey and pulled him to his feet.

Cupping his jaw, Grey staggered out of Matt's grip. "Goddammit! I think you broke my jaw!"

Matt stepped toward Grey, his fist pulled back to punch him again, but Grey held out his hand. "You're right," Grey groaned through the pain. "I deserved that, but it's the last free one you'll get. Understand?" Grey ducked when Matt threw another punch at his head.

Grey tackled Matt around the waist, shouldering him to the ground. Matt kicked and tried to roll away, but Grey was on top of him before he could move, socking him in the eye with a powerful right hook of his own. As he pulled back to land another, Mason pulled him off Matt and dragged him backwards toward the door.

"That's enough," Mason growled when Grey threw him off.

"Enough my ass." He lunged at Matt again, who was scraping himself off the dirt floor. Turning on his heel, Matt twisted out of Grey's path and swung his elbow back, but instead of hitting Grey, he nailed Mason square in the nose.

Mason stumbled back, clutching his face. When he looked down and saw the blood running through his fingers he'd had just about all he was going to take. He thought about walking over and grabbing the water hose, cooling them off like their mom used to do, but where was the fun in that?

"What the hell." Mason tossed his own Stetson onto the nearby bale of hay and jumped into the fray.

Mason didn't know how long they spent tearing the hell out of the barn or beating the shit out of each other, but when it was over, he found himself slouched on the ground, leaning against a bale of hay between his brothers.

Each of them sporting various cuts and bruises, and fighting for their next breath, no one spoke for several long minutes. Finally, Matt pushed himself up to a sitting position and used the hem of his tee-shirt to wipe the blood from his left eye. "Fuck, I think that one's gonna need stitches."

Mason leaned forward and took a look at the cut above Matt's eyebrow. "Na, you're just a big pussy."

Grey chuckled and cupped the side of his face, trying to wiggle his lower jaw. "I think I'll get by with not having my jaw wired shut, but it hurts like a son of a bitch. We're getting too old for this shit."

"Speak for yourself," Mason huffed, flexing his right hand. His knuckles were raw and bleeding and he thought he might have sprained his wrist, but he'd never admit it to them.

"Too bad they won't wire your jaw shut permanently," Matt said as he ripped his shirt over his head and held it to his brow to stem the flow of blood. "Maybe it would keep you from spewin' off at the mouth so much."

Grey huffed and the small grin he managed turned into a wince when it pulled at the cut on his lower lip. "Probably a good idea. I don't know why I hadn't thought of it before."

"I could hit you again and see if we can't make that happen." Mason knew that Matt was only half joking.

When Grey didn't respond, they waited him out. The silence stretched out for so long, Mason was about to give up when Grey finally spoke.

"I can't remember her eyes." Grey's tortured sigh betrayed his weak attempt to hold back the words.

Matt lowered the blood-stained shirt from his face and turned to look at Grey, the cut on his brow stinging like hell from the sweat that ran from his forehead. "Is that what all this is about? You can't remember Sarah's eyes?" He choked out an incredulous huff and shook his head. "Fuck, Grey. We have a million pictures in that house to remind us of what she looked like. I have a dozen of em' in my room."

Mason stared blankly at the stall door across from him, his arms resting over his bent knees. "At least you don't have to watch our wedding DVD to remember what her laugh sounded like."

For a moment the pain in Grey's jaw subsided as a small wave of shock poured over him. "You lost her laugh?" He couldn't imagine he'd ever forget the way Sarah's laugh would wrap around him like a warm blanket in the winter. He'd also never imagined that his brothers had lost pieces of her, too.

Mason nodded. "About three years ago, I guess."

"At least now I know where the DVD went." Matt stretched out his legs and propped his elbows up on the bale of hay behind him, wincing when a stab of pain shot through his shoulder. He jerked his arm back and cupped the tender muscle. "Gaw-dammit! When did you two learn how to wrestle like that?"

Mason chuckled and wiped his bloody hand on his jeans, then dared to touch the swollen lump on his face that used to be his nose. "About the same time as you learned how to punch my lights out. *Fuck* that hurts!"

"Now who's bein' a pussy?" Matt tossed Mason's words back at him.

"Speaking of pussy." Mason let his words trail off, not sure if he should have raised the subject of his time with Claira around Grey. They would have to talk about her sooner or later. Mason shrugged. Maybe it was time to test the waters.

Before he said another word, Grey's head fell back against the bale of hay. "I knew I smelled her when I walked in here."

Mason and Matt shared a shocked glance. "You fucker!" Matt growled. "You told me to go slow! How the hell is eatin' her out on the first date goin' slow?"

Mason couldn't help but laugh, a triumphant smirk on his face. "I didn't *dine*, exactly. I just…tasted. And I've never tasted anything sweeter." The mutinous look on Matt's face said he was considering finishing the job he'd done on his nose.

With his head still lolled back as he stared at the ceiling, Grey released an agonizing groan. "You two are killing me."

"Sorry, bro," Matt said when Mason shot him a warning glance. Matt ignored him and gave Grey a nudge with his shoulder. "You feel it too, don't you?"

Grey lifted his head and released an irritated sigh. Feel it? Hell, he was eat, sleep and drinking it. Didn't mean it was right, or that he deserved anything Claira had to offer. "Yeah, I feel it."

"Is that what's got you all torn up? That you're attracted to Claira?" Mason pushed. He knew Matt thought Grey had grieved Sarah, but now he wasn't so sure. If Grey still hadn't let her go, then their plans with Claira may be in trouble no matter how right they felt about her. They would push him, but in the end if Grey wasn't ready, they couldn't or wouldn't move on without him.

"It's natural to forget some things, Grey," Matt said. "We all have things we can't remember about her, but she'd want us to be happy, man."

Grey sat up with a groan and pushed himself to his feet. "I'm hearing you. I really am." He raked his hand through his hair as he bent and scooped up his hat. After slapping it on his leg a few times to knock off the dust, he flipped it onto his head. "I don't think I'm ready for this."

Matt shook his head and sprang to his feet, tossing his bloody shirt to the waste basket down the aisle. "You know you feel what we do. You're not alone in this, Grey. I'm not sayin' it'll be easy. She's got somethin' she's hidin', somethin' she's scared of. Hell, we all have issues, but I'm tellin' ya she's worth it, bro. You gotta give her, and yourself, a chance."

Mason was in awe of his twin at that moment. He couldn't have said it better himself, except for one thing. He wrapped his arms around his knees and looked up at Grey. "Just so you understand, Grey. We're serious about her. We want you to want her, too, but not just to get your rocks off."

Grey had no problem with that. He'd been shooting pool with a rope for so long after Sarah's death that when the urge did finally hit him, he'd made a damn fool out of himself with some cheeky waitress in Billings. Since then he'd stuck to impregnating the shower when the urge got to be unbearable, which wasn't often, until now.

The feelings he had for this woman he scarcely knew had him running in circles. He didn't like it, and he sure as hell didn't know what he was going to do about it. Lately he'd been nursing a case of blue balls from sun up to sun down, but he'd never use a woman like Claira just to drain the swamp. Grey pushed the thought away and offered a hand down to Mason, pulling him to his feet. "Duly noted, but I'm not making any promises," he said.

Mason retrieved his hat and slapped his brothers on the back as they headed for the door. "So, what kind of mess are we facing with the twins?"

Matt shot Grey a mean look and Grey hung his head in apology. "For Con, nothing two puppies won't fix, I hope, but I think I have a shit load of work cut out for me with Car."

"Two puppies?" Mason let out a low whistle as he flipped the barn light off then closed and latched the door. "That bad, huh?"

Grey shrugged. "Considering I wasn't aware we were even keeping one, I think it's a damn good compromise."

"You'll give em' the whole damn litter if that's what it takes," Matt swore as he cleared the front steps in two strides.

Grey shook his head and grabbed for the front door handle. "I think you're right, but let's not tell them that unless it's our last option."

Chapter Eleven

Sweat beaded on Lucien Moretti's skin and trickled along the deep, muscled V that ran along his spine. His blood burned through his veins at an exhilarating pace, his lungs pumping air through his flared nostrils as he tightened his grip on her hips and pounded her pussy.

His need increased with each pulse of blood that ran through his cock. Her strangled cries of ecstasy drove him to a place hidden deep within. A place where he could smell her light, exotic scent and feel the silkiness of her rich mocha hair wrapped around his fist. He could hear her sultry voice, feel her breath on his skin as her angelic cries danced around him like a warm summer breeze.

"Gabriella!" He shouted her name as the force of his climax pushed him into that euphoric world where only they existed. "Gabriella, mine. Always and only, mine," he chanted as he spilled himself inside her, filling her over and over until he was fully spent.

When he was but scarcely recovered, he pushed himself up to hover above her, unable to wait to see his love for her echoed in her own eyes. As his vision cleared and fantasy withered, what appeared before him was nothing but the tear-stained, haggard face of a common whore.

"What the—." Lucien recoiled from the offensive reality, growling a curse as he wrapped his hands around the girl's neck and wrenched her off his bed. He studied her face, his features twisting in revulsion as images of Gabriella's flawless face merged with the inferior imitation that stood before him. "Putanna!" He shouted as he drew back his fist and struck her across her face, sending her crashing to the floor at his feet.

She was a fucking whore! His Gabriella had betrayed him. After all the years he'd waited for her, all the things he'd given her, she'd betrayed him! She'd spit on his love for her and left him to...to what?

She couldn't possibly want a life without him. She was promised to him! *She's mine!*

When the whore tried to stand, he shackled her wrist and jerked her to her feet. Her pleas for mercy filled his ears, triggering his wicked grin and sending a familiar euphoric rush through his veins. She would beg him. Before he was through, Gabriella would beg. Like the common whore in his arms, she would plead for him to love her.

"Shh, mi cielo." He pulled the whore against him, cupping her face in his hands as he fluttered gentle kisses against her closed eyes, her forehead. After ten years she would finally be his.

The whore's sobs echoed against his bare chest. "Shh-shh. It will be ok, love." Their noses touched and then he skimmed his lips against hers, her trembling breaths hot against his skin. His fingertips slid along the back of her scalp, anchoring in her long, ebony locks before he tugged her head back to look at her. The look of fear and confusion in her eyes fed his anger and desire. His pulse pounded in his temples and hummed through his veins. Although he'd just fucked her, his cock stiffened in anticipation, seconds before he snapped her neck.

"Soon, mi cielo." He lowered the whore's lifeless body to the floor, reaching to his king size bed to retrieve the sweat-sodden sheet. "Sleep now." The white Egyptian cotton billowed in the night air as it floated down like a spotless cloud to cover her broken body.

Lucien walked to his bedroom door and flung it open. Ramos stood at his post across the expansive hallway and jumped to attention when he heard Lucien's voice. "Take her away," he ordered his guard and paced lazily to the cellaret near the window.

Without a sound, the burly footman hurried in behind him and scooped the heap from the floor, sparing not a glance or a question as he quietly left the room and clicked the door closed behind him.

Lucien poured a finger of fire and slammed it back, smashing the glass against the floor. It had been a week since he'd heard from *The Lieutenant*. What a ridiculous name for someone who was supposed to be the most feared, elusive hunter on the planet. He'd owned dogs with names more menacing.

"A fucking week!" He marched to the bedside table and flipped on the lamp. He stared at his cellphone willing the assassin to call. He'd call the man himself, tear his fucking head off, if he had the bastard's number. His gut had churned with uneasiness when he'd turned over the down payment and the asshole wouldn't even give him a phone number to reach him. '*You'll hear from me when I have her*,' was all he'd said before walking off into the sunset, with a million of his fucking dollars.

He didn't care if Gabriella's father had *highly* recommended him. It wasn't her father's money anymore. It was his. All his, and soon, Gabriella would be as well. With or without *The Lieutenant*, he was going to find her. Gabriella's incarcerated fool of a father wasn't the only one with lowlife friends in high places.

He picked up his cellphone, his hands trembling with anger, and punched at the display until the number he was looking for scrolled into view. He tapped the dial button and waited. When the familiar voice on the other end barked a curt greeting, calm poured over Lucien like warm honey. He could see a new plan falling into place. Fuck the million dollars. Some things you had to do yourself.

~*~*~*~*~

Claira's heart was in the clouds, soaring with the angels, fueled by unfamiliar feelings. Good feelings, she'd decided. Her mind, however, was fully entrenched in the gutter, where it had been since her visit to Falcon Ridge. The visions the twins had inspired had haunted her dreams throughout the night.

Matt's mouth sliding across her skin, his tongue tracing her lips, along her jaw until his teeth nipped at the tender shell of her ear. His ragged breath puffed hot against her neck, one hand slipping beneath the collar of her shirt as the other began unbuttoning the buttons at a slow, torturous pace. She tried to stay calm. She didn't want them to notice her inexperience, but when she felt Mason's hard, lean body press against her back and fold around her as he traced the other side of her neck with his tongue, her heart nearly exploded.

She'd awoken from the dream with her pulse pounding in her head, her throat and other areas that left her otherwise breathless.

She'd tossed off the covers, embarrassingly aware of the uncommon wetness between her thighs that seemed to flow on command when she thought of Matt or Mason. She understood her arousal. She wasn't ignorant of the mechanics of sex. She'd simply never appreciated the importance of it. Or the urgency that everyone else on the planet seemed to have toward it. Now that her body demanded what her analytic brain had denied it for all her years, she didn't know how to process it all.

Once she'd finally fallen back to sleep, the dreams started all over again, her sex-deprived body taking control once more. The trend continued the next morning. Her memories of her time in the barn with Mason were so hot that she'd barely noticed the cold water sputtering from the showerhead.

He'd been so endearing with the puppies. The concern in his eyes when he told her about the puppies' mother recovering at the vet's made her heart ache for them. He'd told her about the day they found her at death's door and saving the tiny puppy when it couldn't take its first breath.

With anyone else she'd have thought they might have been bragging a little, but when she'd lost her balance while reaching for one of the puppies and skinned her bare knee against the dirt floor, she'd seen his true nurturing quality.

He'd picked her up with little effort and set her on a nearby table before retrieving a small first aid kit from one of the stalls. After he'd cleaned the wound with a careful, steady hand, he'd lowered to his haunches in front of her and blew a cool puff of air against the stinging cut, sending a shiver dancing along her heated skin.

The small bandage in place, the tips of his fingers traveled up her thighs, tracing small circles beneath the hem of her skirt. She swallowed back a moan as she stared at his hands. Big and strong, they covered her thighs, thick tendons rolling beneath his tanned skin.

"Claira."

Like iron to a magnet, her gaze was drawn to his. The electric-blue desire she saw pulled her further into their depths.

She tried to look away, but she couldn't. He leaned in and pressed his lips to her bandage then stood and towered over her, spreading her thighs with his manly hands. He stepped between them and lowered his head, capturing her lips with his own.

His kiss was every bit as stirring as Matt's, but different in so many ways. Matt had been charming and teasing, slowly tasting her as she grew comfortable with his caresses. Mason consumed her. His lean body crowded against her, his calloused hands kneading her thighs as he plundered her mouth, holding nothing in reserve.

Passion she'd once thought only fantasy, flowed from his lips, his tongue and infused with her own need for human contact, emboldening her to take more, to drink from him. Her hands found their way to his work-hardened chest. With every stroke of his hands on her thighs, her hands echoed the movement across his chest and down his rippled abdomen.

The higher his hands traveled up her thighs, the lower hers explored. When his fingers grazed across the hot, damp cotton of her panties, he mumbled a curse and deepened their kiss. Her fingers trembled against his shirt and over his belt as she dared them to do what she so desperately wanted.

Her fingertips made contact with the starchy denim of his jeans and a tremor of desire rocked her entire body. Mason's finger tested and teased the edge of her panties. As her hand caressed over his bulging erection, he slipped two fingers under the elastic and stroked them against her slit, swirling them through her wet heat. A deep moan tore from Mason's throat and an equally aroused whimper escaped from her when the tip of his fingers pressed at her entrance.

Uncertainty flooded her thoughts. Suddenly she wasn't so confident in her own boldness. Mason must have sensed her hesitation because he pulled his hands from beneath her skirt and tore his lips away, panting as he leaned his forehead against hers. His hands came up to frame her face, his fingers caressing her cheeks.

"I knew it would be like this," he said, his breath's measured and forced. "I want you, Claira. Hell, I *need* you, but I know it's too soon. I can wait. We can wait, as long as you need us to, sweetheart."

Whatever thoughts she'd begun to have about the 'we' portion of his statement were obliterated when Mason pulled back and traced her lips with his fingers. She could smell herself on his fingertips. What she once thought embarrassing suddenly became a most erotic pleasure.

The tip of her tongue snaked across her bottom lip, tasting herself for the first time. Mason brought his fingers to his lips and tasted her, licked her essence from his calloused digits then kissed her senseless again. She couldn't remember who broke the kiss, but they were both breathless and panting when he'd finally released her and helped her down from the table.

What was left of her senses had evidently malfunctioned because, when he'd asked her to come back for Sunday supper to finalize their plans for Connor, she'd agreed without hesitation. When he'd walked her to her car, she felt a twinge of guilt about not saying goodbye to Matt, followed by a wave of disbelief as she realized she'd just been making out with his brother.

Something similar to shame had fought for space in her head. His kiss had felt so unbelievably right when she knew it shouldn't. She should have never let things go so far, with either of them.

Standing in the canned goods aisle of the local supermarket twelve hours later, she battled with the decision to call them and back out of their Sunday plans. She'd studied every label on every can of beans, peas, corn and tomatoes on the shelves, twice, and hadn't really seen any of them.

Her mind kept reliving their kisses and caresses, mingling them with blurred memories of blood and death. That part of her life was supposed to be over, but she couldn't allow herself to believe in her new freedom enough to live out the fantasies; the hope that Mason and Matt had given her.

She needed a therapist. She understood doctor-patient confidentiality, had lived by it at one time herself, but she'd never been able to bring herself to trust in it. If her father or Lucien ever wanted the doctor to talk, he or she would, no doubt, telling them everything they wanted to know. She could never trust anyone with her secrets.

She reached out for a can of green beans and fumbled it, sending the ones stacked precariously around it tumbling to the floor. When she tried to catch one, it bounced off her fingertips and crashed into the shelf, knocking more cans to the floor and sending them rolling down the aisle.

Painfully aware of her sudden lack of coordination, she stooped to pick up the closest of the wayward cans when a hand landed on top of hers. Her head shot up as the hand jerked back and she found herself face to face with a stranger.

"Let me help," the man offered with a shy smile and began to gather the cans. He stacked them back on the shelf as she grabbed for the few still at her feet. The stranger stood and slid a few clumsy steps down the aisle to gather those that had rolled away, reaching low under the bottom shelf for one in particular. When he returned, he added it to the shelf behind her then held one out to her.

When she didn't move he pushed it toward her, urging her to take it. "The one you were after, I believe." His eyes were sincere and his tone friendly. Still, she didn't move. "Surely you want it. I've never seen someone study a can of beans for so long."

Her eyes darted to the can in his hand and then back to him. Her mouth went dry and her insides began to shake. Who was he? "You...you were watching me?"

~*~*~*~*~

His smile turned shy again and he blushed. Blushing on command had been one of the more difficult deceptions he'd mastered, but he'd used it so often it seemed effortless now. And it always worked.

He reached over and grabbed a can of baby peas. "Um, actually, I was waiting for you to choose one so I could grab these."

She glanced down at the can his hand and then back at him, her eyes nervously scanning her surroundings. When she relaxed her shoulders and her eyes closed on a sigh, he knew his efforts had been a success. She reached out, her hand trembling so slightly he wouldn't have noticed if he'd been anyone else but who he was. She took the green beans from his hand and thanked him for his help.

Watching her place the can in her cart, he reached out and offered his hand. "Grant Kendal." He smiled, making sure it reached his eyes.

Everything about him had been chosen by design to make her feel comfortable. From his name to his conservative but relaxed haircut, even his nondescript, brown eyes and common aftershave had been thoroughly researched and pieced together to garner him all the trust he needed to manipulate her in a hundred different ways and keep her where he wanted her.

If all went according to plan he wouldn't need her to trust him; wouldn't need to get that close. But in his experience, very few things ever went exactly as planned, and he had to cover all his bases on this one. When she took his offered hand in hers and gave it a firm shake, then looked him in the eyes, he was only half convinced it had worked.

"Claira Robbins," she smiled confidently.

She looked different than the photos he'd seen of her, dressed differently, too. When he'd first arrived in town and began putting his plan into action, he'd had to study her carefully before he was convinced he'd found his mark.

By all accounts she was the mousy, conflicted creature that others believed her to be, until that handshake. In his line of work, he found that few people ever made eye contact, even when they shook hands. The sudden confidence in her eyes and body language was surprising, betraying his own confidence in his preparations. The sloppy bastard that wanted her seemed completely clueless of her true nature, something that *didn't* surprise him at all.

Chapter Twelve

Claira closed her eyes and censured herself for her panic-laced reaction to a common stranger. She was *not* that woman anymore. If she was going to live a normal life, the life she deserved, then she needed to start acting like a normal person. Meeting a nice, somewhat plainly-handsome stranger that had only been trying to help her was normal. Wasn't that what normal people in small towns did? Help other normal people?

Tossing off her defensive posture, she met his warm brown eyes and couldn't help but smile. He was an average-looking man, broad in the shoulders with a comfortable quality about him. Not near as handsome as her cowboys, though. *Her cowboys.* She snorted at the thought, then cleared her throat. She could do this.

Standing in the middle of the aisle, she chatted amiably with Grant, where she learned that he, too, was new in town. He'd been staying with his grandmother in Dillon, a small town about a hundred miles west of Billings, until she'd passed away a month ago. The strain in his voice when he spoke of her was enough to convince Claira of his sincerity. He was a nice guy, looking for a fresh start, something she could relate to.

Moments later they said goodbye. He waved her down the aisle as he headed for one of the cashier lines with his can of baby peas. A bit of pride bubbled up from her chest as a muted giggle. She'd done it. The new found freedom of talking with a random stranger felt good.

Keys in hand, she paused at the trunk of her car as an even more bizarre thought occurred to her. Spending time with Mason, Matt and even their family hadn't triggered her anxiety; not in the way talking to Grant had.

Sure, she'd been nervous and more than a little uncomfortable, but she'd never doubted their sincerity and hadn't once considered herself in danger around them. Maybe not the sort of danger she'd become accustomed to, anyway.

If she counted their ruggedly handsome faces, their gorgeous sapphire eyes, substantially immense muscles, and the way they touched her? Oh, yeah. She was definitely in danger alright.

Grinning at the goose bump-inducing tingle that ricocheted through her, she lowered the last of the three bags into her trunk and slammed the lid. This kind of danger she could handle. Well, she doubted she could handle all of it at once, but....

Sliding behind the wheel, she closed the door and clicked her seatbelt into place. A chirping giggle escaped into the quiet that surrounded her as she pondered the ridiculousness of it all. She, Claira Robbins, a quiet, simple, teacher, homebody and disaster magnet extraordinaire, was being seduced by two beautiful men. Twins! And she was attracted to them. *Them! Plural!*

She could spend an entire month psychoanalyzing why this was happening, or shouldn't be happening. In fact, she should drive straight to Billings and sit herself down on the first couch in the first therapist's office she came to.

She'd lost her ever-loving mind to think she was capable of handling what they proposed, but when she pulled into her small driveway and clicked off the engine, she found herself looking forward to her Sunday dinner plans. She'd survived talking with a complete stranger, after all. She could do this!

With uncontainable excitement, Claira pulled her purse strap over her shoulder and started up her front stairs. Keys in hand, she froze in mid-stride, her feet anchored to the second and third steps.

Her eyes locked onto the overhead porch lamp, ominously void of light, and stared hard at the dark globe, unbelieving she hadn't noticed it when she first pulled up. The light had been on when she left. She never turned it off; ever.

She couldn't see over the top steps to know if the string was still attached to the thumbtack at the bottom of the door. She wouldn't know for sure if the door had been opened until she could get close enough to see if the toothpick or the paperclip were still there. One more step up and she'd know, but she couldn't make her legs take the step. Instead, she leaned forward and braced her hands on the step above her. Breathless she lowered her head and squeezed her eyes closed, willing her panicked tears away.

It's only a blown bulb, she chanted over and over in her head.

Sweat began to drip from her forehead and she realized she hadn't taken a breath. Her lungs burned with need. She clenched her jaw, forcing the much needed oxygen through her nose. With a moan of sheer panic, she forced her head to turn, looking back over her shoulder to the bottom step. Prying open her eyes, she searched for the last thread of hope. A helpless squeak of relief escaped her throat when she saw the thin line of pebbles on the first step, undisturbed.

Just a blown bulb. Just a blown bulb.

Turning her head back toward the front door, her lungs seizing with dread, she forced her legs to push her up the last step she'd need to be able to see the paperclip.

One more step. It's only a blown bulb. No one has been here. No one is *here.* He *isn't here.* She heard Marshal Gregory's voice in her head. *Stay calm. Be ready.*

Paralyzed with fear, visions of a madman flashed through her mind, but she pushed them away. She had to maintain control. She lifted her head, her eyes burning from tears and sweat. Her hand moved on its own, wiping the sting from her eyes, but her heart stopped when her vision cleared and the paperclip and toothpick came into view, lying together on the porch floor beneath the door.

Black spots swarmed her vision. The roar in her ears drowned out every other sound and the world turned eerily silent as it swirled around her. Everything moved in slow motion as she slowly crept back down the stairs to her car.

Her limbs numb, she stumbled over something she couldn't see. Tunnel vision blocked her attempts to find something to grasp on to. She fell hard against the ground, a sharp pain exploding in her leg and her palms. The pain snapped her from her panic, her vision clearing enough to see her car tire beside her.

Gasping for her next breath of air, she pushed herself up, her hands grasping for the door handle. Tears blurred her vision again.

Please! Please open!

When the latch flipped up but the door didn't budge, a desperate sob escaped her aching throat. Her hands shook so hard she couldn't focus on them. She turned and slid down the side of her car into the gravel, sobs wracking her chest. Where were her keys?

The loud bang of a slamming door caught her attention. She jerked her head up, listening. She held her breath as the faint sound of footsteps echoed from the direction of her back porch. *He's here.*

Her gaze darted around the ground in front of her. She lunged for the clump of keys lying in the grass near the bottom step, skidding across the grass on her knees. She didn't know where the sudden calm had come from, but she was grateful none the less for the surge of adrenaline that propelled her back to her car.

Opening the door, she threw herself into the front seat and locked the door behind her. Frantically she searched through her purse and clutched her cellphone. Dialing 9-1-1 while her other trembling hand tried desperately to insert the key into the ignition, she cried when the keys fell from her grasp and landed somewhere near her feet.

"9-1-1, what is your emergency?"

"Oh God!" She said, her throat so tight she could barely speak. "He's in my house!" She kicked her legs out, frantically searching the floor with her feet for her keys. *Where are they?*

"Ma'am. You said someone was in your house? Are you there now?"

"Yes!" She folded herself beneath the steering wheel to search the dark floorboard with her hands.

"What is your name and address, ma'am?" The emergency operator's calm voice asked.

"Uh," Claira had to stop and think. "198 Harvest," she groaned again as she reached under her seat and felt the cold, sharp edge of one of the keys. She couldn't reach them without getting out.

"Are you in the house, ma'am? Can you see the person?"

"Um, no." Claira blew out a frantic breath and held in a sob. She needed those keys. She needed to focus. "I'm in the driveway, in my car. Someone is inside! Please, send someone. I can't reach my keys!"

"Stay in your car and lock the doors, ma'am. Can you see the person in your home?" The emergency operator prodded.

Claira sat up and glanced at the house, abandoning her search for her keys. Movement on the right side of the house caught her attention. Her focus sharpened and she recognized the figure walking toward her from the small pathway between her house and the neighbor's fence.

"Matt?" Or Mason? In truth, through her tears she couldn't tell. "Oh, no!" Chills ran down her spine and her hands flew to the door handle, dropping the phone. She had to get him away from there. She pulled on the handle but the door wouldn't budge. *The locks!* She ran her fingers over the control panel, pushing all the different buttons.

Come on! Come on! Open!

"Matt! Run!" She shoved her shoulder against the door at the same time her fingers found the release and she fell out of the car, catching herself on the armrest.

"Claira?" Matt called out as he picked up his pace and jogged toward her car. "Darlin', what's wrong?"

Claira grabbed his hand and dragged him toward the street, her thoughts fogged with panic. She had to get him as far away from there as possible.

"Claira!" Matt said, stopping and pulling her into his arms. "Shh, honey, calm down. It's okay. Whatever it is, it's okay."

"No. You have to run. He won't stop," Claira pleaded, writhing in his grasp.

"Who, darlin'? Who won't stop?"

~*~*~*~*~

"It's okay. No one is going to hurt you." Matt sat on the ground, almost in shock himself, and rocked a pleading, sobbing Claira in his arms as he listened to the approaching sirens. A growl rumbled in his chest when he noticed the trickle of blood running down her calf. What the hell was going on? He didn't have a clue, but he sure as hell planned on finding out.

"It's okay, darlin'. The police are here. We'll be fine. Breathe for me."

He tipped her chin and wiped away her tears with his thumb. Her chest rose and fell so rapidly, she was going to pass out if he couldn't calm her down. *Who did this to her?*

When her eyes rolled back in her head and her short, rapid breaths stopped, Matt shook her. "Claira, breathe!" He shook her again. "Claira!" He recognized the officer peeling out of his patrol car at the end of her driveway, gun drawn, and shouted over her limp body. "Call an ambulance, Benton! She's stopped breathing!"

"They're on their way, Matt. What the hell happened?" He dropped to one knee and laid his fingers across her neck, checking for a pulse, his gun held to his side as he glanced at the house.

"I have no idea."

Officer Benton Dryson shouted something else, but he didn't hear what it was. All of his attention was focused on Claira. She had to breathe!

Nearing a full-on panic attack himself, he laid Claira flat on her back and propped her head back. He held his ear to her mouth, hoping for even a small sound when she sucked in a shuddering breath, exhaling it out with a broken groan and a cough.

"That's it, darlin'. Breathe for me. You can do it." His hands bracketed her head as he leaned over and looked down into her terror-filled eyes. "Follow me, Claira; in through your nose, out through your mouth." Matt breathed in deep through his nose and pressed his lips out as he exhaled, coaching her. Her eyes focused on his and each breath she took came a little easier.

"Sir?" A voice called from somewhere next to him as a hand clamped over his shoulder. He shrugged it off and continued to breathe with Claira. "Sir, you need to move so we can help her." Matt didn't move until he heard Benton's voice calling him.

"Matt, you need to let them check her out," Benton said and held out his hand to help him from the grass. Matt raised his head and saw the EMTs crowding in around them. He moved to Claira's side but didn't leave her. "I'm right here, darlin'. They're going to help you, but I'm not leavin' you alone."

Her eyes followed him when he moved to let the paramedics move closer. When they crowded around her, blocking their gazes, Matt stood to his feet and mumbled a curse. Someone was going to pay for this.

"Matt?" Benton called over to where he stood near his patrol car. He jerked his head up, taking in Benton and the scene around them, wondering when the hell all the other officers and bystanders had shown up. Benton walked to him and stood with his arms crossed. "The house is clear. Want to tell me what the hell happened here?"

Matt turned to watch as they moved Claira onto a stretcher, clamping his hand against the back of his neck as he shrugged. "Damn if I know, Benton. Mason and I, we called your dad about her water heater and met him here about an hour ago to take a look at it. Claira wasn't here. Frank and Mason took off to the hardware store to pick up a new one while I stayed here to disconnect the old one. I stepped out back for a minute and heard a car door slam. When I rounded the corner, Claira fell out of her car screaming for me to get away. She was frantic, Benton. What the hell happened?" Matt didn't think he would ever forget the look of sheer terror in her eyes.

"She called in a B&E and then dispatch lost her call after she screamed your name into the phone," Benton explained. "The house is clear, no signs of forced entry. Is it possible she mistook you for an intruder?"

Matt paused, playing back as much as he could remember. "It's possible, I guess, but Benton I've never seen anyone that scared. And why would she get out of her car and run to me if she thought I was the one who'd broken in?"

Benton unfolded his arms and placed one fist on his hip, the other palm resting on the butt of his holstered gun. He cocked his head and motioned for Matt to follow him. "I don't know, but I want to show you something."

Matt shook his head, his eyes following the swarm of people around Claira. "I don't want to leave her."

"She's fine, Matt. She's probably just in shock. It will only take a minute."

Matt fought the urge to push his way past the EMTs to make sure she was okay. He shoved his hands into his pockets to keep from punching something, or someone, and followed Benton up the stairs and into the house. The rooms were flooded with light and there were several officers milling around the living room. Benton paused as they passed through the front doorway.

"What do you make of this?" He turned and pointed to a thin, braided string running down the wall.

Matt knelt to his haunches and followed it through a row of tiny hooks to the bottom of the door. No matter how he looked at it he couldn't make sense of it. "What is it?"

Benton flipped on the nearby light switch, closed the front door and looped the end of the string over the switch. "Open the door," he ordered, nodding for Matt to follow his lead.

Matt opened the door and the switch promptly fell into the 'off' position. "What the hell?"

"Yeah, took me a few minutes to figure it out myself." Benton scratched his head. "I know my dad wouldn't have put this up like this before he rented the place out."

"Why would Claira do something like this?" Matt asked, feeling an uneasy stir in his gut.

Benton cocked his brow and then shrugged his shoulders. He flipped the switch a few times, peered through the front window at the globe outside. "The bulb must be blown. My guess is, she's rigged it for some kind of advanced warning system and panicked when she saw it wasn't on. I was hoping you might be able to fill me in as to why she'd think up something like this."

Matt shook his head. "I have no idea, but I'm going to find out."

"She mention anything to you about being in trouble?" Benton asked him after they stepped back out onto the front porch.

Matt shook his head. "Mason thought she might be hidin' from somethin', someone, but, no. She hasn't said a word. We only met her a few days ago. There hasn't been time."

"You and your brothers seeing her?" Twin emotions played in Benton's eyes. Shock and approval gleamed back from his cousin's expression.

Matt nodded. "Sort of." He didn't know if declaring their intentions to the local PD before talking to her about it was the smartest move, even if Benton was family.

"I'll try to blow off the report since this isn't technically a crime, but watch your back, cuz. If she is runnin' from an ex-boyfriend or some psycho…"

A loud voice crackled over the radio at Benton's side, rattling off a string of numeric codes before he could finish his warning. Benton responded with a string of his own and motioned for Matt to get moving. "She hyperventilated; a bit of mild shock, but they're taking her to the hospital to be sure. I'll call Mason and Grey if you want to go with her."

Matt didn't hesitate, his feet carrying him at a dead run toward the ambulance before he could utter a response.

Chapter Thirteen

A light flashed and flooded the dark room long enough for Claira to see that she was in her father's study. The pounding thunder vibrated the polished hardwood beneath her bones, prodding her to move. Her hip ached and her head was spinning, trying desperately to make sense of the darkness.

Another flash of light sparked, this one brighter than the last and the thunder closer behind it. Shadows danced along the dark walls, creating a mystic play against the sounds of the storm. Fragmented memories filled her mind faster than she could make sense of them. Her brother! Stephan and her father were arguing. Shouts of rage filled the room and helplessness ripped at her chest. He would kill Stephan if she didn't do something.

Stephan! Claira pushed against the floor, bracing herself on the nearby footrest, almost fainting at the pain that wracked her body. Holding a trembling hand to her stomach, she braced her other forearm on the footstool as she waited for another flash of light.

Stephan!

When the next flash came, she crouched on her hands and knees and crawled through the surrounding darkness toward the door. Her hand landed in something sticky and wet, sliding out from under her. With a crack, her chin hit the floor and she rolled to her side. The smell was horrid and the nausea tripled in force causing her to wretch, losing the meager contents of her stomach.

Stephan!

Gasping for air she pushed forward, slipping again. She felt a hard bundle under her breasts. Her hands grasped the long, heavy object and a scream tore from her lungs as she felt the crisp hair along its surface. Hands trembling, she followed the limp limb, feeling her way to the man's chest.

Stephan?

She prayed it wasn't him, but somewhere in her shattered heart she knew it was. As if to deliver the final line of a tragic poem, another flash of light spilled through the windows and her eyes met the cold, dead stare of her only brother's lifeless eyes.

"Stephan! Noooo!"

"Claira, sweetheart. Wake up." A familiar soothing voice echoed through her nightmare. "Wake up, Claira. You're safe, sweetheart. We have you now."

"We won't let anything happen to you, darlin'. You're safe here with us."

Claira's sobs stopped. She jolted from the bed as consciousness settled in around her. Through puffy eyes she searched the darkness until her gaze settled on Matt, and then Mason lying on the bed on either side of where she'd been.

"Where am I?" Before the words were out, more broken memories flooded her fuzzy thoughts and filled in a few of the gaps. "I'm at your house. How...?" She squeezed her eyes closed, trying to remember how she'd gotten there.

Mason sat up beside her, cupping her shoulders with his big palms, his eyes searching to connect with her confused gaze. "Lie back down, sweetheart. You're in Matt's room. We brought you home from the hospital so you can rest."

"Hospital?" *Oh God.* They'd taken her to the hospital. Being admitted into a hospital was like waving a white flag. He would know where to find her. *Wait.* She hadn't been admitted, if she was here. And even if she was, Lucien didn't know her new name. All of her identification was in order. No one would question it, would they? Claira tensed, her eyes darting around the dark room. "Where's my purse?"

"It's on the table in the hall," Mason spoke in hushed tones, trying to soothe her sudden panic. "Would you like me to get it for you?"

Claira studied him for a moment, both concern and helplessness evident in his expression. She shook her head. She was safe there, for the moment. "Where are the twins?" She couldn't let them find her in their fathers' bed.

"They're at our parent's for the night, sweetheart. The doctors said you needed rest."

She remembered snippets of the EMTs treating her in her front yard, and Matt's eyes staring down at her. She turned to look at Matt, reaching out to touch his face as her memory crystallized. He was okay. "I'm so sorry," she sighed, her lips trembling to hold back a sob. "I should never have—"

"Darlin', don't say that." Matt sat up behind her, wrapped his arms around her shoulders. "You did nothin' to be sorry for. We should've called you before we came over to look at the water heater. Frank said it would be days if he had to do it on his own, so Mason and I met him there this mornin' to help. He wanted to wait for you to come home, but I didn't think you'd mind. I'm the one who's sorry, Claira. It was my fault they didn't wait for you."

Claira tensed at the thought of Matt inside the house alone with that monster. "But how did you get in? I changed the locks and Frank didn't have a key."

"The door was unlocked when we got there. Sweetheart, this is a small town, but not that small. And you live in the city proper. You should lock your doors when you're not there." Mason met Matt's stare over Claira's head, but she didn't understand the look they shared.

"It wasn't locked?" She didn't understand. She always locked her door, as well as completed all of the other steps she'd incorporated into her routine. Had she been so distracted by her thoughts of them that she'd forgotten to lock the door?

"What about the alarm?" She asked with a yawn. Feeling a bit dizzy, she reached up and massaged her throbbing temples.

"Frank punched in the code," Matt said pulling her down to the mattress to lie beside him. He snuggled her to his chest and pressed his lips to the top of her forehead. "Just relax, darlin'. It was all a big misunderstanding. We didn't mean to scare you. We can talk about it in the mornin'."

That sounded right. Frank knew the security code. She couldn't believe she hadn't locked the door. Her lungs filled with fresh air on another deep yawn.

"The sedative the nurse gave you is still making you groggy, sweetheart. Sleep and we'll talk about all this in the morning." Mason stretched out behind her and settled his chin on her shoulder, pressing a light kiss to her neck.

"What time is it?" She asked on another yawn, unable to resist snuggling into their comforting warmth.

"Eight thirty, I guess." Matt's hand caressed her arm. Mason's hand lay heavily against her hip, drawing small, soothing circles that seemed to dull her nerves and heighten her awareness of them at the same time.

"I've been sleeping that long?" She mumbled against Matt's chest, feeling the moisture of her hot breath against her cold nose.

"Mmm-hmm," he nuzzled her closer. "We've got you, darlin'. Close your eyes and let us hold you a while."

She'd obviously forgotten to lock the door, and in her panicked state never once considered that Matt or Mason, or even Frank had been in her house to help her. That was all.

Their warm hands caressed her skin. She was cold. So cold. The feel of their skin against hers felt so good. So warm. She was safe, for now.

~*~*~*~*~

From his bedroom doorway, Grey listened as Matt and Mason crept down the stairs, leaving Claira asleep in Matt's room. When they disappeared into the kitchen, he snuck to the foot of the stairs and listened as Matt relayed all of the details of what had happened at Claira's. By the time Matt was through, Grey was seething. Having heard enough, he turned without a sound and crept up the stairs.

He'd heard Claira's sobs earlier that evening and had slipped into Mason's room next door, listening to the sounds of their voices, wishing he could join them. Knowing the beautiful, helpless creature was alone and frightened beyond belief, not ten feet above his own bed, he couldn't bear the thought of leaving her.

Grey paused in the doorway and studied her pale complexion as the moonlight flirted with the shiny strands of her curls. She lay still, curled in a tight ball, her hands and knees drawn into her chest. She was so small and defenseless, like a baby bird that had fallen from her nest. *My baby bird.*

Only the sound of her steady breaths filled the room, calling to him like a whispered prayer. Without thought, his feet shifted silently across the hardwood floor. He pulled off his tee-shirt and slid slowly onto the mattress behind her.

Stretching out beside her, he froze when she turned in his arms and snuggled into his chest. He lowered his arm, his hand skimming across the silken skin of her shoulder.

The tense knot in his chest relaxed for the first time since he met her, allowing him to take his first deep breath in days. He would never forget this moment, when he first touched her. The softness of her curves against his rough, calloused hands felt magical as he stroked her skin. Lost in the sensation of her touch, he didn't notice her soulful, brown eyes staring at him until his hand had trailed the length of her arm and began its journey back to the top of her delicate shoulder.

Neither of them said a word when their gazes met and held for what seemed like an eternity. Finally, Claira's eyes fluttered closed and she lowered her head into the crook of his arm, her soft, angelic face resting against his chest. Grey released a strangled breath as her arm circled around him and hugged him closer.

He didn't know how to explain it, but at that moment he would have given his life for her to never have to feel afraid again. What sick fuck would want to hurt such a tiny, delicate being? His arms folded around her and he rested his hand against her cheek. The last piece of his broken heart fall away and a new rhythm sounded in its place.

He knew then that he was lost to her, before he'd ever truly found himself after Sarah's death. Somehow he would have to reconcile the finality of it all or he'd lose Claira, too.

The sounds of hushed footfalls ascended the stairs and he met his brothers' gazes over Claira's shoulder when they paused in the darkened doorway. "She shouldn't be alone," he whispered. He knew his brothers would understand the meaning behind the words he couldn't yet say. They lingered there a moment, taking in the sight of her curled securely in his embrace before they turned and left them alone together.

Chapter Fourteen

The scent of pine and something definitively masculine whirled around Claira like a summer breeze, filling her lungs and sending warm waves of desire through her limbs. She'd awoken twice during the night, once with Grey's strong arms around her, holding and caressing her while she slept. Before dawn, she rose again to use the bathroom, gulping down a much needed cup of water and taking a swig of the mouthwash that sat on the bathroom counter to wash away the sticky cotton in her mouth.

To her disappointment, Grey was gone when she awoke that last time, but Mason had been snuggled against her in his place. Now she could feel the unmistakable strength of not one but two warm, male bodies pressed against her, along with two quite intimidating erections. She felt a flush of heat rise to her cheeks and ricochet down between her thighs.

"Good morning, sweetheart." Mason smoothed the hair away from her face as she opened her eyes, his deep, comforting voice as soothing as his touch. Her breath caught when she found his baby blues staring back at her, his blond lashes so long they nearly concealed the creases at the corners of his eyes when he smiled.

He leaned in and placed a chaste kiss on her forehead then buried his nose in her hair and took a long, lingering breath. "Christ, you smell good."

She felt Matt's arm encircle her waist from behind and she turned to see his identical glorious smile. From the angle of the sun's early morning light shining through the window, she could see a hint of hazel flecks near the edges of his blue eyes and wondered if Mason's had them, too.

"Good mornin', darlin'," Matt said, his smile widening before he leaned in and captured her bottom lip between his. His kiss was gentle and playful, but ended as quickly as it began. "You scared me yesterday, Claira," he said, brushing his knuckles over her cheek.

"I'm sorry," she sighed. Matt tried to interrupt her, but she pushed ahead, determined to make him understand that she wasn't the raving lunatic she'd morphed into the day before. "I overreacted. I saw that the porch lamp was out and I got scared. My mind made a mountain out of nothing, and I'm sorry I put you through that."

"What I don't understand is why?" Mason asked, turning her chin so that she was forced to look at him. "Who are you running from, Claira, that you have to go to such extreme and archaic measures?"

She tried to look away, but Mason wouldn't let her. He pulled her chin up a little more and pressed his lips to hers in a reassuring kiss. "Tell us who's done this to you, sweetheart. We won't let them hurt you again, ever."

She would be lying if she said she hadn't been tempted to tell them everything. She couldn't explain why, but she trusted them explicitly, without question. The less they knew the better. There was nothing to tell, really. That life was over. After the complete fiasco the day before, she was ready to let go, put her past away for good and start her new life over, hopefully with them in it.

"It doesn't matter." She shrugged, looking back at Matt. "That part of my life is over. Please let it go." She leaned back and looked at Matt, the need to kiss him overwhelming her shyness. "Kiss me," she whispered, her voice shuddering with uncertainty as she pressed her lips to his.

"Claira," Matt breathed, brushing his tongue over her bottom lip. When she opened her mouth to him, he slid his tongue deep inside and tangled it with hers. His erection thickened and pressed against her lower back. When his hips flexed hard against her, she couldn't contain the moan that clawed its way from her chest.

~*~*~*~*~

Matt's pulse surged in response. He knew he should demand more answers, but he couldn't stop the raging need to possess her. The mewling sounds she made in the back of her throat were like electricity pulsing through his bloodstream, pushing him precariously close to the edge. She made him feel like an untried teenager.

He lifted himself above her and nudged her knees apart with his own, settling comfortably into the cradle of her thighs. Wrapping his forearms beneath her shoulders, he buried his hands in her hair, holding her as he deepened their kiss.

His hips rolled against her pelvis, the zipper on his jeans pressing painfully against his swollen cock. They both released a tortured groan, and he felt the bed dip beside them. Breathless, Matt broke the kiss and turned to see Mason leaving the room.

"Don't go," Claira pleaded, her spoken declaration sending shivers down his spine. She'd accepted them; both of them.

Mason turned and propped his hip on the side of the mattress. Stretching out across the top of the bed, he traced his thumb across her kiss-swollen lips. "Are you sure, sweetheart? Are you sure you want both of us?"

Claira nodded and Matt's cock jumped in response. Her chocolate eyes shifted between them and then closed on a sigh. "I don't know if it's right or wrong, and…and I don't care about that anymore. I want you. Both of you."

"Ah, Claira, sweetheart, we want you, too." Mason leaned down and kissed her.

Matt pulled back and unzipped his jeans, rolling them past his hips, but left his boxers on. He tossed his jeans to the floor and resumed his position between her outstretched thighs.

"Is this what you really want, darlin'?" Matt had to make sure. He sensed her hesitancy. He would never do anything to hurt her, but he didn't think he could stop once he was skin to skin with her, the need to connect with her so strong after the chaos of the day before.

Claira nodded, worrying her bottom lip between her teeth. "I'm sorry, but I haven't…"

Matt and Mason shared a worried glance. Mason gave him a little shrug. "Are you a virgin, sweetheart?" Mason asked, trying to tamp down the surprise in his voice. There was no freaking way she could be. If she was, then Matt could kiss his position between her legs goodbye, because there was no way in hell he was he giving that gift to his brother without a fight, twin or not.

"I…no…I just…" Claira stumbled over her words, her cheeks turning rosy with her innocent blush.

Reading her body, Matt snuggled closer and pressed his swollen cock against the spot he knew would bring her the most pleasure.

He'd make damn sure she enjoyed every moment of this. "There's nothing to be embarrassed about, darlin'. Show us what you like and we'll make you feel good."

Claira closed her eyes and shook her head. God, she wished they had just kept moving. She didn't want to have to tell them. "That's just it," she said after an unbearable silence. "I don't really know. I've only done this once and I wasn't very good at it."

Matt swallowed, hard. He hated to ask but he had to know. "Do you mean with two men, or once, period?"

"Oh—only once, period," she stammered. "I was in college. It was a long time ago, and I…"

Mason grinned at Matt and then turned and captured her lips again in a gentle kiss. When he pulled away, she opened her eyes and Matt could see the hidden desires there.

"Sweetheart, no one is good at this their first time. Well, except for me," Mason said. Matt rolled his eyes and Claira giggled. "We'll teach you how to love us."

"And we'll have an incredibly fun time learning what you like," Matt teased, his hips rolling against hers again, his eyebrows bouncing mischievously above his laughing eyes.

Matt was rewarded with another one of her giggles. Man, he could listen to that sound for an eternity and never get tired of hearing it. He disappeared beneath the sheet and drew her panties down her legs, sending them flying over his shoulder where they landed on the dresser behind him.

"Oh Jesus! You smell good." His muffled groan vibrated against her wet, sensitive cleft and her back arched from a pleasure she'd never known.

"Told you." Mason threw off the sheet, revealing Matt's position between her thighs. He never thought he would experience this with his brothers again. Being with a woman on his own had satisfied his carnal needs, but never fulfilled him the way making love to a woman they all loved together had. He could feel Grey's absence, but after seeing him with her the night before, he knew it was only a matter of time before Grey would join them; completing them.

Mason skimmed his hand along Claira's hip and feathered his fingers along the curves and valleys leading to her ripe, lush breasts.

As Matt's tongue danced along her folds then disappeared into her hot, wet core, Mason pushed her shirt over her breasts and circled his tongue around one taut, bronze nipple, eliciting another desperate moan from her lips before moving to the other. He couldn't wait to have those rosy lips wrapped around his throbbing cock, but not yet. This was about her pleasure and learning her body's needs and desires.

Claira writhed beneath them. Matt was teetering on the edge, the need to claim her so intense. "You like that?" He folded his tongue and pushed it further into her sweet pussy, gathering her thick, fragrant arousal. "Fuck, Claira. You taste sweeter than honey and somethin' else completely indescribable. I can't get enough of you."

Claira pressed her thighs together around Matt's head as her back arched against the bed, pressing her breast harder against Mason's incredible tongue. The things they were doing to her with just their mouths made her world spin. She didn't understand the force that hummed through her body. She needed something, anything….

"Please," she begged, unsure of what she was begging for.

"Please, what?" Matt looked up at her, his lips glistening with her essence. He recognized the need in her eyes. "You need to come, darlin'? Is that what you want?"

"I…oh don't stop. I don't know." She arched her hips against Matt's face, urging him to continue, her body seeking what she didn't know to ask for.

"Don't worry, sweetheart. He'll give you what you need." Mason traced the globe of her breast with the tip of his tongue one final time before he nipped her nipple. His bite blazed a fire that shot straight to her core as Matt sucked on the sensitive place at the top of her sex and hummed his approval.

Claira flew apart, floating up and out, a million pieces in a million different directions into a whole new world where light shined brighter than the sun and a warmth like she'd never felt melted her bones into a fiery lava. She floated there in an unknown heaven, her body humming and pulsing until she heard a silken voice calling to her.

"Claira," Matt whispered, crooning in her ear. "Sweet Claira. You're so beautiful when you're flyin'." He peppered her face with small, sweet kisses as her breathing calmed and she drifted back to Earth.

"I…I've never…it's too much, so wonderful," she panted, her heart lurching in her chest as her body continued to shake with her release.

"Was that your first orgasm?" Matt was stunned they were her first. It was too much to hope for.

"I'm hoping that's what that was," she giggled, unable to hold back her smile. "Because I don't think I could handle anything better than that."

"Oh, it gets *way* better than that, darlin'. I promise." Matt chuckled and covered her mouth, devouring her laughter as he drank from her lips. She could taste herself heavily on his tongue before he broke away and kissed a trail down to her breasts. "I've yet to taste these beauties," he continued to tease, caressing the tip of one taut nipple with his thumb before he sucked it into his mouth.

"He's a breast man." Mason chuckled and tilted her mouth toward him, releasing a primal growl of his own when the taste of her pussy exploded on this tongue, firing his taste buds to life. "God, I've missed your taste." Tipping his head to the side, he deepened their kiss, his teeth lightly nicking against hers as he explored her mouth, gathering her unique flavor before retreating to skim her lips and plunging in again.

She tensed when she felt Matt's penis nudge at her opening. "Relax, darlin'. Let me in."

Mason trailed his fingertips over her collarbone, down to the valley between her breasts and cupped one in his big palm, kneading her soft flesh. As Matt rolled his hips, nudging the swollen head of his cock into her slick, wet passage, Mason pinched her nipple and rolled it between his thumb and forefinger, simultaneously deepening their kiss again.

Claira cries of pleasure mingled with Matt's, her back arching off the bed with the same pleasured responses as before. "God, Claira! So tight." Matt groaned, his efforts to hold back his release evident in the taut, corded muscles in his neck, the sheen of sweat blooming from his pores and hoarse cries clawing from his chest.

"Look at him, Claira." Mason pulled away from her lips and nodded to Matt hovering above her. "Look at the way his arms are shaking with the pleasure and pain of holding back his release. He wants it to last, sweetheart, but you're making it so good for him he's fighting not to let go."

The sensual picture Mason was painting with his erotic words and the sight of pure, male rapture in Matt's expression sent a spike of need and lust straight to Claira's womb. Her stomach muscles quivered and contracted. Her hips jolted up as Matt began a slight forward roll of his hips. His rock-hard cock pushed through her delicate, tight passage much deeper and faster than he'd intended.

"*Fuuuck!*" Matt's curse came on the heels of Claira's scream. "Darlin', I'm sorry. I'm so sorry." Trembling, Matt began to pull out, afraid he'd hurt her, but the thick, hot arousal that flowed through her tight, pulsing passage soothed his worry and spurred him toward his own spine melting orgasm.

Deeper and faster, he fed from her breathless moans as he moved inside her. Her whole body quivered around him as he lost control, pumping once, twice then roaring as he held himself stiff inside her. He could feel his cock pulse against the tip of her womb as his seed spilled in endless wave after endless wave.

Just as he thought he wouldn't be able to come again for the rest of his life—as he lay on top of her, their chests heaving together in breathless abandon—Claira's velvet sheath contracted around him again, sending a shock wave through his still half-hard cock. His hips pulsed against hers, triggering a secondary orgasm in them both. He cried out into the crook of Claira's neck, his teeth scraping against her shoulder as his dick pulsed to life inside her again. *Dear sweet God in heaven*, he didn't think it was possible to come twice in the same lay.

Matt laid his sweaty forehead against hers, his eyes closed, a smile on his face as they continued to pant through every breath. "Oh, you are so never leavin' this bed," he chuckled, bracing himself on his elbows.

"Hmmm," Claira hummed and turned her head toward the soft hand that caressed her cheek. She opened her eyes to see Mason's staring back at her in wonder, his eyes as dark as the deepest ocean.

"That was one of the most beautiful sights I've ever seen." His thumb slid over her lips, tracing along the seam as Matt continued to pepper slow, sensual kisses along her neck and shoulder.

Claira couldn't help the guilty feeling that pushed at the edges of the euphoria surrounding them. She glanced down at the apparent bulge tenting the front of Mason's black boxers and a frown pulled at the corner of her lips.

As if reading her thought's, Mason slid a finger under her chin and tipped her face back to his, pressing a soothing kiss against her swollen lips. He kissed the tip of her nose then pulled back to look at her. "It's okay, sweetheart. There will be plenty of time to get to that."

"But you didn't..." She chanced a timid glance back down to his groin. She was utterly boneless. She had nothing left to give. How could she physically satisfy two men?

Mason chuckled, reaching out to trace her cheekbone. "Oh, but I did, in a way. I felt every pulse, every sensation that passed between the two of you. It was incredible." The expression on her face told him she wasn't quite buying it. "We'll have our time, sweetheart, when you've had time to recover. There will be times when we're all together, and other times when each of us has you all to ourselves. But no matter what, you get the final say. We don't ever want you to feel pressured to be with any one or all of us."

Claira was astounded at what she felt swelling in her heart for this man; for both of them. Was this love? She didn't know, but all the wants and needs she'd held back her entire life seemed to burst through the dam she'd built to keep them at bay. "I want you, though. I want to feel you with me like this."

Mason placed another kiss on her nose and tweaked her nipple, eliciting a squeal from her and a laugh from Matt. "Believe me, sweetheart. I want you too. Let's get you into a warm bath and we'll see what happens after that."

Matt pushed up, both of them wincing as he pulled out of her tender sheath. He sat on the edge of the bed and slid the full condom from his spent cock. Claira gasped as the realization dawned. She hadn't once thought about protection. How was she supposed to remember all the do's and don'ts of something as elementary as sex when every brain cell in her head was liquefied every time they touched her.

Matt heard her shocked gasp and turned to see her staring at the wad of tissue in his hand. He grinned and patted her bare thigh with his empty one. "We'll always protect you, darlin'. You aren't on the pill, are you?"

She shook her head, worrying her lip between her teeth in that way that made him want to eat her alive.

"Don't worry about a thing, then. It's our job to always protect you, Claira." Matt stared into her sated, brown eyes, hoping she understood how serious they took that responsibility.

Chapter Fifteen

Billowy puffs of bubbles swirled around her sated and relaxed body as she reclined neck-deep in what had to be the largest bathtub known to man. The thin mat of coarse hair in the center of Mason's chest tickled her back when Matt, sitting across from her, lifted her legs and draped them over his thighs. "Feelin' better, darlin'?"

Claira giggled when he teased the arch of her foot with a light squeeze. "If I felt any better I'd be the elemental equivalent of Jell-*Oh*—that feels good." Her head fell back on a moan as Mason pressed his thumbs into the sore flesh between her shoulders. "I think I might have pulled something yesterday."

Matt exchanged a look with his brother, another silent message she didn't understand. "Who's Stephan?" he asked. His hand never ceased its soothing caresses on her foot, but his brows furrowed with concern when she hesitated to answer his question.

"Is—was he the one you told us about earlier?" Mason asked, placing his lips against the slow curve of her neck. "Your first?"

Claira pulled her legs from Matt's lap and drew her knees into her chest, resting her chin on top of them. She scooped up a handful of bubbles as she thought about what to tell them. Stephan had been her world after their mother left. Now that she didn't even have a picture of him, her memories were all that was left. The possibility of never sharing them with someone left a cold hollow in her chest. He deserved to be remembered.

"He was my brother," she finally said, scooping up another handful of bubbles, unable to look at either of them. "He died in an accident the day before my twenty-first birthday."

An accident she'd caused. Her memories of what happened that night were still fractured at best. The only thing she knew for sure was that, before she'd found him lying dead on her father's library floor, she'd held the gun that had shot him.

She'd taken the gun from her father's desk to protect him. He was so angry with their father, and the screaming wouldn't stop. Lucien had been marching toward Stephan with a look she knew all too well meant that Stephan was dead if she didn't do something. That's where her memories faded into nothingness. She woke up to a police officer standing over her, reading her rights. Her father had her arrested for murdering her own brother and her life as she knew it had fallen apart from there. But she couldn't tell them any of it. She couldn't tell anyone.

"I'm so sorry." Mason wrapped his strong arms around her. "What happened? Can you talk about it with us?"

Claira shook her head. "I..." She bit down hard on her cheek, determined not to cry. "He was my hero, my world. I miss him terribly, but I can't."

"That's ok, sweetheart. We understand, believe me," Mason said in a near whisper. "It's still hard to talk about Sarah sometimes."

"You loved her very much, didn't you?" A heavy guilt settled across her shoulders. She had no right to use their love for Sarah to divert their questioning about her brother. She simply couldn't tell them about what had happened the night Stephan died.

"We did," Matt said, grabbing the shampoo and pouring a generous amount into his palm. He motioned for Claira to lean back into Mason's arm and began massaging the clean smelling soap into her wet hair. "She died giving birth to Con and Car. She had a heart condition that had gone undiagnosed throughout her pregnancy and went into cardiac arrest minutes after Car was delivered." Matt's nostrils flared when his chest expanded on a deep, wrenching breath. "The doctors said she died instantly."

Mason looked down into her eyes as Matt scooped up a handful of water and drizzled it over her scalp. "It was the best and worst day of our lives."

Her heart seized for a beat and her chest began to ache. Some of the families of the children she'd worked with had splintered under the stress of such trivial things like a few missed car payments, or a string of late nights at the office. Their family had not only made it through one of the hardest tragedies the world could have thrown at them, they were still strong and bound by a love she'd thought only existed in fairytales.

"Can you tell me about her?" Claira knew it wasn't fair to ask it of them, especially when she'd avoided their questions about Stephan, but she felt an inexplicable desire to know the woman who had held these strong, wonderful men's hearts. When Mason nodded, but didn't continue, she asked what seemed like the least painful question she could think of. "How did you meet her?"

Matt chuckled as he rinsed the last of the shampoo from her hair. "She took my bottle away and gave it to her kitten."

"What?" Claira giggled at the unexpected image.

"We grew up together," Mason shrugged, smiling as he lifted her from the water and drew her back against his chest, his hands cupping her breasts and lifting them until her taught nipples peaked above the bubbles. "Our mothers were best friends. It was sort of expected for us to be together. We never expected anyone else to capture our hearts." His thumbs circled her nipples as he leaned in and caught her earlobe between his lips, sucking off a drop of water. "Until now," he whispered, his tongue flicking against the soft lobe, summoning the newly familiar ache between her thighs.

"Mason." She sighed and arched against his chest. Matt slid closer, his eyes fixed to Mason's hands on her breasts. She leaned her head back against Mason's shoulder as his hands left her sensitive nipples and slid over her ribs to her hips. He cupped her bare ass cheeks then continued up the back of her thighs to the bends of her knees, lifting and separated her legs, lowering her heels onto Matt's shoulders.

"Have I ever told you how gorgeous your legs are? So slender and perfectly toned."

"Ah, so he's the breast man and you're the leg man." Claira laughed as Mason tickled the back of her knees, sending cold shivers over her wet skin and hot spikes of need to her core.

Matt's hands appeared through the puffy suds and cupped her breasts. "Getting cold?" He asked, his heated gaze focusing on her rigid nipples.

Claira shook her head, unable to form the necessary syllables for a verbal response. Mason's fingers trailed over her shins, stopping to circle her kneecaps before tracing twin paths up her inner thighs. When his thumbs came together over her slit and spread her lower lips, Claira's back arched on a moan. Her heels slid from Matt's shoulders, her legs falling open and draping over the crooks of Matt's arms.

Matt leaned forward, spreading her legs wider for his brother as he sucked a hard nipple between his teeth. Mason's thick fingers traced her folds, exploring and caressing before pressing one into the depths of her tight, sensitive channel.

"Still sore, sweetheart?" Mason's voice rumbled in her ear. She sucked in a ragged breath through her teeth and tightened around his finger.

"Not much," she panted as his finger slid out and then slowly back in. She was a little tender, but not enough to want them to stop. She wanted—needed to feel them touch her.

One of Matt's hands left her breasts and found her hand under the water. He circled her wrist and brought her hand to his groin, wrapping her fingers around his engorged cock. She flinched when she touched him, but he covered her hand with his own and tightened his grip. "I'll show you," he said, dragging his lips across one nipple to the valley between her breasts.

Claira licked her lips, wishing she could see what they were doing, yet grateful for the cover the thick bubbles provided. She wasn't sure how to react or move and the distraction Mason was causing with his hands between her legs didn't help her already handicapped coordination. When Matt's hand moved hers up his thick shaft to the mushroom tip, they both moaned with pleasure.

~*~*~*~*~

Mason thought he'd go out of his mind with need. His dick was so hard it was going to rupture if something didn't happen soon. He'd already tested the limits of his control when he passed up her earlier offer. He hadn't wanted to make their first time unpleasant for her, but damn he didn't think he could take any more.

One finger in her pussy, he moved his free hand between him and Claira and gripped his own dick. He pumped in time with his fingered thrusts into Claira's scorching hot sheath and the motion of her hand on Matt. Dammit, he needed her heat around his cock and those legs around his waist!

When Claira's passage began to tighten like a vise around his fingers and her back arched into a tight bow, he knew she was close. He deepened his thrusts, crooking his fingers to find that special spot, at the same time easing his pinky down toward her back passage. His dick pulsed in his hand when he circled the tiny, smooth pucker, expecting her to tense against the unexpected sensation. Her husky groan spurred his desire and he sank the tip of his pinky past her tight ring of muscles on the next inward plunge. She soared, shouting her release as she bucked against his hand.

Joining her in his own explosive release, Mason's head fell back, his lips stretched tight across his teeth as he cried out behind her, his fist pumping in time with her inner spasms. Matt had to be close behind them.

He saw something shift behind them and looked past Matt to see Grey leaning against the doorframe, his right hand aggressively massaging the bulge behind his zipper.

Coming down from his high, Matt opened his eyes to see his telling gaze fixed to something behind him. He and Claira turned at the same time to look for themselves at what had captured Mason's attention.

"Oh God." Claira's hand drew back from Matt's cock as she flailed against Mason, trying to sit up. When she looked down and saw that her breasts were on full display for Grey to look his fill, she slid back down beneath the bubbles, hoping there was enough to cover her.

"It's okay, sweetheart." Mason pulled her back to his chest and wrapped his arms around her shoulders, covering her bare breasts. As if *that* was any better.

She was humiliated. She knew it was silly. These three men had once shared a wife. Grey seemed to look straight through her. She didn't think he liked what he saw. The protective and caring way he'd held her the night before, adding to the safety she'd felt for the first time in so long, warred with the almost hostile and brooding way he was staring at her now. She suddenly felt like an interloper; like she was treading on hallowed ground, and all for reasons she could easily understand.

Before the embarrassment could claim her life as she'd silently prayed it would, Grey's hands dropped to his sides, drawing out her desire to look at him. She'd only seen him in a business suit. Dressed in faded, worn, blue jeans, a hunter-green button up that made his angry, green eyes look like glowing jewels, he looked…hard. Everything about him seemed strong and tough. His sleeves rolled up to his elbows, his muscles bunched and flexed; his stance rigid and tense.

His expression as unyielding as his posture, he cleared his throat with a growl and crossed his arms over his broad chest. Tearing his gaze from her virtually naked form, he looked first at Mason, then Matt.

"We have a heifer down, up on Logan Bluff. Sheriff Long called it in about ten minutes ago. Saw it when he flew over on his way back from a trip to Missoula."

He glanced back at Claira and then down at his boots, toeing the bottom of the doorframe with his boot. He shoved his hands into his pockets and turned to go, but then stopped, pausing in the doorway.

All she could see was his broad back as he leaned a shoulder against the doorframe. His slumped shoulders rose on a breath. She thought for a moment he was going to turn back around, but he dropped his head and pushed off the open frame again. "We need to ride up there now while we still have plenty of light." Without a look back, Grey stepped away from the door and disappeared.

Chapter Sixteen

Ten minutes later Matt met Grey at the top of the stairs and they raced down to the main floor together. When Grey pulled up short and darted into the kitchen, Matt paused in the hallway, a little confused. He turned to see what his big brother was doing. Thinking he'd maybe gone to get a thermos of coffee for the long ride ahead of them, Matt was a little puzzled to see Grey bent over in the pantry, the upper half of his body buried in the chest freezer.

"What the…?" When Grey reemerged with a large bag and paced past him toward the front door, Matt had to ask. "What's with the frozen peas?"

Grey paused in the hall and grabbed his Stetson from the hook near the front door. "It's been a long time since I've been in the saddle with a hard-on, but I'm sure it still hurts like a sonofabitch."

Fuck! Grey was right. As Grey headed out the door toward the barn, Matt turned and ran back to the pantry. He stirred the frozen contents in the overstuffed freezer until his hand landed on another bag and pulled it from the pile. "Carrots." He slammed the freezer door shut and tore out to meet Grey. Who the hell cared what vegetable it was, as long as they numbed his dick enough to survive the trek to Logan Bluff and back.

They were saddled up, iced down and about an hour into the two and a half hour trip before Matt broke the silence between them. "What did Benton have to say this mornin' when you went over to meet him and his dad at Claira's?"

Grey shifted in his saddle. "Frank changed out the porch lamp while Benton and I cleaned up the mess in the front yard."

Matt peered at Grey and scratched at his eyebrow. "That was thoughtful, but you still didn't answer my question."

Grey slowed as he guided his paint over a precarious section of rock. Once they were both safely around the hazard, he turned in his saddle and looked back at Matt. "She's not going back there."

"Dammit, Grey. Would you just spit it out?" Matt was about two seconds from pulling Grey off his damn horse and beating it out of him, again.

"Benton's called in a favor with one of his Ranger buddies down in Fort Worth. He's running a check on Claira with the information he already has, but he's asking this guy to dig around, see what he comes up with."

Matt pulled his horse up short. "What the hell? You're runnin' a check on *her*? Shouldn't we be focusin' on whoever this bastard is that has her scared out of her mind?"

"Goddammit!" Grey turned his horse around to face him. "You were there! She's not talking. We start with what we know, and right now all I know is that some sick bastard is tormenting a sweet, innocent school teacher that makes my dick so hard I can't think straight. I know we're not letting her go back there. I know we're not letting her go anywhere or do anything that doesn't include one of us until we figure out what the fuck is going on. We'll talk to Uncle Cade, too. He might still have access to some of his old contacts with the Feds. He can start looking at whatever this guy in Fort Worth digs up."

Grey straightened in his saddle and spurred his horse back around toward the trail. Matt clicked his tongue and his horse trotted up beside him. "So you were watchin' us this mornin'? You were listenin' and watchin' but you didn't have the balls to—"

"Fuck you, asshole." Grey shot back.

"You like her, a lot. Admit it." Matt didn't need Grey to confirm a damn thing. He could sit up there on his *high horse* as long as he wanted, but it was going to be fucking awesome to see him fall off the damn thing and straight into Claira's heart.

When Grey didn't bite at his bait, Matt decided to let it go and focus on a different piece of the puzzle. "We can't keep her locked up at the farm, Grey. She's sweet, and *very* innocent, but she's got a job. And who says she wants us bossin' her around?"

"If she doesn't like it then she can start talking. She seems to like you two well enough to make the effort." He stood up in the stirrups, adjusting himself with a curse. "Fuck, these peas are thawed."

"She'll want you, too, when you stop bein' an ass and give her a chance." Matt squirmed, his saddle was feeling more and more like a frozen torture chair to his balls. At least he'd had some release this morning. God had he ever. He didn't know how Mason had held back and he sure as hell didn't know why Grey's balls hadn't imploded already. It wasn't just because Claira was so beautiful. This thing inside him that pulled him to her was brutal and relentless.

Grey grunted a cryptic response and heeled his paint to a brisk trot once they hit the clearing at the top of the bluff. Wondering what Mason and Claira were doing back at the ranch, Matt spurred his horse to a gallop and caught up with his brother, the ache in his groin growing more punishing with every stride. Whatever it was, it had to be more fun than this. Good-time Charlie wasn't having a very good time, at all.

D.L. Roan

Chapter Seventeen

Mason smiled at Claira when she walked into the barn, his hand slowing to a stop on top of the horse he was grooming. When the door closed behind her, it took a moment for her eyes to adjust to the dim light inside. His gaze swept over her and her cheeks heated with her blush.

"Thanks for the tee-shirt." She said, fingering the hem that hung to her knees.

"It looks good on you," he said with a flirty wink.

She took a few cautious steps, shying away from the big animal between them, watching the horse warily from where she stopped a few stalls down. The beast was enormous. Seeing Mason petting it as if it were no bigger than a dog gave her a strange sense of pride and awe.

His big hands looked small moving across the massive expanse of its back and shoulders, yet he exuded such a sense of control and mastery in his touch. She wondered if the horse felt the same calm as she did when he touched her.

"He's beautiful," she said, stepping back when the horse turned its head and looked at her.

"Easy, boy." Mason crooned to the horse in a soft soothing tone as he slid his hands around the horse's chest and up his neck. He stepped around to the other side and reached for her hand.

Claira froze for a second, but something in Mason's eyes and gentle way eased her anxiety. She reached out and took his hand. He held onto the halter along the horse's head and brought her hand up to the horse's nose.

"No sudden movements," he said calmly. "Just let him smell you."

Claira's heart raced with anxious excitement when the animal brushed his nose against her palm, its hot breath dampening her skin when it took in an inquisitive, powerful sniff and snorted it back out again. The whiskers on his nose tickled her skin as she raised her hand to feel the gray-black fur on his chin.

"It's so soft," she gasped in surprise, running her fingertips along the wrinkled velvet, taking care not to get too close to its mouth. When she dropped her hand, afraid to push her luck, the horse dropped his head and nudged her hand with his snout.

"He likes that," Mason laughed and guided her hand back to the horse. "I think you found another new friend."

"What's his name?" she asked, feeling as if she were touching some mystical creature, sensing the leashed power that stirred within.

Mason rubbed the spot between the horse's eyes and smiled. "He has an official name as long as my arm that reflects his bloodline, but I've yet to find a suitable barn name for him. He has an intriguing personality and I can't quite pin down a name that fits."

Claira lowered her hand and took a cautious step back, her gaze moving over the horse's massive form. She felt so small and insignificant standing next to two such majestic beings. Something about the way Mason moved around the horse made her stare in awe. It was like he was part of the animal; two halves of a whole.

Mason caught her watching him and she snapped her gaze back to the horse. "His color is almost like a gray mist, with a little blue mixed in. Like a ghost. It's very unique."

Mason chuckled and picked up a brush from a nearby table. "He's a roan." He reached out and took Claira's hand, placing the thin round comb in her hand.

"What's that mean? Is it a breed?" Claira let him guide her to the horse's side. Placing his hand on top of hers he began stroking the horse's coat.

"It's his coloring," Mason explained. "He's technically black, but a rare gene causes his coat to lose its pigment at the end of the strands, turning them white. They've never been able to isolate the gene that causes it, so it's not something that can be controlled with breeding. It's one of nature's little surprises that mankind has yet to find a way to manipulate. I think that's part of what makes him special."

Claira studied the way the beast's color changed as they moved. "It's like magic."

Mason's free arm wrapped around her waist, pulling her against him as he guided her hand in long, sensuous strokes over the horse's coat. The rhythm of their movement was timed perfectly with the horse's deep breaths and it wasn't long before Claira found herself wrapped in a magical spell.

Neither of them spoke as they moved. The sounds of the brush raking across the coarse coat and the horse's strong lungs pumping one deep breath after another were the only sounds filling the large space. She took a deep breath, inhaling the unique scents of horse and hay, closing her eyes as she leaned into Mason's arms and let him guide her body with his. They moved as one, caressing and flowing together like a dance they'd practiced a hundred times. *Magic.*

Claira felt like she was in a dream, weightless and floating along on a cloud, when Mason's grip on her loosened. She opened her eyes as he lowered her onto a bed of hay in one of the stalls, his warm hands roaming and caressing her skin; just as they'd moved along the horse. His bright blue eyes were darker than they'd been earlier, swirling with desire.

She reached out and touched his cheek and he turned into her caress, kissing her palm. "I need you," he whispered softly, his breath tickling her skin. "Can you take me?"

Her stomach flipped and her heart fluttered. Feeling swept along in a tide she couldn't control, she lowered her hand and tugged at his belt. She needed him too.

Claira worked at the buttons on his jeans with both hands, groaning in frustration when the second button snagged. Mason stood and made quick work of freeing his cock. Toeing off his boots, he shed his jeans and boxers in one swift movement then reached for Claira, but she swatted him away.

"I want to taste you," she said as she stared in fascination, eye level with his swollen cock. She reached up and ran her finger through the pearly drop of fluid on his tip. Curious, she brought it to her lips, tasting it with the tip of her tongue. His taste was different than she'd expected, salty with a faint bitter tint.

~*~*~*~*~

Mason grabbed his dick and circled the base in a tight fist. "*Jesus,*" he moaned, torn between the need to sink into her tight pussy for the first time, and the desire to fill her mouth with more of his seed. Did she have any idea how sexy that was?

He knew he wouldn't last a minute in that hot, sweet mouth of hers, but he couldn't deny her pleading expression. He took a step closer and brushed the swollen head across her plump lips. "Lick it, sweetheart. Oh, yeah, that's it."

Claira tilted her head and twirled her tongue around the bulbous head. Mason's breath hissed through his teeth when her tongue pushed against the hole, retrieving another drop and swirling it around and down his shaft.

When her tongue flattened out and wiggled along his shaft on her way back to his tip, Mason thought he'd bust a nut if he didn't get inside her one way or another. "Open up, sweetheart. Wrap your lips over your teeth." Mason placed his hand on the top of her head and guided his cock over her lips. "Oh, fuck yeah! That's it. Suck me."

Her lips stretched around his girth as he pushed a little deeper and tapped the back of her throat. He palmed her cheeks and tilted her head up a little. "Look at me, sweetheart."

When she looked up and saw the ecstasy in his eyes, a feeling of power overwhelmed her. She was doing that to him, giving him pleasure the way he and Matt had done for her. When he bumped the back of her throat again she tensed, but he didn't push any further. He pulled back again and she tightened her lips, swirling the tip of her tongue along the underside of his shaft, sucking on the tip as the rounded edge caught on her lips.

"*Ahhh!*" Mason cried out and pushed back in, his grip tightening in her hair. "So good. I can't—! He pulled out of her hot mouth and gathered her up into his arms, consuming her mouth with his own.

Their mouths met in a ferocious duel, their tongues clashing in a heated battle for more. Their hands were everywhere, pulling and tugging at clothes until they were both naked as the day they were born and tangled together from toes to nose.

Mason ripped himself from her arms and reached for his jeans, removing a foil packet from his front pocket. He sheathed his cock and then wrapped his trembling body around her again, devouring every part he could get his mouth on.

"Must get inside you," he panted into her ear as he reached down and cupped her ass, pulling her up into his arms.

Claira locked her legs around his hips and rocked her slit against the head of his shaft as he walked to the other side of the stall. Pinning her against the wall, he fisted his cock and placed it at her opening, driving home in one hard thrust, sending cries of ecstasy tearing from them both.

Mason was blown away by her sensual responses to him. She was on fire, consumed and controlled by a passion so fierce he thought they would burn alive if he didn't claim her, taste her, make her his. She groaned aloud when he broke their kiss and leaned back to look down at where they joined.

"Look at us, Claira. Watch as you take me deep inside you."

Their breathing quickened as she lowered her forehead against his, watching as he slid out and pushed back in, the friction of his forceful thrusts sending more blood to his already aching cock.

The sight of what they were doing, being able to feel her every move as he watched himself sink deep inside flung him to the very edge of ecstasy. The musky scents of their arousal, sounds of wet skin slapping against wet skin all swirled around him, overwhelming his senses until they all merged into one overpowering need to come inside her.

"Mason," she moaned, pleading. "I need..." She gripped his shoulders as he tightened his hold on her bare ass, bucking against him when he slid his fingers down the valley between her cheeks.

"I've got you, sweetheart. I know what you need. Let me give it to you." Tapping on her back passage, Mason fucked her hard. Pressing her against the wall, he devoured her mouth as it opened on a cry.

Claira bucked against him again when the tip of his finger pressed into her ass.

"Oh God. Mason! It burns." It was too much, not enough. She squeezed her eyes shut, every muscle in her body pulled tight and centered on the place where Mason claimed her over and over.

He inserted another finger, stretching her with each long stroke. When he felt her inner muscles tighten around his cock and fingers, a primal groan ripped from his chest and echoed through the room.

"Ah fuck! Sweetheart, I'm coming!" His hips bucked against her uncontrollably, his balls tightening as streaks of hot and cold ran along his spine. His scalp tingled and his toes curled as the first stream of his cum erupted from his cock, filling her over and over as her own orgasmic cries filled his ears.

She slumped against him, her body trembling around him. She sank her teeth into his sweaty shoulder as another wave of tremors rocked between them. Mason tightened his arm around her to hold her steady. He wasn't ready to let her go.

Puffs of hot, steamy air billowed between them as he struggled to catch his breath. They remained there for a while, joined together and panting for each breath before he shifted and pulled back to look at her.

Claira's sweaty, pale skin glistened in the soft light that filtered through the wood-planked walls of the stall. Her soft, brown curls clung to the tiny beads of perspiration along her rosy cheeks, one small strand caught in the corner of her mouth. Her brown eyes, glazed with passion, closed on a sigh as she leaned her forehead against his.

"How do you know?" she asked, her voice laced with an odd mixture of pleasure and uncertainty.

Mason relaxed his grip. She unhooked her legs and he let her slide down his body until she stood on still-trembling legs. "How do I know what, sweetheart?"

Claira clung to him, her arms wrapped around his waist, her hands sliding up to feel the slick muscles in his back. She laid her head on his chest and listened to the pounding of his heartbeat. She couldn't reconcile the feelings that swelled in her own heart. Surely she couldn't be in love with him; with them. It was too soon to feel this way about him, or anyone. Wasn't it?

"Earlier, you said you never thought about someone other than Sarah capturing your hearts until now. How do you know that? You don't even know me."

Mason gathered her close, his hands roaming her bare back. "Don't you feel it?" He pulled back and tilted her chin up so that she was forced to look at him. "Do you think it's like this with just anyone? I can't deny that we're little more than strangers, Claira, but there's something familiar that my soul, our souls recognize in you. We were made to fall in love with you." When she didn't respond he lowered his lips to her ear and whispered. "What is your heart, your body telling you, sweetheart?"

Her head couldn't justify loving and sleeping with two men, and wanting a third. Her mind was also trying to resurrect the guilt and fear she'd always harbored for getting too close to anyone. If she cared for them they would suffer. She shook her head and forced herself to forget the past.

Mason was right. There was a sacred place that had opened up and allowed these men to become more than important. They were rapidly becoming a vital part of her being. But, what was she supposed to do? Where do they go from here?

"Was it like this with Sarah? Is that how you know?"

Mason shook his head and stepped back from her. Reaching down, he pulled off and discarded the condom, tossing it in a nearby trash bin.

"Sarah was different. She'd always been a part of our lives." Mason paused, and then bent to pick up some of their clothes. How did he explain without cheapening what they'd had with Sarah? None of them had felt like this before. How did he explain something that was so new to them, too?

He handed her clothes to her and bent to step through the legs of his jeans. "Our dads knew the feeling. It happened with our mom. They knew she was the one for them, but with Sarah it was more like a comfortable love rather than an overwhelming calling."

Mason slipped on his boots. Swinging his shirt over his shoulder, he studied her as she slipped back into her pants and bra, not even remembering when they'd been discarded. He shook his head as he realized how powerful an effect she had on him. It was mind-blowing to think that less than a full week ago he hadn't known she existed.

When she noticed him watching, she blushed and turned her back to him, as if he hadn't just seen and fucked every beautiful inch of her. He slipped up behind her and wrapped his arms around her waist as she pulled her shirt over her head.

"Don't hide from me, sweetheart." He kissed her ear and her neck, pulling her hair from the collar of her shirt. When she sighed and slumped against him in frustration he knew he hadn't convinced her. "Claira, look at me." He turned her in his arms and stooped down so they were eye to eye. "You do feel something, am I right?"

"Yes," she nodded without hesitation. "But I—"

"Don't over think it. Just give us a chance. That's all I ask."

"All of you?"

"What do you mean?" Mason asked, taking a step back when he noticed the sudden shift in her expression.

"Grey obviously doesn't share this mystical feeling you talk about. He's as much a part of this decision as you and Matt are. This won't work without him."

He could see her struggle to remain detached from her emotions, but her trembling lower lip gave her away. She was falling for them.

He stepped up and took her in his arms, capturing her quivering lip in a quick, sensual kiss. "You're both right and wrong, sweetheart. This won't work without him, but the good news is that he's totally overwhelmed by what he feels for you." His thumbs wiped away the tears that had formed at the outside corners of her eyes. "He's stubborn, but he'll come around. And man, when he does, you'd better watch out." He chuckled.

Claira froze. "Why?"

Mason chuckled again, his chest rumbling beneath her cheek. He slid one hand down and caressed her ass, then gave it a playful pat, startling her enough to pull back and give him a questioning glance. He kissed her forehead and moved his other hand down, cupping her ass and pulling her against his groin. "You'll see soon enough, sweetheart."

Chapter Eighteen

"What the fuck were you thinking?" Grey shouted at Mason as he and Matt stormed through the front door of the small town Sheriff's office, his long strides eating up the sidewalk as he stomped toward Mason's truck.

"What was *I* thinking? I'm not the one who just got his ass arrested for assault. You two are lucky Tom Grunion dropped the charges against you."

"She shouldn't be home alone, Mace!" Grey grumbled as he reached up and caught the wad of keys Mason tossed him from across the hood. "She shouldn't be there at all! I can't believe you let her go!"

"What was I supposed to do, tie her up?" Mason caught the heated flash of approval in Grey's eyes but ignored it. "After waiting on you guys for two hours after dinner, she wanted to go home. I checked the house before I left. She's fine, which is more than I can say for the two of you! What the hell happened?"

"You won't believe it," Matt said as Grey backed his truck out of the angled parking slot and pulled onto Main Street. "Damn heifer was cut up worse than a butchered catfish." Matt's fists tightened and he struck out at the truck's dashboard. "Damn that bastard!"

"Who? Grunion? Was he there?" Mason knew they had been picked up at Grunion's ranch after checking out the downed heifer at Logan's Bluff, but he had no idea why they'd gone there in the first place.

Grey shook his head in disgust. "No one was there but the dead heifer." Sending a sideways glance at Matt he said, "I tried to stop his crazy ass from riding over to the Grunion's, but he was gone before I could mount up and catch him."

"Again," Mason growled. "What the fuck happened up there?"

"We spotted the downed line of fence before we spotted the heifer," Grey snarled, still focused on the road ahead of them as they made their way through town. "When we saw the cuts on her we thought, at first, she'd gotten tangled up in the razor wire. When we got close enough to dismount, I almost lost my lunch. She was mutilated, Mace!" Grey pounded his fists on the steering wheel. "Her throat was cut and she'd bled out, but not before they carved up her flanks. Some bastard carved the word *'mine'* into her hide like some sick message."

"What the—? Grunion carved her up? How do you know it was him?" Mason pushed at Matt's shoulder for an answer. "Did you see him, or any of his men there?"

Matt shook his head. "Didn't need to see em'. It was Grunion, or his crooked cowhands. You can bet the farm he ordered it done. He wanted that stallion. He wants Falcon Ridge, too. Always has. I know he cut Bernie up, too."

"He's bitter," Grey said, "but he wouldn't do this. This was sick. You saw the look of surprise in his eyes when you flew off your horse and decked him. Speaking of which, have you completely lost your fucking mind? Pull that shit again and you won't have to bet the farm. With his greedy lawyers, he'll own Falcon Ridge for sure if you keep that shit up."

"Sheriff says Dirk's going to file trespassing charges." Mason didn't like old man Grunion. He'd never been one to latch onto an emotion as destructive as hatred, but he hated Tom Grunion's son, Dirk. They were a bigoted and a cold-hearted bunch, but surely they wouldn't resort to butchering their cattle and slaying their pets.

"He, or any of his fuckin' family or cowhands show their coward-ass faces on our land again, I'll show em' trespassin' charges. Dead men can't file charges." Matt made to punch at the truck's dash again but pulled the punch at the last minute.

"Goddammit, Matt!" Grey growled. "This isn't the wild west. You can't go around threatening to kill people."

"Who's threatenin'?" Matt scoffed.

"The Sheriff will have a team up there at first light to take a look. Let the law handle this." Grey had other things on his mind besides keeping his hot-tempered brother from getting his hands on a Grunion, even if they did deserve it.

"Where we goin'?" Matt asked as Grey turned onto one of the dark side streets before they reached the end of Main Street.

"We're going to get Claira," Grey said as he turned onto one street after another, weaving his way through the older community until he pulled onto the small lane where Claira lived.

"It's after midnight!" Mason said, pulling himself to the edge of the back seat to peer out the windshield. "She has to work tomorrow, Grey. You can't just show up at her door in the middle of the night and drag her out of her house like a freaking cave man. You'll push her too far!"

The truck slowed to a quiet stop when they came to Claira's little house.

"Grey?" Matt questioned when he threw the gearshift into park and opened his door.

"Come pick me up in the morning when you bring the boys to school," Grey said as he left the keys in the ignition and loped through the dew-covered grass of Claira's front lawn and disappeared into the darkness as he headed around back.

"What do you think he's doin'?" Matt asked as he slid into the driver's seat and stared after Grey.

Mason watched his big brother disappear, his heart swelling to life with what he felt and saw happening to Grey. With a weary smile on his face, he swung his legs over the center console and plopped down into the passenger seat, clicking his seat belt into place. "He's protecting our woman," he nodded as Matt slowly pulled away. "Let's go get our boys and go home."

"I have to meet up with the Sheriff first thing, and we have a lot of fence to fix. Can you take the boys in tomorrow and pick up Grey?" Matt asked.

"You bet. I'll take any excuse to see Claira again." Mason was already feeling her absence, even if it had only been a few hours. In a way, Grey was right. She belonged at Falcon Ridge, with all of them. She just didn't know it yet.

~*~*~*~*~

Raising his head, Grant Kendal cautiously peered through the windshield. He ducked again before the red glow of the truck's brake lights illuminated the inside of his non-descript sedan. When the crimson glow dispersed, he straightened slowly and watched as the McLendon's truck disappeared around the corner.

He'd been a little surprised when they pulled up and stopped right in front of him. There were a few other cars parked on the otherwise quiet street, but it would have been more than suspicious if they'd seen him sitting there in the middle of the night, only a few yards from Miss Robbins's house.

From his hidden position inside the car, he watched as the older of the McLendon brothers exited the vehicle and crept into the darkness toward her house. He was confident they hadn't seen him, nor had they been suspicious of his car. He shook his head in disgust. People could be so ignorant of their surroundings. He wasn't complaining. It only made his job easier.

Two subtle movements on either side of the street caught Grant's attention. Within a millisecond, he dismissed the prowling tabby and zeroed in on the dark form that approached the front steps of his mark's home. Motionless, he watched as Grey McLendon took a seat in one of the two rockers on the front porch, the glow from the overhead light falling across his rugged features.

"Looks like Miss Robbins has her own private security detail," he mumbled to himself as he settled back into his reclined seat and watched Grey McLendon do the same in the rocker.

Unable to start the car and pull away without attracting unwanted attention, he resigned to get comfortable for the next few hours, glad that he'd just taken a piss when the McLendon brothers pulled up.

He wondered again why he'd taken this job in the first place. Goddamn his mentor for calling in that last chit. Grant owed him one, so he'd damn sure pay up, but he sure as hell didn't have to like it.

He cringed at the word *owe*; hated the meaning of it even more. Thank fuck this was the last favor he owed anyone. He'd sworn off private contracts a long time ago. Hell, he was tired of the legit ones, too, truth be known. He was tired, period.

He had enough money to buy his own private island and retire in comfortable silence, not a soul around he'd have to talk to and placate with fairy tales of what they thought real life was.

In his line of work, he'd found that most people cocooned themselves in white picket fences and golden retrievers. They lived in total denial of what a shithole the world around them had become. None of them knew how the world really worked, nor did they care as long as people like him didn't knock on their door.

His fists tightened and relaxed repeatedly. He needed a break. That was exactly what he intended to do when this clusterfuck was over. He'd pick one of his many aliases, start over one final time, away from all the gore and bullshit. He wasn't sure there was much humanity left inside him, but if there was, he needed to find it quick before the darkness swallowed him whole.

Chapter Nineteen

Claira's heart jumped out of her chest when she stepped out into the pre-dawn air and saw a dark figure out of the corner of her eye. As she turned to run, she caught the familiar profile, a startled squeak her first reaction. "Mr. McLendon? What…what are you doing here?"

Grey pried his numb and aching body from the miniature torture rack he'd all but slept in for the last five hours and met Clara's startled gaze. "We need to talk. And call me Grey."

"How long have you been out here?" Claira glanced out at her driveway, her brow furrowing in confusion when she didn't see any of the McLendon's trucks parked in her driveway. "How did you get here?"

Grey pulled off his Stetson and turned it in his hands a few times before he scrubbed a hand over his stubble-covered jaw and motioned to the door she still held half ajar. "Got any coffee?"

She tried to ignore the butterflies that had replaced the nauseating panic knotting her stomach. He was so ruggedly handsome, even when he was half asleep on his feet. His dark hair was mussed, his green eyes languid and unfocused, his movements slow and a little stiff. He was adorable, like a big, grumpy teddy bear.

If she could only find out why he was here, she might feel a little sorry for him. In his disheveled state he wasn't near as intimidating. She almost felt comfortable enough to tease him. Almost.

"No, I'm sorry." She shook her head and closed the door behind her. "The coffee maker is broken. I haven't had time to get a new one since…" She paused, her cheeks reddening with the thought of what she'd put them through the past weekend. What she'd done with his brothers. *What is he doing here?*

"Do you always leave this early for work?" Grey asked, his hat still clutched in his hand.

"No. I...It was late when Mason dropped me off. I haven't done any lesson plans for the week so I'm going in early to catch up."

"Look, Claira," Grey's voice came out a little scratchy after sitting in the night air for the past few hours. He cleared his throat, stalling a little longer. Now that he'd had time to calm down, asking Claira to come home with him was a little more difficult than he'd expected.

He was still adamant about her not staying there alone, but common sense had won out over anger sometime during the night. He knew he couldn't force her to go. God, how did he talk to her? It had been a long time since he'd been interested in a woman, much less asked one out for coffee. He'd never had those awkward dating moments with Sarah.

He watched as she turned the key, locking the two deadbolts, and then cleared his throat again. "Can we go get some coffee?"

Claira studied him for a moment, long enough to make him feel like an ass. "Grey? Why are you here?"

"As I said, we need to talk." Grey shoved a hand through his mass of unruly hair. When he caught her staring, he shoved his hat back onto his head. "It's about what happened Saturday and I'd like for us to be coherent and sitting down when we talk about it."

He watched as her blush raced from her cheeks to cover her neck. He couldn't help but wonder how much more of her was turning the same shade of tempting pink. It was too early to get a hard-on that he had no hope of remedying any time soon.

"It was a misunderstanding, Mr. McLen—"

"Grey," he reminded her.

"Grey," she stammered. "I'm sorry I intruded on your family, with your brothers. I…It won't happen again. I was just…I shouldn't have gotten involved with my students' parents and I—"

"Miss Robbins. Claira. Will you just shut up and listen for a minute?"

Whatever she was about to say was derailed by his testy rebuke. Grey grumbled a curse as he took a stride toward her. When she tensed and flinched he paused. "I'm sorry. I've normally had half a dozen cups of coffee before now. I'm a little grouchy and beat up from the long ride out to the ridge yesterday. My ass is numb from sitting in that torture rack you call a rocking chair and I've got one hell of a headache. I didn't mean to startle or upset you."

"A *little* grouchy?" Claira arched a brow and watched as he struggled to rein in his obvious inner grump.

"Please, can we go grab a fresh cup at the diner on Main? I'll pay and promise not to growl at you again if you'll just get me there."

Claira giggled and, before she could come up with a reason not to, she'd nodded her agreement. Grey grabbed her keys from her hand and hastily urged her down the front steps to her car. "I'll drive." He said as he opened her door and waited for her to get in.

"But—"

He ignored her protest and nudged her into the passenger seat.

"Impatient, much?" She asked, pulling her legs inside.

"Always." Grey closed the passenger door and ran around to the driver's side.

It took three tries before he finally gave up and squatted between the open door and the driver's seat. He hung his head in defeat, blowing out a frustrated breath with a muted curse. "Claira, baby, where is the lever to move the seat back?"

Claira couldn't hold back her snort. Seeing a man the size of a small horse trying to squeeze himself into her tiny car was by far the funniest thing she'd ever seen. "It's broken," she snorted again, covering her smile with her hand.

Grey was at his breaking point. Lack of sleep, lack of coffee and the innate need to protect Claira from some unknown lunatic while battling his own inner turmoil over his sudden *feelings* for her had all begun to take their toll. Oh, and let's not forget the incessant prick in his jeans. If it weren't for that constant reminder, he'd think she was turning him into a fucking girl!

Pressing his lips together to keep the curses from flying, he stood and marched to the passenger side as she exited and took the driver's seat. Reaching down, Grey slid the passenger seat back as far as it would go—which wasn't near far enough—and then folded himself into the still overly cramped space.

When he pulled the door closed, his knees were crammed against the dash, his thighs pressing against his chest. His shoulders were bunched together between Claira's seat and the passenger door. It was official. He was the main attraction in a clown car at a rodeo.

"Not one word," he warned when he caught her watching him, still choking back a train of giggles. Claira snorted again as he tried to turn and grab his seatbelt. It was no use. "They'll need the Jaws of Life to pry me out of this death trap you call a car, even if we don't crash."

Claira shook her head and started the car, trying her best not to laugh at him as she pulled onto the quiet, still dark street and headed toward Main Street. "Don't pick on my little car," she patted the dash as if it were a pet. "It's a smart, little car."

She'd completely lost her senses. "Baby, this is the *stupidest* car I have ever laid eyes on in my entire life. Papa Joe was wrong," he said as he twisted, grunted and jerked in his seat, already losing feeling in his feet. "There isn't enough room left in this thing for a goddamn hamster."

~*~*~*~*~

Grant Kendal watched as the small car rolled away and disappeared around the corner. *Stupid car.* As he crept silently across her lawn and up the front steps, he noticed that Miss Robbins hadn't engaged her extra efforts at securing her home, not that they mattered much to him. Before the first sliver of the sun's rays arced across the sky, he was inside her home, alarm disengaged and the door bolted behind him. With her having finally hooked up with the McLendon's, it was time to put the second phase of his plan into action.

~*~*~*~*~

Grey leaned over his cup and inhaled the fresh, life-saving aroma. His eyes opened and looked beyond the rim of his cup to notice Claira was doing the same. When her sleepy gaze met his he grinned, recognizing the same desperation for caffeine. Neither spoke a word until the second cup was delivered by an overly chipper waitress, earning herself a disgusted eye roll from Claira and a warning growl from Grey when she tried to take his empty cup.

"Just fill it up and leave it," he ordered.

He watched as Claira slowly awakened and found it endearing that she shared his same morning coffee habit. She took a deep breath. A small smile pulled at the corner of her lips.

"You look tired," Grey said before he took another long sip of coffee.

Claira balked at his remark. "Is that what you dragged me here to say?"

Shit. Grey shook his head and cleared his throat. "No, that came out wrong. You look beautiful, but also weary. Who are you running from?"

Claira's face paled at the sudden and unexpected change in subject. Her gaze dropped to her cup. *What was she hiding?* "Nothing, no one."

She was a terrible liar. Her shy guilty expression gave her away as quick as her blushing cheeks.

"If that's the way you want to play it," Grey grumbled and sat back in his seat. He studied her for a few moments and then leaned his elbows on the edge of the table. "Tell me or don't tell me, it's your choice, but you're not staying in that house alone. You can come to the ranch or I can move in until whatever is going on with you is over, but make no mistake, you don't have any other choices."

"I can't stay at your house!" Claira screeched, drawing the attention and scowls of other nearby caffeine addicts. Her glance darted around the small café and then back to Grey as she steeled her posture and lowered her voice. "That's ridiculous! I don't need a babysitter. I'm perfectly fine." When he didn't relent, she tried another approach. "I can't stay there while I'm teaching your children. It's inappropriate and unprofessional!"

"Fine," Grey nodded. "I'll pack a bag and pick you up after school is released. What time do you leave?"

"No. I can't...You don't understand. There's—"

"There's no further argument to be had, Claira. School is out in a week and then the boys are going to stay at Sarah's parents for a while. I'll stay at your house until then. When school is out you'll stay at the ranch."

She appeared to be taken aback by his command. That was too bad. She could talk, or put up with an unwanted houseguest.

"You can't stay with me. I'm not staying at your home, either. There's no reason for it. You're crazy for even suggesting such a thing."

Grey chuckled and took a relaxed sip of his coffee, confident in his decision. "I've been called worse."

Settling back against her seat, Claira shook her head in frustration. She waved to the waitress and pulled her purse into her lap. "I'll have one of these to go and the check, please," she said and pulled out her wallet.

Unaffected by her denial, Grey drained his cup and picked up the other full one. "So what time do I need to pick you up?"

Claira paused and then dropped her hands to her lap in defeat. "Why are you doing this? You don't even like me."

Grey started counting. *One Mississippi. Don't like her? She's eating me alive from the inside out and she doesn't think I like her? Fuck that! Two Mississippi. Three Mississippi.*

I spent the night on her porch, sitting in a chair built for a freaking doll house no less. I took out—four Mississippi—five Mississippi—breathe. I took out a knee cap on the dashboard of that fucked-up, deathtrap she calls a car when she slammed on the brakes for some stupid, confused squirrel. Damn thing was probably trying to mate with the hamster under the hood.

Six Mississippi—I haven't showered, shaved or—breathe, or had near enough coffee to make even the slightest dent in this ass-kicking headache. She doesn't think I like her? How about the hard-on pressing against my zipper? That should give her a fucking clue! Seven Mississippi, eight Mississippi! To hell with Mississippi!

He slid out of the booth and stood before her, towering over her so close she had to lean back to look up into his eyes. When she did, the ominous cloud that had hung in his gaze moments earlier was gone, replaced by steel determination and that same flash of desire she'd seen that first day in class. Only this time it was more than a fleeting flash, it was a flash flood of boiling lava. He pulled a chair from a nearby table and straddled it, his face mere inches from hers.

"Grey."

On her one word protest, her lips parted, his hands cupped her face. He pulled her to him with lightning speed and crushed his mouth to hers. Claira tensed as the taste of coffee and Grey burst over her tongue and short circuited her nervous system. She forgot how to breathe. Her heart rate hit the stratosphere. Her skin felt like it had melted from the friction of her blood running through her veins at such a frantic pace.

She didn't know what she expected Grey's kiss to feel like; had barely dared to imagine him kissing her at all. She certainly didn't expect the gentle, commanding presence that flowed around and through her, bending her will to his own as his tongue slid beyond her lips and glided smoothly over hers.

Just like that, she surrendered to his command. Her spine arched toward him, air filled her burning lungs at a frantic pace. When his tongue retreated, she leaned in and chased it back, unwilling to let him go so soon. She wasn't sure how they got there, but when her fingers slid through his thick, silky hair at the base of his neck a helpless whimper squeaked in her throat and she drew him closer. His hands moved from her face to her shoulders, and then suddenly he was pushing her away. He tensed before he tore his mouth from hers, his breaths coming in erratic pants.

The dark cloud was back in his eyes, intense and piercing, making her flinch as he pulled back and focused his cold gaze on her. She couldn't read him. Was he angry?

Before Claira could consider it further, Grey jumped to his feet, the movement so fast the chair he was sitting in tilted and wobbled on one leg, nearly falling over before he caught it and swung it back to the table behind him. "I'll pick you up at three," he nodded, turned on his heel and stormed through the front door of the diner, ringing the life out of the little bell hanging at the top.

Chapter Twenty

Grey was gone. Claira's gaze moved precariously around the small diner, noticing half a dozen people staring at her with mixed reactions on their faces. With her wits returning from the little vacation they had taken while Grey's tongue was down her throat, she felt her cheeks heat with another flush of embarrassment and frustration. Who did he think he was, kissing her like that and then pushing her away? It wasn't as if she'd asked him to kiss her.

Claira picked up her wallet, pausing when she noticed the ten dollar bill already lying on the table. When had he done that? She shook her head and stuffed her wallet back in her purse. She needed to get out of there and get to work. And under no circumstances was she letting Mr. Grey McLendon pick her up from school or stay at her house.

Okay, so she may have a deadly, pissed off mobster looking for her. No, there was no maybe about it. Lucien was looking, but it didn't mean he'd find her. And what made Grey think he knew her? He didn't know anything about her. No one did.

Claira Robbins had no history. Her birthday, even her credit score was made up for crying out loud. You'd think they could have given her a score above six hundred, not that she needed credit. That was her; no history, no family, no friends and three outrageously frustrating and beautiful men that were driving her slowly insane. *Pathetic*.

Claira stormed out the door, forgetting her coffee-to-go order, and made her way back to her car. Her smart, little car. She couldn't stop the smile that erupted when she remembered Grey's big body stuffed into her passenger seat like a smashed loaf of bread. Just as quick, her smile faded, her brows furrowing together when the vision of his cold, angry stare flashed through her mind as he pushed her away from him. *Frustrating man!*

Her cellphone's shrill ring pulled her from her confusing thoughts. She hurried to dig it from her purse with one hand as she unlocked her car with the other. Glancing at the caller ID, not recognizing the number, she clicked the talk button.

"Hello?" When no one answered she pulled the phone back to look at it. "Hello?" She tried again. Nothing. She hung up, tossed her phone back into her purse and started the car, clicking her seatbelt into place. As she was pulling away from the diner, the phone began to ring again. "Not again." She didn't think she could take another day of anonymous hang-ups. She'd already changed her number once.

As soon as her phone stopped ringing it started again. Keeping her eyes on the road, she fished out her phone and answered it. "Look, if you're not going to say anything, then stop calling me!"

"Claira? Are you ok?"

Claira's shoulders slumped when she heard Mason's calming voice. "Mason," she sighed as she pulled into the faculty parking lot and shut off her car.

"Good morning, sweetheart. What was that all about?"

She slumped in her seat and released another long breath. It felt so good to hear his strong, soothing voice. "Sorry," she smiled into the phone as if he could see it. "I've been getting a lot of hang up calls lately. I need to change my number."

"Prank calls?"

"I guess," she huffed. "They never say anything. They either hang up or wait until I do."

Mason wanted to confront her, ask her who she was running from. But the last thing he wanted to do was upset her even more before she went into work. Based on the call he'd just gotten, Grey had already done quite a job of that. "I think you should change your number if they don't stop. Just be sure to give me the new one."

She smiled again at his teasing tone. Not wanting to worry him, she decided not to say anything about changing it the first time. "I will." Another thought occurred to her as she looked out the windshield and noticed the first few students being dropped off. She'd been hoping to get an earlier start, and would have if Grey hadn't ambushed her. "Who's dropping the boys off today since Grey decided to stay the night on my front porch? Aren't Monday's his day to drive them?"

"Look out your window."

Claira turned and saw Mason in Matt's truck pulling into the parking lot. "You're here." The breathless sigh of relief and excitement caught her a little off guard. Was it possible to feel so many things for someone she'd just met? It didn't make sense. She felt like she was losing control of everything. She couldn't afford to lose control, but she didn't seem to be able to stop any of it from happening.

Mason backed the truck in next to her. She winced when she saw the huge dent in the rear door before it opened and the twins spilled out. Mason ran around the front of the truck and squatted in front of Con and Car as she opened her car door.

"Hey, Miss Robbins," Car turned and waved, his smile as bright as the morning sun. Con was still wiping the sleep from his eyes, his greeting more of a grunt, like someone else she knew.

Claira smiled, intent on hiding her frustrations and confusion. She was sure it fooled everyone but Mason. "Hi," she smiled as she watched the boys run off to her class.

"Hi, yourself." The look on Mason's face made her weak in the knees. Where Grey was sleepy and grumpy, Mason looked like he'd just rolled off the cover of a magazine instead of a bed. He took the few steps needed to close the space between them and wrapped her in a warm embrace. "I want to kiss you really, really badly, but I know it would make you feel uncomfortable here at the school. So I'll settle for a hug."

Claira wanted to jump in his arms and beg him to take her home, but he was right. It wouldn't be proper and God only knew what kind of gossip it would start, not that she cared that much about wagging tongues. Instead, she relaxed in his arms and released the rest of the tension that had knotted inside her. When she thought about Grey's kiss and the way he acted afterward, the conflicting emotions sent a shiver down her spine.

"Are you cold?" Matt asked as he squeezed her tighter in his arms. "I have a sweatshirt in the truck you can borrow. It'll warm up by lunch, I'm sure."

Claira shook her head and pulled back from his embrace. "It's not that. I just…" How did she explain it? Grey was contradicting on so many levels. His kiss was so warm and commanding, she couldn't deny how wonderful and surprising it felt. She'd thought for one brief moment she'd read him wrong and maybe he did like her the way his brothers did, but he clearly wasn't ready for whatever this was they were doing. Either that or he didn't like her kiss. *Oh, no!* What if that was it. What if he'd pushed himself to give her a chance and he didn't find what he was looking for?

"Hey." Mason's soft voice broke her panic and her eyes snapped up to his. "Don't over think what happened this morning." Mason smiled and cupped her face in his big warm hands.

"He called you, huh?"

"Yeah." Mason nodded. "You've turned his comfortable, controlled, self-loathing world completely upside down and he's trying to find his footing. He's overreaching a bit with this whole moving in thing, but it's his way. He protects what's his. We all do."

Claira slumped in his arms. *I'm not his. I'm not anyone's.* Knowing it was a losing battle, she tried anyway to dissuade their feelings about her needing protecting. She didn't want them to worry or start prying around for answers she couldn't give them. Or worse, get hurt because of her. "I'm not in any danger."

Still not wanting to upset her day, Mason decided to wait a few more hours before he started demanding the truth. "Go make geniuses out of our sons," he smiled and gave her a pat on the rear, fighting to keep a respectable distance. "I'll be over with dinner later and we'll talk."

Claira fought her own urges not to lean in and reach for a quick kiss. Pushing her warring emotions aside, she grabbed her books and purse from the car then ran in to greet the twins and her other students for a fresh start to a new week.

Half a dozen hang-ups and six hours later she stepped out of her classroom and locked the door behind her. "Shhhoot!" She jumped when Grey's hand landed on her shoulder. God, she needed to calm down, or drink less coffee. How was she going to convince them nothing was wrong when she couldn't convince herself?

"Sorry," Grey whispered. "I didn't mean to startle you."

Claira released a ragged breath and shook off her rioting nerves as she took in his polished, yet rugged appearance. Wearing a pair of black jeans that melded to his strong, lean thighs, and another green button-up that mirrored the color of his eyes, she couldn't help but noticed the trickle of jet black hair that peeked out from the open collar. His presence was both comforting and alarming. She knew he'd never harm her, even felt safe with him—not to mention aroused—but he saw too much and made her feel too many conflicting emotions. And he was a stubborn *ass.*

"Ready to go?" He asked, his hand laying claim to her lower back. The heat from his touch radiated through the thin material of her shirt and made her want to push back against it.

She straightened her shoulders and shook her head. "You don't take no for an answer, do you?"

Grey's lips quirked up into a mischievous grin and one brow arched up to match the sentiment behind his words. "You just now figuring that out?"

"Jackass," she whispered as she fell into step next to him.

"Now you're getting closer," he chuckled and ushered her down the long, dim hallway toward the exit.

"Miss Robbins! Oh, Miss Robbins! This was left for you—oh!"

Claira cringed when she'd heard the stuffy, aristocratic voice calling her name through the halls. When Grey turned her to face the man that had forever ruined the sound of her new name, she had to cover her mouth to keep the laugh from bubbling out uninvited. The sourpuss look on Principal Dawes's face as he heel-toed it down the hall after them was priceless. You could almost hear the squeak from the stick up his butt when he walked.

~*~*~*~*~

"Mr. McLendon, how nice to see you." Principal Dawes' surprised and confused expression never left Claira as he extended a hand to Grey. "Is everything ok with our Miss Robbins?"

Grey held back a groan as he reached for the man's limp-wristed attempt at a greeting. *Not yours, asshole.* "You'll have to ask her." He despised the sniveling, little bug and he'd be damned if he'd let him belittle her again.

Dawes ignored the retort. With a snarl he handed Claira a legal-sized envelope. "This was left at the office for you today, Miss Robbins. In the future, we'd appreciate if you restrict your personal deliveries to your home."

Grey's hands twitched with the need to bend the little prick over and shove his size thirteen boot up the guy's tight ass. He grabbed the envelope from Claira's hand and tucked it under his arm. "I had that sent here and I had expected it to be delivered before now. My time is in short supply, Mr. Dawes. I'd expected her to have my schedule available for review before our meeting this afternoon."

"Meeting?" Dawes choked on his question, his eyes fixed on the envelope.

Grey crossed his arms over his chest and leaned toward the little shit, causing him to take a step back. He knew he was being a dick, but he didn't care. "*Miss* Robbins will be tutoring my sons this summer. I'll expect your cooperation in the future if the need should arise."

"Of course." Dawes nodded aggressively, looking more like a spring-challenged bobble head. He turned a panicked smile to Claira. "Anything you need, Miss Robbins, you let me know." With that, he turned and rushed back down the hall toward his office.

Chapter Twenty-One

Claira's heart pumped fiercely as it expanded against her chest. No one had ever stood up for her the way Grey just had, except for Stephan. She looked up at him, studying his hard expression as he stared after Principal Dawes. *Like he's the bug to be squashed instead of me.*

Grey was the most stubborn, mercurial, sometimes infuriating, tenderhearted and protective man she'd ever known, and all of a sudden she found herself in the safe fold of his protectiveness instead of being on the outside.

It was a heady sensation; an honor, really. Her insides fluttered with mixed emotions, again. Was he really trying to protect her? Why? Why did he walk away from her at the coffee shop? Why did he look at her like he could eat her alive one minute, and then like he wanted to tie her to the bumper of his truck and take off down the road the next?

She was so confused. How was she supposed to know which way was up with him? She was nowhere near close to figuring any of those things out when he ushered her out into the sunbathed parking lot and she got her first glimpse of her car, and all four flat tires.

Claira stood dumbstruck in the middle of the school parking lot staring at her crippled car. Grey was pacing around, talking to someone on his cellphone. It wasn't until she heard the tail end of a snarl that she realized who he was talking to.

"I don't give a damn if *all* your men are at Falcon Ridge inspecting my herd! I don't care if you have to deputize half the goddamn county. Get someone out here to inspect her car, now! And Sheriff, I want someone at her house before we get there! Harvest Lane. Yeah, ten minutes, fifteen tops."

With another growl he shoved his phone into his front pocket and marched toward her, taking her by her hand and pulling her to his truck. "Where are we going? I have to wait for the police!"

She tried to turn back to her poor little car, but Grey kept a tight hold on her as he opened his passenger door and, like a sack of potatoes without a mind or will of her own, picked her up by her waist and deposited her onto the front seat. When he tried to close the door, still not having said a single word to her, she jammed her foot against the panel and pushed it back open. "Grey, what are you doing? I can't leave."

~*~*~*~*~

Grey paused and checked his innate need for control. He released a frustrated breath and stepped up to her, settling himself between her thighs as much as her long skirt would allow. *Big mistake.* The feel of her wrapped around him, her intoxicating scent and worried expression, along with the sheer terror that ran through his veins at what he'd seen in that envelope had his every sense on overdrive.

"Claira, baby, we need to get you home. The Sheriff will take care of your car."

He didn't want to tell her about the pictures until he had her tucked safely away at the ranch. He didn't want her to see them at all. He could feel the worry and confusion, mingled with weariness rolling off her in waves. Seeing that vile filth would only make it worse.

"I'm sorry about this morning," he sighed.

After he'd left her sitting in the diner that morning, he'd kicked himself down the street, not having a clue where he was going, but he knew why he'd left. It was the same fucked up reason everything else in his life was a mess. Sarah.

Never once, in the twenty-four years he'd known her, not even in the three of those years they'd been married, had she overwhelmed him the way Claira had with one kiss. Everything inside him ached for Claira in a way that was completely unfair to the memory of his wife.

It wasn't bad enough that she'd died because of him. Now it seemed his traitorous body was hell-bent to destroy the very essence of what Sarah had meant to him. How could he be more attracted to someone, need someone, love the taste and the feel of someone more than he ever had his own wife?

He'd called Mason, told him about what had happened at the restaurant and then asked him to pick him up at the cemetery. A year had passed since his last visit to Sarah's grave. When he sat beside her headstone, he'd pleaded for answers, but none came. No answers ever came.

Grey felt himself changing inside while he glared at the words scripted across the top of the polished granite stone that stood in front of him.

Three hearts beat as one, for one. Always.

He'd always known he and his brothers would share a wife, and that person had always been Sarah. As far back as he could remember she'd always been theirs. They could never love separately. It wasn't who they were. Was it possible for the three of them to love two different women in such different ways, together, without losing Sarah completely?

By the time Mason pulled up alongside the curb and got out of his truck, he'd just about made himself sick trying to reconcile his feelings for Claira against those he'd had for Sarah.

Mason didn't say a word when he'd walked by him, his hands tucked into his jean pockets as he bent down and brushed a kiss over the top of Sarah's headstone. A moment later he slapped Grey on the shoulder and nudged him toward his truck. When they were both seated in the silent cab, Grey looked over and noticed the overconfident expression on his face.

"You know how fucked up I am right now, right?"

Mason had smiled and started the truck. He paused, his hand on the gear shift, and looked over at him with those soulful eyes that always seemed to see right through him. He hoped to God he couldn't see the truth.

"Yep," Mason nodded and threw the truck into drive. "But I know you, Grey. You're as stubborn as the day is long, but you're not a coward. You'll get it all figured out soon enough."

Now, standing in the parking lot with a scared and frantic Claira, somewhere deep inside Grey knew things would never be the same. He had to get her home safe and keep her that way. At least until he could work through his fucked up thoughts.

"I have a lot of things I'm trying to work out in my head, Claira. I need to…I need to talk to you, about a lot of things, but I need for you to trust me. Just for a little while. Can you do that?"

She did trust him. Strange, but there it was. He was so different from Matt and Mason, yet similar, almost an exact mix of the two, with a twist of uncommon dominance and darkness added into the mix. She nodded wordlessly and turned in her seat to allow Grey to close the door.

When Grey slid into the driver's seat and closed the door, he reached over and wrapped his long arm around her waist and drew her across the bench seat until she was snuggled up beside him. With a strained smile and a wink, he started the truck and pulled away from the school.

A throng of neighbors, a fire engine and two Sheriff's cars filled Claira's little yard when they pulled alongside her driveway. Claira stiffened against him as he shut off the engine and opened the driver's door.

Their cousin Benton came rushing down the front steps, the Sheriff in tow. "Stay here," he patted Claira's thigh and stepped out of the truck. Claira leaned forward to watch as her landlord drove up and ran over to join them.

Ohmygodohmygodohmygod! He'd found her. It was starting all over again. She didn't want to believe it. It was supposed to be over. How could he have gotten to her this quickly? The phone calls, the tires, and now her house was on fire?

Claira tried to think through the paralyzing fear that gripped her. Something was off. If this was Lucien, there would be no house left. Flat tires and prank calls weren't his style. It had to be him, didn't it? No one else knew enough about her to hate her this much. Had she run over something on the way to work? Had she been so distracted by Grey's frustrating behavior and the prank calls that she hadn't noticed? Could this be a coincidence? She hadn't ironed anything. She hadn't left the coffee pot on, because there wasn't one to leave on. God, would this day ever end?

Grey ambled back to the truck and offered his hand to help her out, but he stopped her as she reached the edge of the seat, his arms bracketing her thighs. "Looks like my brothers crossed a wire installing the water heater."

"Grey, I'm telling you they didn't."

"Not now!" Grey turned and shouted over his shoulder at his cousin Frank, the owner of her now charred, little rental.

When Frank stifled his rebuttal, Grey turned and faced Claira again. "The neighbors called it in before it got too bad, but the back half of the place is a total loss. We can salvage a few things from your room and office, but it will take weeks to clean the place up and make it livable again. Looks like you'll be moving in with us after all."

"I…" Ugh, Claira felt like screaming, crying, yelling, anything but the wordless nod she gave Grey.

What else could she do? She didn't know anyone else she could stay with. There wasn't a hotel for fifty miles and the only bed and breakfast in town was booked through the fall. She knew because she'd checked there when she'd first arrived in town.

Without a car, or any other friends, she didn't have a choice. That was what chafed her the most. She'd come all this way to gain her freedom, and she still didn't have any more choices than she ever had before.

Grey helped her pack the things that weren't ruined by the fire, water or smoke and loaded both moderately stuffed bags into his truck. It was pretty sad, really. Even with the things she didn't take, her meager possessions didn't amount to much. She'd left it all behind before. At least she had a few things of her own this time.

Each time an involuntary protest erupted from her mouth on the way to Falcon Ridge, Grey had an easy reply and assured her she was more than welcome at their ranch. She ached to see Matt and Mason; to be with them.

When they pulled into the ranch, Mason greeted her with his disarming smile, a tight hug and a kiss on her cheek. "Hey, gorgeous. Rough day?"

She didn't know why, but the moment Mason touched her, tears welled in her eyes and her throat burned from holding them back. Mason hugged her tighter. "Hey, it's going to be okay, sweetheart. Let it out. I'm so sorry about your place."

Before Claira could release the first sob, the twins came running from the house and she pushed from Mason's embrace. "Daddy Grey!" Con screeched as he ran and jumped into Grey's arms. "I missed you, daddy. Where were you all night?"

He reached over and ruffled Car's hair as he hugged Con in his arms. "I had some ranching business to take care of with Daddy Matt and we kind of got stuck up on the mountain. Sorry I missed tucking my two favorite boys in last night. Did you have fun with Daddy Mason?"

Both boys nodded. Claira watched the byplay between Car and Grey and wondered what sort of battle was waging between those two. Grey let Con slip from his grip and reached out for her hand. "Miss Claira had a fire at her house today. Will it be okay if she stays with us for a while until her house is fixed?"

"Oh, cool. Did you get to ride in the fire truck, Miss Claira?" Car rushed to her side. He took her hand from Grey's and led her toward the house. "Was the fire big or was it just a little one, with lots of smoke? I want to be a fireman like our cousin, Hal. Not a policeman like our other cousin, Benton. Firemen get to do way cooler stuff."

"No way," Con protested behind him. "Cousin Benton gets to carry a gun and drives a fast car. That beats a big ol' clunky fire truck any day!"

Claira glanced helplessly over her shoulder at Mason and Grey as she was escorted up the stairs by the two impish little boys.

Chapter Twenty-Two

The next week passed in a blinding blur. Claira's tires were re-inflated and her car dropped off at the ranch after the Sheriff's men had had time to go over the damage. Seems someone had let the air out rather than slashing them. Could have been a kid playing games, but Grey didn't think so.

After seeing the photos of Claira curled up on her bed reading a book, some others of her coming and going from school in her car, mingled with others of the mutilated heifer they found on the ridge, he knew there was a threat to contend with and it was somehow tied to them. Whoever was fucking with them had turned their attention to Claira and that was unacceptable.

They shuttled her and their boys off to school each morning and worried like hell until they arrived back home every evening, even though they knew their Uncle Cade was watching over her while she was away.

Cade was a former Fed. A spook. No one knew with certainty what his true profession was exactly, but they all knew he was the last person you'd ever want to piss off when it came to messing with their family. *Was Claira family?* That thought only added another layer to Grey's confusion.

Still, even with Cade on covert protection duty, they worried. What they'd heard from Benton's contacts was less than helpful. Nothing. They hadn't found a single shred of data on Miss Claira Robbins. Uncle Cade had shrugged it off and said he'd call in a favor, see what he could dig up, but he didn't sound hopeful.

In the meantime, Claira had taken to cooking breakfast and dinner and helping the boys do their homework while Grey and his brothers dealt with the everyday ranch work, as well as the mess up on the ridge. They still had a mile of fence to repair and had given up a dozen ranch hands to sit watch on the ridge for any of Grunion's men.

With each day that passed that week, Claira seemed to nestle further into their family fold. Taking a spot at the Chutes and Ladders game they played on game night, snuggling into the single recliner with a blanket, looking cute and vulnerable while Grey tried to focus on whatever cartoon movie they'd chosen for movie night. Like they were *one—big—happy—family.*

His brothers hadn't touched Claira in a week and Grey was going out of his ever-loving mind. Having her there and not actually *having* her, was about the worst thing he'd ever endured. Fate was a bitch. His gut clenched every time he saw Claira in the kitchen, which, to him, was still Sarah's kitchen. Combine that with the incessant need to touch her and he was an absolute wreck. His heart, mind and body were waged in a brutal three way war with their separate needs and wants.

His parents weren't helping matters, either. His mom had practically adopted Claira that first night they'd met in the kitchen. Claira was even talking about going Christmas shopping with her, for crying out loud. It was June! And the dads! They were like three stooges fighting over a pork chop when it came to her. Always telling embarrassing stories about him and his brothers, and winking at him every time she came into a room. What the fuck was that all about?

Holding his temper and wayward emotions in check was getting harder every day she was there, along with a very persistent body part. He needed a break. They all did.

He hadn't hesitated when Uncle Cade recommended someone to take over rebuilding the feed barn. Although a newcomer to the area, Grey had liked the man from the onset. Now that school was out and the boys were headed to Sarah's parents for a few weeks, he and his brothers were going to get this thing with Claira settled. Not having to finish the feed shed would give them the time. A firm handshake and two days later, he was walking the new man out to the old feed shed site when Claira and the boys came rambling out of the barn.

"Daddy, look! Bernie's playing with her puppies! She's going to be okay!" Grey smiled when Car reached for one of the puppies and held the squirming ball of fur out to him.

The vet had pronounced Bernie well enough to come home and Mason had picked her up on the way back from town that afternoon.

"This is the one I'm keeping. His name is Snipe cause' I caught him taking one of the other puppy's toys away."

"Seems like the name fits, son." Grey chuckled as the puppy pulled at Car's hat and squirmed in his arms. "I hope he doesn't take a liking to your pants, or my socks."

"Mr. Kendal, it's nice to see you again." Claira reached out to shake the new man's hand.

Grey felt the hair on the back of his neck stand on end. How the hell did Claira know his new hired hand? He was supposed to be new in town.

"Hi, Miss Robbins. It's nice to see you again, too. You live out this way?"

"Well, I…"

Oh, no fucking hell way! "She lives here…with me…and my brothers." Grey said, daring Claira to contradict him. His reaction and gruff tone had shocked even him. Grey didn't like the big green monster any more than he liked Kendal touching Claira, but damn if he could stop it from possessing him.

"I met Grant in the grocery store the day I…well, when Matt and Mason came to install the water heater. I sort of caused an avalanche in the canned vegetable aisle and he helped me clean it up." Turning her gaze to Grant, she ignored Grey's piercing stare. "What are you doing here, Grant?"

She's blushing? For this wandering loser? Grey knew he wasn't exactly being fair. He'd liked the guy no less than three minutes ago, but that was before he started flirting with his woman. *His woman?* Was she? *Hell, yes! No. Fuck!* "I hired Mr. Kendal to rebuild the feed shed. He'll be staying in the bunkhouse with the other hands."

Grey felt ridiculous for being jealous but somehow, throughout all his internal battles, he hadn't imagined Claira meeting anyone else; flirting with anyone else. Not that she was flirting exactly, just…ah, hell! He was a possessive sonofabitch and he didn't like the idea of her meeting some stranger in a supermarket. Especially with everything else that was going on. He knew he didn't have any claim on her, but hell if he could stop himself.

~*~*~*~*~

Later that evening, while she was washing the dinner dishes, Matt snagged Claira's arm and whisked her into the dark pantry just off the kitchen, closing the door behind them. Before she could protest, Matt covered her mouth in a frenzied kiss, his warm, talented tongue filling her head with all sorts of ideas while his hard body folded in around her, his swollen erection grinding against her belly.

"I can't wait another minute. I'm going crazy not being able to touch you." His mouth covered hers again, sucking her bottom lip between his teeth. "Kiss you." He lifted her shirt and traced the smooth skin of her abdomen up and under her bra, pushing it out of his way. "Love you," he panted against her neck before he lifted her shirt and stole a taste of her budded nipple, drawing out a muted moan when he nipped and pulled on the taught nub. "I love your breasts. Silky, smooth peaks that fit in my palm perfectly, mmm." He lapped and suckled at her nipple before pushing away the rest of her confining bra.

"Matt," Claira sighed and slumped against him, her knees buckling beneath her.

"Daddy Matt?" Con's small voice called from beyond their dark hiding spot, jerking Claira out of her lust induced euphoria.

Matt slumped against her, his hot breath spilling over her exposed skin as a rumble of frustration vibrated through him. He righted Claira's clothes and nuzzled her neck, kissing his way to her ear. "Meet me in the barn after we put the boys to bed."

Claira's heart stuttered. Over the last few days she'd almost convinced herself she'd imagined what had happened between them before the fire. At first she'd been relieved when the brothers had given her some space. They had set up a comfortable routine.

She hadn't felt right about not paying them for allowing her to stay in their home, and of course they refused such an outlandish offer. She'd decided that taking care of the twins and the things that needed done around their house was a fair trade as they managed the unbelievable, everyday demands of running a working ranch.

She'd had no idea how demanding ranching could be. Some days the brothers came home so exhausted they'd eaten dinner and gone straight to bed after tucking their boys into bed. Con and Car had virtually adopted her, showing her more than two six year olds should know about ranching and had adapted well to having her in their home.

She'd even managed to arrange a schedule to give Con extra attention to his studies, tutoring him as they'd planned in Grey's office, which Grey would promptly vacate the moment they got home, not to surface again until dinner and sometimes not even then. *Frustrating, confusing man.* He was avoiding her. Other than the one game on game night and half a movie on movie night, she'd scarcely seen him.

She wasn't sure he'd want to continue Con's tutoring when her house was habitable again. She'd spent enough time with both the boys to know that they were both bright boys and neither needed a full time tutor.

She had a suspicion that Con's lacking academic performance had very little to do with academics and more to do with some unintended, unidentified family dynamic.

Something felt off about the way they interacted with Con; Grey in particular. He treated Con with kid gloves and Car was feeling slighted. She couldn't quite put her finger on why. Who knew? It wasn't as if Grey would ever talk to her about it anyway.

Seeing Grey come in that evening, eat the dinner she'd prepared for them, and then leave without a word to her, had her blood running cold. Matt and Mason had been as accommodating and gentle with her as ever, but hadn't touched her the way they had before she'd come to stay with them. By the time Matt had pulled her into the pantry, she'd been consumed with doubt.

She didn't know where this was leading, or if it was the right thing, but then and there she decided she couldn't push aside her feelings for them any longer. They were all proud, good, respectable men and fathers. More honorable than any man she'd ever met in her previous life. In truth, she never knew such men existed outside of romance novels, which she rarely read. Who was she to turn down three, well, make that *two*, cowboy princes?

She needed them; needed to trust them and believe that everything would work out. Since she'd come to the ranch, the calls had stopped and she no longer felt as though someone was watching her. Lucien didn't know where she was, Claira was almost certain of it. She would just have to have faith in Matt and Mason, and their faith that Grey would come around. She hoped.

"Daddy Matt?" Con called again as he passed through the kitchen once more, still searching for the man wrapped around her, making her blood sizzle.

"Say yes, darlin'. I need you." Matt's arms constricted around her, pulling her against his work-hardened frame. "If you don't say yes, Con's gonna' find us makin' out in here. I'm not lettin' you go until you agree," he chuckled.

Claira nodded, afraid that Con would hear her if she tried to speak. With one more fierce but quick kiss, Matt left her in the dark pantry, her heart still beating a mile a minute.

Chapter Twenty-Three

An hour later Claira snuck out to the barn, the light within calling her to join her new lover, or lovers. Would Matt ask Mason to join them as well? God she hoped so. It felt like a lifetime since she'd felt Mason's brand of passion envelop her in a cocoon that only he could spin around her.

When the heavy barn door closed behind her, she peered down the dark aisle between the stalls to the far end of the barn.

"Matt?" She waited, but didn't hear anything except the rustling of a few of the horses.

They're not here. Had they changed their minds? The boys had been particularly rambunctious after dinner. Maybe they were reading an extra story to get them settled.

A shuffling noise from one of the stalls caught Claira's attention. One of the puppies snarled and yelped. Such a fierce sound from the small, innocent creature made her giggle. "What a little bully you are." She peeked over the stall door in time to see the little black fur ball pounce on one of its unsuspecting siblings.

"He's the alpha."

Claira jumped back from the stall, her gasp echoing through the dank, cool air. "Grey, you scared me." She noticed the still, somber expression on his face and hugged her arms around herself to keep out the chill of his glare.

"So I gathered." Grey's insides churned as he looked at the petite, slip of a woman that had turned him inside out. He'd made up his mind. He wasn't going down this road again. Seeing Claira cooking in Sarah's kitchen every goddamn day was pure torture. Between the ache in his chest and constant throbbing in his groin, he was done for. Something had to give.

Claira saw the ghosts in Grey's eyes and her heart broke. Matt and Mason's plans for them all would never work. She had to leave. The past weeks had shown her what a dynamic family they were. Car and Con would never want for anything and the love that flowed between them all was something she could only dream of sharing one day. Their family was a tight-knit unit she would never fit into no matter how much Matt and Mason wanted her. Without Grey the entire idea was hopeless.

Grey would never love her as he once loved Sarah. She was only hurting him. She wished she could comfort him somehow, let him know that she would never want to erase Sarah from their lives. She couldn't stay and torture him any longer. All the feelings she'd resolved within herself no more than an hour ago in Matt's arms, suddenly became so small and unimportant. She couldn't, she wouldn't, come between Grey and his family.

"I…I should go." Claira turned to leave him to his ghosts. She would find someplace else to stay. Maybe it was time to move on from Grassland. She wasn't sure she wanted to keep working at a small private school that stifled the personalities of children the way Grassland Academy did. Other than the McLendon brothers, well, Matt and Mason anyway, her temporary job, which was now officially over, was all that held her there.

"Don't go." Grey's voice was as rough as sandpaper and flittered up Claira's spine as she turned back to face him.

Grey took a step in her direction but froze as she took a step back. "We…" Grey's voice crackled and he cleared his throat. "Claira, we need to talk."

Claira shook her head, pulling her arms tighter around herself, hoping it would keep her wayward emotions from overwhelming her resolve. "That's not necessary, Grey. I see the pain I'm causing. I'll leave first thing in the morning, after I say goodbye to Con and Car, if that's…" she swallowed back the tight knot in her throat. "If that's alright with you."

Grey heard the pain in her voice, saw the sadness and fear in her big brown eyes. He'd never understood the saying quite as clearly as he did at that moment, but wild horses could not have kept him from her, not even ghostly ones. Before he'd completed the thought, his feet had taken the half dozen steps toward her and his whole body folded around her tiny frame.

"I don't want you to go."

Claira fought the unyielding need to melt against him. He felt so strong and warm. His clean, woodsy scent filled her senses. Mixed with the musty smell of the barn, she knew she would never forget it. No matter where she went, she would never forget Grey and his brothers.

"But…you don't want me to stay, either." When he didn't respond, she clenched the back of his shirt into her fists and took one last deep breath to pocket away a little more of his scent for her memories before she released him. She forced herself to look up into his sparkling green eyes and cradled his chiseled face in her hands. "You're a good man, Grey McLendon. Thank you for allowing me even this short time with your amazing family."

Grey wrapped his long fingers around her wrists. Claira flinched at his touch. She didn't think she could stand another moment of the brokenness she saw in his eyes or the feel of him against her skin.

She turned to leave, but his fingers tightened around her wrists. "Don't go," Grey choked out.

Claira's heartbeat filled her ears and her chest felt as though it would burst from aching. She couldn't breathe. She had to go. "Please let me go. There's nothing more to say."

"Just wait a minute. Please." Grey firmed his grip on her wrist and threw his head back, taking in a deep, shuddering breath. He didn't know what the hell he was doing, but he couldn't let her walk out of their lives.

"Please, let me go, Grey." Claira twisted her wrist against his grip, but he wouldn't release her. Tears sprang unwanted to her eyes. She was losing the tenuous grip on her emotions with every second that he held her there.

Grey released her and she stumbled backwards. Before she could catch her balance, she found herself crushed against his chest, enveloped in his strong arms. A possessive rumble rolled through his chest as he reached out and pulled her into his embrace, capturing her lips in a searing kiss that stole her wits and her breath.

His hand smoothed a path up her spine and burrowed under her hair at the nape of her neck, stroking her scalp with such tenderness it made her knees buckle. When she swayed in his arms, he groaned and loosened his grip around her, his hands stroking up and down her back, her arm, everywhere he could touch.

The empty chill that had invaded her bones vanished, replaced by a warm, languid feeling that she'd never experienced before. Her head lolled against his chest, her thoughts drifting along a whispering current of surrender. How could such a guarded man possess such commanding passion and gentleness?

He pulled away a little, taking her chin and tilting her face up toward his. When she opened her eyes, she was stunned at the raw emotions swirling in there green depths.

~*~*~*~*~

"You're not leaving," he said and crushed his lips to hers in another bruising kiss, his tongue sliding long and deep alongside hers. Her mewling whimper set a fever loose in his blood that burned up every other thought but Claira. Her rich taste, her hot mouth, her soft skin and sweet smelling aroma that was only Claira filled every pore of his being. He had to have her. *Now.*

Buttons flew in every direction as he ripped her shirt open from top to bottom. He groaned when his knuckles grazed her bare nipples. *No bra!* How had he not noticed that before? When she reached up and began to unbutton his own shirt, he stilled her efforts to undress him, imprisoning her wrists in a firm grip. He lowered her hands and pinned them behind her back. "Leave them there."

When she opened her mouth to protest he filled it again with another invading kiss. If she so much as touched him he'd go off like a roman candle on the fourth of July. After six years of emotionally enforced abstinence, he wasn't about to fire his load into his pants. He wanted to be buried to the hilt inside her. Needed it like he needed air to breathe.

Her hands crept up to the back of his neck once more and he couldn't hold back his frustrated growl. Pulling her arms from around his neck, he pushed her torn shirt over her shoulders and down her arms, tying the thin fabric in a sloppy knot around her wrists.

"Grey, I need…." Claira struggled to free her hands. Grey laid his forefinger over her lips to silence her protests.

"I know what you need, baby bird." He leaned down and nuzzled her ear, sucking her earlobe between his lips. *So tiny and soft.* "I'll let you touch me all you want, once I'm buried so deep inside you, you can taste me. Not one moment sooner."

He dipped a hand beneath the hem of the short, little skirt that had driven him crazy all night. He gripped her panties and gave them a stiff yank, extracting a surprised squeak from her and exposing her soft curls to his probing touch. His finger slipped over her clit and slid unimpeded through her slick folds. *Fuck!* "You're soaked."

Claira whimpered as he pulled his finger back and circled her clit again, her eager response fueling his pride.

He gathered her in his arms and walked to the blanket covered bed of fresh hay Matt had set up for them. When Mason had asked him to check on their newly acquired stallion after dinner, he knew it was a set-up. His brothers had forced his hand and, despite his best efforts to resist their plot, he was helpless to the visceral pull Claira had on him.

He laid her out on the bed of hay and pinned her beneath him, his hand working between them to free his cock. When he lifted his head and peered down at her naked breasts, she chased his kiss, her lips leaving a trail of fire along his jaw and neck. He took one quick taste of her nipple before he was drawn back to her mouth. She kissed like a wet dream and he couldn't get enough of her.

Her thighs parted and hugged his hips as he positioned his cock against her pussy. Before he could push inside, she dug her heels into his ass and pulled him inside her in one long thrust.

Grey couldn't contain the animalistic need that roared through his veins. *Mine! Ours!* She was theirs and he would make sure she'd never doubt it again.

Something snapped loose inside his chest when he felt her body bow and arch beneath his. Her hot, tight pussy hugged his cock in an embrace that forever bonded him to her. Nothing had ever felt more right, more real than having her in his arms as he buried himself deep inside her.

"I need to touch you, please," Claira begged and struggled beneath him.

"I've got you, baby bird." He reached behind her and freed her hands from the knotted shirt. "Touch me, Claira." He tucked his forearms beneath her shoulders and buried his hands in her hair.

With a firm grip, he pulled her head back and thrust his tongue into her hot mouth as he flexed his hips and buried his cock in her pussy again and again. He swallowed her whimpers of pleasure, biting and licking at her supple lips until his lungs screamed for air.

Sweat dripped from his chin. She licked the salty offering from his skin as her hands roamed down his shoulders, her tiny fingers curling around his thick bicep. The rasp of his bare chest against her sensitive nipples added another sensual layer to his torturous need. More sweat glued them together; her skirt hiked up to her waist the only barrier between them. His heart pounded against his chest as he looked down at the woman beneath him; the woman who had both broken and healed him.

"Look at me." Grey stopped moving, waiting for her to open her eyes. "Claira, baby, open your eyes and look at me." He needed to look into her eyes as he came inside her.

Claira sluggishly obeyed his command. Her brown eyes fluttered open and he was caught. He didn't deserve her, but he was hers and he'd never let her go again.

He began to move, this time agonizingly slow as he stared down at her. His hips rolled against her as he pulled out slowly, almost completely, and then thrust hard against her, the tip of his cock bumping against her womb.

She whimpered at the jarring pressure. He stilled inside her, not wanting to cause her any more pain. "Please don't stop," she begged with a breathless whisper.

That was all Grey needed to stake his claim. He would mark her forever as his, as theirs. He'd been so wrong to deny his brothers this treasure. They all belonged to her, body and soul.

"So…fucking…beautiful." Grey thrust deep and hard, feeling the tip of his cock tap the end of her velvet channel with each stroke. He was drowning in her eyes, losing himself in her wet, hot depths.

"Grey! Oh-God!"

The sound of his name on her lips made the hair on the back of his neck stand on end. His scalp began to tingle and his balls drew up tight. The muscles in his arms and legs bunched and burned with the force and speed he demanded from them.

His! Theirs! His! Mine!

When her teeth sank into the skin of his left bicep and her pussy pulsed around him with her release, he reached the end of his control. Over and over he plunged, emptying himself deep inside her as she marked him, claimed him as her own.

"Fuck, baby," he panted, his hips still convulsing in response to her own residual spasms. His frantic breaths mingled with hers. Collapsing over her, his quivering arms gave out under his own weight. "That was—I—you feel so good."

"Grey." Claira whimpered against his sweat-slickened neck, her hands still clutching the tight muscles in his back.

"Hey, don't cry." Grey's thumb wiped away a tear that had escaped. "Did I hurt you?"

Claira shook her head, not trusting herself to speak. She'd never felt this complete in her entire life. She loved him, with all her heart.

She was about to tell him that very thing when something shifted in his expression. With a muted curse, he rolled off her. "Fuck!" He jumped to his feet, his legs tangling in his Wranglers piled around his knees.

"Goddammit! I can't believe I did that!" He pulled up his pants, not bothering to button them. "Claira, I'm so sorry."

Claira froze, her heart taking a nose dive. He was rejecting her. She'd never felt more loved or happy in her entire life and he was *sorry?* How could she be so stupid?

His mouth kept moving, saying something in the way of an apology if his expression matched his words, but she didn't hear anything over the pounding of her breaking heartbeat in her ears. She'd been stupid to think she could ever compete with a ghost.

She scrambled to her feet and pulled her skirt down. Reaching for her tattered shirt, she jerked away from Grey as he tried to take it from her grasping hand.

"Please, don't touch me." She clasped the tattered ribbons that were all that was left of her shirt to her chest, trying desperately to reclaim some small piece of her dignity.

"Claira?"

She turned to see Matt and Mason standing inside the barn, their faces marred by confusion and outrage. They took in her disheveled state and their eyes burned like lasers, cutting through the air as they turned their sights on Grey.

She couldn't do this. She'd been so selfish and stupid. This was never going to work. Falcon Ridge could never be her home. She could see that now. Everything was so clear. Grey must hate her to be so cruel. No, he hadn't meant to be. His regret had been genuine. It was her fault for thinking she deserved a life with them. A sudden memory of her father's henchmen carrying her dead brother away from her flashed through her mind. No. She didn't deserve them.

Claira stifled a sob and ran past Matt and Mason, making a beeline for their house. She had everything she needed in her bag upstairs. She would hate not saying goodbye to Con and Car, but it was all she could do to make things right. She had to leave. Now.

Chapter Twenty-Four

"What the fuck just happened?" Grey stood frozen in the cool barn as he watched their frantic woman run past his brothers.

"That's exactly what we'd like to know." Mason stalked up to him.

Grey shook his head, cursing his own stupidity. "I…I didn't use a condom."

He hadn't even had the class to take off his boots before he fucked her senseless. *And he forgot to wear a damn condom!* How could he, of all people, forget something so vitally important? He wouldn't survive having another child; losing his heart all over again. It would kill him. He was such a stupid, sorry ass!

He buttoned up his jeans and paced to the other end of the aisle. God, he hadn't used a condom. He couldn't be much more of an idiot if he'd tried, but damn if he could make sense of her running out like that.

"Surely she knows we'd take care of her if something happens."

"If something happens?" Matt stalked up to stand next to Mason. "You mean if she gets pregnant?" He pushed Grey back a step. "Right, Grey? Because God forbid we go through *that* again."

"Damn right I don't want to go through that again, but I'd never abandon her because of something I did! I need to go to her!" Grey pushed past Matt but Mason stepped in front of him, blocking his exit. "What the fuck is your problem?" Grey asked.

Mason stared at him, shaking his head in disbelief. "If she saw the same look on your face that we just did, I'd say you are the last person she wants to see right now."

Grey's head snapped back. "What look?"

Mason stepped around him and Grey followed his movements. He didn't have time for this shit. He needed to get to Claira and find out what he'd done wrong.

"Did you really regret fucking her, Grey?" Matt asked and crossed his arms over his chest.

"What?" If his little brother didn't shut the hell up, and quick, he was going to regret being born. Why the hell would he ask such a question?

"That's what it looked like to me," Matt said.

"You don't know what you're talking about." Grey turned to go after Claira but stopped when he heard Mason mumble something behind him. He turned back and stalked up to Mason. "What did you say?"

"You used her." Mason didn't mumble this time. He stared right into his brothers guilty eyes. "You sorry sonofabitch. You used her. Now you feel guilty and you think you can say you're *sorry* and everything will just go back to the way it was? As if you didn't just *fuck* her, and us, over the coals?"

They had it all wrong! "It wasn't like that! I said I was sorry for not using a condom! Not that I was sorry I fucked her! And I didn't just *fuck* her, okay! Quit saying it like that! Goddammit, I'm in love with her!"

"That's bullshit!" Matt snapped and pointed to the nest of hay on the floor. "If you loved her she would be wrapped in your arms on that blanket right now and not in her room crying her eyes out! Why are you so damn determined to fuck this up, Grey? Why?"

When Grey didn't move or even attempt to deny it, Mason made one final push. "Why do you hate yourself so much that you can't allow her in?"

Everything inside Grey felt like it was breaking all over again, like it did when they lost Sarah. Only this time it was a hundred times worse. His chest ached, his skin felt like it was too small for his body, his eyes burned with tears he had no way of fighting. If only they knew what a bastard he really was; the bastard that had killed their wife and nearly killed their unborn sons!

"Answer me, *goddammit*!" Mason demanded. "We can't go on as a family like this any longer!"

"I killed Sarah!" The second the words were spoken Grey's blood turned to ice. It was over. All of it. He couldn't carry the weight of his lies another second.

A single tear flowed from the corner of his left eye, down his cheek. His jaw clenched tighter than his fists at his side. "I killed her. Is that good enough for you? "

Claira gasped, his admission hitting her with the force of a freight train. An invisible hand clamped around her heart and squeezed. Three sets of eyes turned to see her standing in the doorway. She'd heard them arguing as she walked to her car, bag in hand, and couldn't stand the thought of them fighting over her. She looked into Grey's tortured eyes and gasped at the pain she saw there. "What do you mean, you killed her?"

Grey shook his head and another tear escaped, followed by more. Disgusted with his weakness, he turned his back to hide his ugly guilt. He should have never said a word, but something had broken loose inside him, while he was inside of her, and he could no longer hold any of it back, not even his fucking tears.

"You know, I prayed to die. I prayed for God to take me instead of her." Grey paced to the other side of the aisle, his hands fisted in his hair. "No matter what happened, she didn't deserve to die. She deserved so much better than a bastard like me."

"Grey, you're talking nonsense." Matt tried to step in front of him, but Grey turned and paced in the other direction.

Claira stood frozen in the doorway, her heart skipping every other beat, her breaths catching in her throat as she watched Grey fall apart right in front of her.

"She knew she had a heart condition," Grey said, his feet rooted in place a meager three feet away from her. He might as well have been a million miles away as he re-lived the worst day of his life.

"That morning, I was standing in the kitchen watching our beautiful, pregnant wife butter toast, thinking how incredible it was that she carried our sons in her swollen belly. She'd been distant since her latest check-up and I was afraid something was wrong with her or the babies, but she kept telling us everything was fine.

"I pressed her again that morning to tell me what was wrong and she broke down in tears. That's when she told me. She was scared because the doctor had warned her not to get pregnant. She'd ignored his advice and pushed us to start a family, never *once* telling us about the risks."

"Son of a bitch," Mason growled under his breath.

Grey's fist came back and plowed into one of the stall doors across from them. He slid to his knees holding his bleeding hand to his chest, his shoulders shaking with his silent sobs.

Claira ran to his side and tried to wrap herself around him. "Grey, please let me," she begged when he flinched and pulled away from her. "It wasn't your fault. She knew the risks she took. It was a bad choice to get pregnant, and a huge mistake not to tell you, but it was her mistake, Grey, not yours."

Grey's head shook in violent denial. "No!" He pushed her away and tried to stand, but fell on his ass in the dirt. "One minute I was watching my own miracle making fucking breakfast, and then I watched it all slip away.

"I was so pissed at her. I'd never felt more betrayed. She'd lied to me, to all of us. I said some of the worst things I've ever said to anyone." He felt his heart stop when the memory of his hurtful words came back to him. *Why didn't you just kill yourself and save us all the worry?*

"How could she put herself at risk like that?" Matt leaned against the barn wall and slid to the floor next to Grey. "I would have—we *all* would have been okay with adopting, or even *no* children!"

"It wasn't your fault, Grey. It was her decision to hide the truth from us. Maybe not your words, but your anger was justified." Mason crouched down in front of Grey, feeling every bit as if he was going to pass out. He took in a deep breath and blew it out slowly, not believing what he was hearing. "Hell, I'm in total shock right now, but I'm sure I'm going to be pissed when that passes."

Grey shook his head again. "You don't understand." His eyes were no longer filled with tears, but the wet tracks on his cheeks glistened in the harsh glow of the bare overhead lights. "She became so upset during our argument she went into labor, a month early. Her water broke right there in our kitchen. If I hadn't said those awful things, made her so upset, she wouldn't have gone into labor so soon."

"Oh, Grey." Claira's heart ached for him. She reached over and traced her fingers over his broken and aching heart, inching her way closer to him like she would an injured animal. She wished she could take the pain and guilt away from him. She knew how it felt to think you were responsible for someone's death; someone you loved more than your own life.

"Grey, you can't..."

"We could have made arrangements for a C-section, anything that would have been less stressful on her," Grey insisted. He ran his fingers through his hair and pulled in frustration. "Her heart exploded after Car was born and Con nearly suffocated before they ripped him from her lifeless body. I can't go through that again, Claira. I can't lose you like that."

"You won't lose me." She threw herself into his arms. Ignoring the dirt floor and the fine sheen of sweat that coated his strong body, she wrapped herself around him. She didn't know what this meant for her or what had just happened between them, but she couldn't stand to see him torturing himself another second.

"You can't keep blaming yourself, Grey. I could never hold you responsible for something like that. I'm sure Matt and Mason don't blame you."

Another wave of guilt rolled through Grey as he thought of the pain he'd caused his brothers. He would die a thousand deaths to keep them from having to live through the loss he'd caused them.

Matt got to his feet and stumbled across the aisle to his brothers. "She's right, Grey. We would never have blamed you for what happened."

"We'd have been pissed as hell, too," Mason said, his bright blue eyes shining with his own unshed tears. He wanted to go to Sarah's grave and kick her damn headstone he was so pissed at her for doing this to their family. He couldn't imagine the weight of the guilt Grey had been carrying around all these years. *No wonder he's been such a fucking mess.*

"I should have never said the things I said to her. I'm so sorry." Grey rocked his forehead against Claira's shoulder as he tried to control his breathing. He'd never been such a big pussy and shed so many tears in all his life. He didn't care anymore. His head was pounding and nose was running, but the ache that had lived in his chest for the past six years had subsided more than he'd ever thought possible. He was mildly comforted when he felt his brother's hands squeeze his shoulders and he looked up to see they were both choking back their own pussy tears.

He wiped the back of his arm across his burning eyes and cleared away the evidence of his weakness. "I'm just so damn sorry I didn't tell you. I couldn't own up to what I'd taken from you."

Mason reached a hand out to Claira and pulled her from Grey's lap. Matt reached down, helped his big brother to his feet then pulled him into his chest. "You didn't take anything from anyone, Grey. She was an incredible woman, and our first love, who we will always love. She was willing to sacrifice her own life to have our children. I wish that she hadn't of lied to us, but we can't change that.

"The only thing you kept from us was the anger and guilt we should've shared with you, you stupid fool of a brother." He pushed Grey away from him and fisted his shirt in his hands. "You were a good husband. You have to let this go. No one's perfect, not even Sarah. You still have us, and our sons. And Claira."

One look at Claira and Grey snatched her into his arms. "I'm so sorry. I wasn't upset about what we did, baby. It was incredible and right and I'd never regret it for one second." He held her away from him then stooped to look her in the eyes. "I didn't use a condom. I know there's no excuse but I…"

"It's ok," Claira shook her head. "I saw the doctor last week during my lunch break and he gave me a birth control shot. They're good for six months, so you don't have to worry."

Grey saw the way she wouldn't meet his gaze and it crushed him. How could he have been so stupid for so long. "Hey," He tilted her chin until she looked up at him. "I meant what I said. I love you. I've just been too much of an ass to see it for what it was."

Claira looked up at him. The ghosts she'd seen in his eyes were no longer there, but she couldn't deny the presence of her own ghosts. She couldn't tell them how much she loved them. Not yet. Not until she told them the truth about everything else.

Chapter Twenty-Five

Mason and Grey whirled around the kitchen putting the finishing touches on the picnic lunch they'd planned for Claira. Since they had no plans of ever letting her go, they'd decided it was time to get her comfortable with ranching life. Lesson number one....ride em' cowgirl!

Judging by her reaction to his roan stallion, which he'd aptly named Magic, Mason knew without a doubt she'd never ridden a horse in her life. They aimed to change that today. A guided tour of Falcon Ridge should give her enough practice for one day, and them enough time to get to the bottom of her skittishness and uncover a few of those secrets she kept under lock and key.

Mason glanced over at his big brother as he slathered mayonnaise on a few slices of bread and noticed the 'cat that ate the canary' grin on his face.

"What?" Grey glanced up from his work to see Mason shaking his head at him, an 'I told you so' smirk on his sorry mug.

"Nothing," Mason chuckled, pushing away from the counter to grab a few sandwich bags. "Guess you figured out a few of those *things* last night, huh?" He closed the cupboard door and walked back to stand by Grey, stuffing the completed sandwiches into the bags. "You know, I never understood why you couldn't stand being in our kitchen after..." He glanced up at Grey and decided not to finish that thought. "Anyway, I'm sorry we gave you so much shit about not taking your fair share of the cooking. I'm just glad to have you back."

Grey finished with the last piece of bread and dropped the knife into the sink beside him, standing there a moment before he turned and faced Mason. He shook his head and leaned back against the counter, crossing his arms over his chest. "I don't have all the answers, yet." He took a deep breath and his smile grew a little bigger. "But I need her."

Mason reached out and pulled his brother in for a back slapping hug. "We all do, man." He pushed Grey back and then snapped him with the damp dishtowel in his hand. "Now let's go show our girl a thing or two about ranching, McLendon style."

An hour and a half later Claira was mounted precariously on top of Biscuit, the gentlest gelding within a three state radius, following Mason and Grey as they ducked out of the barn and made their way toward the lowland pasture. "You're doing fine, sweetheart. Give him a little more head and he'll keep right up with us."

A little more head. Fuck! Grey shifted in his saddle to ease some of the pressure on his balls. *I should have grabbed another bag of those damn peas!*

Waking Claira up had been one of the most erotic experiences of his life. Her sleepy smile greeted them first, followed by the plump swells of her breasts. Her coffee colored nipples beaded to a pair of perfect berries from the sudden rush of cool air that spilled over them when she'd turned over to greet them.

Grey swiped at the drool that slipped out of the corner of his lips before he leaned down and unlatched the first of two cattle gates on their planned route. The memory of how those sweet, mouthwatering berries felt against his tongue had flooded his mouth with saliva so fast it made his jaw ache.

Mason saw him staring at her and smirked. He flipped him a bird when he rode by, mumbling *smartass* under his breath to keep Claira from hearing him.

Claira looked back at the brothers when she heard Mason chuckle and her heart swelled in her chest. Waking up in Grey's bed to two sets of hands caressing every inch of her bare skin was like an erotic dream that she never wanted to end. She thought she *had* been dreaming when she stirred to see both a green and baby blue set of mischievous eyes full of lust and something else she couldn't quite place, staring back at her.

Their deep voices played along her nerves like a bass guitar in a smooth blues song, making every cell in her body hum with arousal. *Now* she understood the carnal fascination with the joys of sex. She would never forget the sights of their bodies entwined together, the sounds of their hearts racing, their breaths mingling together in pants and moans, the musky, sweaty smell of their combined arousal mixed with their salty and all-male flavors budding on her tongue. Just thinking about it sent goosebumps racing over her skin, despite the mid-morning heat.

Even with the emotional upheaval that ensued afterwards, making love to Grey the night before had been better than she'd ever imagined. Making love to Grey and Mason together in Grey's bed....*phenomenal*. She'd never felt more loved or cherished, except with Matt. The only thing lacking about the morning had been the absence of Matt's flirty touch.

She was in love with them. All three of them, and it felt fantastic.

"Too bad Matt's not here." As if he shared her thoughts of missing his twin, Mason's comment conjured up an image of Matt's lazy smile and playful eyes.

"How long did you say the trip to Sarah's parents would take?" Claira couldn't wait until they were all together. She'd decided that it was time to tell them about her past. She dreaded it, feared it, but she couldn't keep it a secret any longer.

Although knowing might dissuade their feelings about her, not knowing could be dangerous for them if Lucien ever found her. After the last few weeks, she felt certain, more than ever, that he would never find her, but couldn't put their family in that kind of danger without giving them the choice.

After Grey had bared his soul, she owed him the truth. They might not look at her the same way after she told them about Stephan, but if Grey could forgive himself, she had to at least give herself the same chance.

"Eight hours round trip, sweetheart." Mason sighed. "Give or take a couple for visiting time and pit-stops."

"Don't worry. He'll be back for supper, baby bird." Grey leaned over and gave her a quick peck on her temple, steadying her in her saddle before he slid back into his own. "You're riding like a pro, by the way. We'll make a ranching cowgirl out of you yet."

"I can think of a few other things I'd rather be riding." Heat flushed her cheeks at her bold statement and her hand shot up to cover her mouth. What had gotten into her?

Mason's loud laughter filled her ears and she whipped her head around to see him doubled over in his saddle. "I think we've created a monster," he said between laughs.

Grey leaned over and plucked her from her saddle. "Hold on, baby," he whispered in her ear, setting her in front of him in his saddle and wrapping a tight arm around her waist. "I intend to give you a few more options the second we get to the creek." He whistled over his shoulder at Mason and then kicked his horse into a gallop, Biscuit struggling to keep up as Grey kept hold on his reins.

Mason raced ahead of them, beating them to the creek bank, and pulled his horse around to greet them. "Thought you'd steal her away from me, did ya?" He chuckled as he leapt down from his saddle and walked over to grab Biscuit's reins from Grey.

"I would have, too, if I hadn't been dragging ol' Biscuit behind me." Grey threw his leg over the back of his horse and hopped to the ground. He reached up for Claira, holding her close as she slid along his body to the ground. He nipped her bottom lip between his teeth in a playful kiss and then lapped at the small bite with his tongue. "Ever been skinny dipping?"

~*~*~*~*~

The morning sun slid beyond high noon and Mason thought he'd died and gone to heaven. Lying on his back, the sunlight glistened off the droplets of water that decorated Claira's naked skin as she lay sprawled on top of him half asleep. Grey was stretched out beside them, tracing her spine with the tips of his fingers, his lips caressing her flank with sultry kisses.

"Did you always want to be a teacher?" Mason asked her, hoping he'd finally get some semblance of information now that she couldn't distract them with sex. Well, she could, but she'd have to stall for a few minutes while he and Grey caught their next wind. He planned to take full advantage of those precious few minutes.

She tensed atop him and he stilled his fingers, waiting to see if she would tell them something, *anything*. They needed her, and that meant all of her. What could be so bad that answering even the most mundane of questions would make her so skittish?

"No," Claira finally mumbled.

Grey glanced up at him when she didn't offer more. "What did you want to be?" he asked, keeping to their plan to extract as much information from her as they could.

She turned her head and looked over at Grey, laying her cheek over Mason's heart. "A child psychologist."

Mason fought not to sigh in relief. Finally they were getting somewhere.

"You said you went to college?" He rose up onto his elbows and kissed her forehead. "Where?"

Claira blinked as she fished for an answer. "Back east." That was the truth. *You didn't answer their question.* It was so hard to switch off the lies. She needed to tell them. "Boston College," she finally forced herself to say.

Grey whistled. "That's a pretty fancy school, baby. Is that where you're from? Boston?"

Claira shook her head and stared at the crisscross pattern on the picnic blanket. "No. I grew up in Maryland, or at least that's where I called home before I came here."

She smiled at the memory of her and her brother playing in the attic of their grandmother's country estate. Mrs. Abbot, the estate manager's wife, would bring cookies and tea and play games with them. She wished they could have spent more time there, away from her father and Lucien.

After their mother left, she and her brother were no longer allowed to visit. She disliked living in the city. She rarely saw their father, but Lucien was always there, lurking in the shadows, watching her. Always. She shivered at the memory of his cold, calculating stare. He was always there, watching and waiting. Waiting for her to *'come of age'*, as she'd heard her father say so many times.

"So is that what you majored in?" Grey asked, bringing her palm to his lips and tickling it with the tip of his tongue.

Claira sighed. The euphoria of their private afternoon had slipped away. She'd never finished her degree. She'd spent her last year of college running from her father, and then running from Lucien. By the time her father was arrested and the trial was over, so was her life. Her teaching degree wasn't real—something the Feds had made up as part of her new identity—but at least she had it.

"I…uh," God she hated the path her thoughts had taken her after feeling so warm and relaxed in their arms. She wanted to hold on to that elusive feeling for a bit longer. "Do we have to talk about this now?"

"Claira, we love you." Grey pressed a finger to her lips when she began to protest. "I know it's hard to think that way so soon, but we do. Baby, we need to know what's going on, what or who you're running from. We won't judge you. We want to help you."

Claira tried to push herself up, but Mason's arms constricted tighter around her naked back. When he didn't say anything, only stared into her soul with those knowing eyes of his, she collapsed back against him and hid her face against his chest.

"You're right. There is something I need to tell you." She reached out and ran her hand along Grey's muscled forearm. "But not here. Not now. Can we please wait until Matt is back, so I only have to go through it once?"

Grey considered her for a moment then glanced at his brother. "Fair enough," he nodded and covered her hand with his own. "It's hard to deny you when you chew on that bottom lip the way you do."

"Thanks, and I know," she giggled, noticing the incredulous look on his face. "Ouch!"

Mason squeezed the soft, perfect globe of her ass that he'd smacked. "Cheeky minx."

Claira squirmed in his grip, but he didn't relinquish his hold. Grey reached into the picnic basket before rising to his knees behind her and she froze. What was he about to do? They didn't keep her guessing long. Mason gripped her bare bottom and spread her cheeks. The look in Grey's eyes stopped her heart.

"While I am helplessly in love with your long, toned legs," Mason said as he stared over her shoulder at Grey. "And Matt trips over his tongue at the very thought of sucking on one of your pebbled, little nipples. Grey has been dying to get his hands on your pretty ass."

Grey got his first look at her perfect, virgin ass and he concurred with his earlier thought. Q and A time was *definitely* over. The look of panic on her face made him pause for a moment and check his raging need.

"Don't be afraid, baby bird. I'd never hurt you." Grey traced a path down her spine with the tip of his finger and his cock flexed at the goose bumps that followed the trail. "I want your ass," he said with a smirk. "Mason tells me you come apart in his hands when he fucks you here with his fingers."

Claira gasped when his finger circled her tight bud, making her flinch and spasm against his touch. *Did they tell each other everything?* "I don't think I'm ready for this." She wanted him there, no doubt, but it also scared the hell out of her. He was so big!

Mason turned her chin so that she was forced to look at him. "Relax, sweetheart. He's just going to play a little; prepare you for tonight when we'll all make love to you together."

Claira swallowed, hard, picturing all of them entwined together like they had been that morning. What did he mean, '*all*'? "All of you? I...how does that work?"

Grey's cock jumped again when her tight ring squeezed around the tip of his finger. His blood raced and sweat beaded along his spine at the thought of that kind of pressure milking his cock. He leaned over her, tracing the curve of her neck with his lips as he whispered in a gravelly growl, "Mason fucking your pussy. Matt sliding into that luscious mouth of yours while I slide into your tight, little ass, baby bird."

An agonizing groan escaped her throat when his finger breached her throbbing tissue. She sucked in a shuddering breath and then blew it out as he moved inside her. Mason tipped her head back to him and plunged them into another toe-curling kiss. She was on fire, writhing on top of him, the erotic picture Grey had described feeding her desire.

"This may be a little cold." Grey flipped the cap on the small bottle of lube and dropped a large dollop at the base of her spine, massaging it down and into her tight rosette. Chills wracked her bones when the pressure increased and she knew he'd added another finger. Her tongue dueled with Mason's as he swallowed her moans, his fingertips digging into the flesh of her backside. His hips rolled beneath her as she pressed herself against his hard length. The fire Grey was creating spread to her legs and up to her breasts making her throb with need.

Mason broke their kiss and cradled her head to his chest as Grey began to stretch her, scissoring his fingers back and forth. "Ohhh." She couldn't hold back the moan as her body began to tremble.

"Hold on, baby." Grey encouraged and then removed his fingers.

"Oh God." Claira froze, pressing her forehead to Mason's chest when something hard and much larger than his finger pressed at her back passage. She wasn't ready for this. She couldn't deny that she liked it when Mason had fingered her there before, but the thought of something bigger scared her. She wanted to try, but she didn't think she could do it.

"Shh, relax, sweetheart. It's just a plug." Mason soothed her. "It will stretch you so you can take us together more easily without us hurting you. Think about what that will feel like. All of our hands caressing you, our cocks filling you over and over, our hearts beating together for you, with you, while we love you and you love us."

Grey was glad Mason was so talkative because he couldn't have forced anything more than a growl past his lips if his life depended on it. It had been so long since he'd felt his control stretched so thin. If he didn't know he would hurt her if he took her now, he would be buried balls deep in her tight, clenching channel. He'd never been more jealous of a piece of silicone in his entire life.

Thank God Matt had had the foresight to stock up on the various items they hadn't had need of in so many years. For the first time in his life he was grateful that his brother's *'live by the seat of his pants'* attitude had taken a back seat and he'd done a little planning, and a little shopping.

"Almost there," Mason watched Grey over Claira's luscious curves and felt the base of the plug slide against the tip of his finger as he held her open for Grey. She was amazing. Knowing they would all share themselves with her tonight, make her theirs forever, made his dick weep. Mason emulated her thrusts, his dick sliding between her slick folds, allowing his climax to take him as she moaned one final time when the plug seated itself deep inside her.

"Ahhh, it burns. Oh… Oh God! Grey!" Claira throbbed around the plug, her inner muscles shuddering, sending her flying. She cried out against Mason's chest as they rocked together in an exquisite rhythm and came together.

"That's it, baby. Feel how good it will be." Grey wrapped a fist around his shaft and stroked, lost in the sound of her voice as his name exploded from her lips. Once, twice. That was all it took until his hot seed sizzled from his balls, through his cock and flowed out over the base of the plug, marking her ass as his. And his it would be before the day was done. God he couldn't wait.

D.L. Roan

Chapter Twenty-Six

Lucien paced the dark alley, the putrid smells of the city churning in the air, offending his senses. Meeting some piss-ant fuck in the sewers where his own shit flowed was beneath him, goddammit!

You will pay for this, Gabriella. You will scream for mercy!

A dark sedan pulled around the corner, steam from a nearby manhole swirling in its wake. *Cut the lights you fucking idiot!* On cue the alley was once again cast in darkness, the only light a faint hue from a flashing caution light at a nearby vacant intersection.

The sedan rolled to a stop a few feet from his own. The back doors opened and four burly men who made his own hired guns look like kindergarten teachers piled out onto the street. No matter. It would be suicide if they so much as breathed in his direction. He was untouchable and planned to keep it that way.

As the goons took their positions around the car, a fifth man emerged into the darkness, straightening his tie and dusting the kinks from his tailored tuxedo.

Cock-sucking politicians. He was in the wrong business. Running smack and smuggling in whores from third world countries paid jack shit compared to the free money these lazy assholes in monkey suits pulled in.

They always thought themselves superior to everyone, like their shit smelled of fucking roses. Still, they always came to him when they wanted something. Well, until recently they went to Gabriella's father, Hector Morganti, but it was all his now and it was time to make a different kind of deal.

He may be the one asking for a favor, but what the slimy bastard didn't know was that Hector kept very detailed records of all his transactions, which he'd worked hard to keep the Feds from acquiring. Regardless of their roles in this little meeting, he would unquestionably be the one calling all the shots.

"Lucien," the slime bag greeted him with a cocky nod.

"Senator."

"I understand that I have something you need. How fortunate for me."

Lucien relaxed when he saw the Senator's cocky smirk. *How fortunate, indeed.* "So I've heard." This man had no idea who he was dealing with.

Lighting a cigarillo, Lucien tossed the match into the street and leaned one hip casually against the front fender of his own sedan.

"Exactly how fortunate, Lucien?" The Senator asked. "I haven't the time or the patience for games."

Lucien took a long draw and expelled the bitter-sweet snuff into the damp night air as he studied the Senator and his men. "Depends on what you have and if it's worth making a deal for what I know you want most."

He held back a grin as he watched the Senator's eye's glaze over. *Always refreshing to know some things never changed.* He tilted his head and took in the Senator's stance.

"Blonde hair, blue eyes, about three, maybe three-foot-two to be exact?" Lucien purred as he sized up exactly how low the perv hung. *Only a bastard would get off on fucking a kid.* Little did the piece of shit know his desires were about to change.

The Senator's twisted libido didn't let him down. "Our latest intel suggests southwest Montana; a hickhole by the name of Grassland. Once the trial concluded she fell off the radar and, as far as I know, no one is looking into it."

Lucien felt a tendril of adrenaline rush through his veins. This was it. He was close and he knew it. Gabriella would be on her knees begging him, fucking his cock with those sweet lips before the week was out.

"I'll expect the delivery by Sunday, Lucien. Not one day later. Understood?"

Lost in his own lustful thoughts, it took a moment for Lucien to comprehend the good Senator's words. "Oh, Senator. One more thing," he said as the Senator turned back toward the open door of his Town Car.

He closed the distance between them, ignoring the two goons that tensed and stepped toward him. "There will be no delivery, this weekend, or any other time, until I receive your usual deposit."

"Now listen here—"

"Ah-ah, Senator. Now is the time for you to listen, not talk." Lucien stepped closer until, even in the dark, he could see the whites of the man's eyes as they widened in shock and anger. "As I was saying. There will be no delivery unless you count the copy of your…let's call it a purchase history, shall we? I'll have a copy hand delivered to you on Monday, so that you know that your account is up to date. Of course, if you have an extra fifty thousand lying around, I could round up something with an ethnic feel to him. We all know little blond boys cost more."

"You son of a bitch. You'll pay for this."

"I highly doubt that, *Senator Collins.* Your desires run deep. I'm sure you and I will be doing a lot of business together, and I will be the only one collecting a fee." Lucien turned on his heel toward his car but stopped and faced the Senator once again. "Of course, if your information leads me to what I seek, I might feel generous enough to give you that blonde trinket after all."

~*~*~*~*~

The ride back to the barn had been torturous if she had to describe it in one word. Between her wet panties and jeans chaffing her thighs, and the constant rocking of Biscuit's saddle against her sensitive backside, Claira was a hot mess of conflicting sensations before the barn came into view.

Her body temperature seemed to be stuck on *inferno*. Her breasts were heavy and swollen, the lacy bra she'd worn raking like talons against her sensitive nipples. Her muscles morphed between languid and tense, relaxed and then pulsing with need until she could feel another climax approaching.

"What the hell?" Mason swung his leg over his saddle and jumped from his horse before they'd stopped at the barn.

"What's wrong?" Claira asked as Grey stopped his horse at the gate and swung down from his saddle.

An uneasy feeling churned in Grey's stomach. He reached up and lifted Claira from the saddle and set her on her feet. "Matt's back already."

A wave of relief washed over her. "That was quicker than eight hours. He must not have made too many stops."

Grey's hand skimmed along the top of the hood of Matt's truck as they passed by on the way to the house. "It's cold. He's been back a while."

Concern replaced her relief as Grey tugged her up the steps and through the front door. The smell of vomit and Clorox filled the air and Claira knew something had gone terribly wrong on their trip.

"Matt, you ok?" Mason rounded the top of the stairs and headed for the upstairs bathroom where miserable retching sounds echoed off the porcelain. "Oh! Oh, that's gross! What the hell happened?"

Matt looked up from his perch beside the toilet as he wiped Con's face with a dampened towel. "I stopped and got the boys some breakfast on the way out of town and within an hour they were puking it back up. I couldn't make the next three hours of the drive." He shrugged and swiped his arm across his forehead. "I didn't want to leave them there sick, so I turned around and came back home. Here, rinse your mouth out, buddy." He handed Con a cup of water and watched him swish and spit in the toilet.

"How long have you been back?" Grey squatted down and put his hand on Car's little forehead. He was sweaty and clammy and looked every bit as pitiful as Con.

"A few hours," Matt shrugged. "Must have pulled in right after you guys rode out. Didn't see much need in interrupting your day." He ran a hand through his own sweaty hair and gave a flirty wink to Claira.

A few hours later Matt stumbled down the stairs and out onto the front porch, freshly showered, but completely drained. After a day like the one he'd had, he wanted nothing more than to sit back in the porch swing in his bare feet and snuggle in close to their woman while Mason and Grey took charge of cleaning up the mess.

Their woman. He didn't believe he would ever be saying that again. It was never something he'd thought about, really. Now that she was there, it amazed him that they had even been able to breathe for the last six years. God knew they hadn't been living. Not like Sarah would have wanted. The anger over what she'd done was still fresh, but somehow it seemed to make sense. It was just like her to stick her chin out to the world and do what she'd wanted to do. He missed that about her. She lived life on her terms, and now it seemed they were getting some of that will to live.

"Hey, darlin'." He blew out a breath as he slid into the swing next to Claira and pulled her legs over his lap. "I'm sorry about our plans tonight."

Claira leaned up and placed a soft kiss on his bare shoulder. He wore only a pair of faded Wranglers, no shirt or shoes. His hair was still damp and he was sporting the stubble of a new goatee. She liked it.

"Please don't be sorry. Your boys come first. Besides, we had all that time to ourselves while you were here by yourself dealing with sick twins. I feel sort of guilty."

Matt chuckled, his fingers massaging gentle circles at the base of her neck. "Well, you shouldn't, but if you insist, I can think of a few ways for you to make it up to me." His eyebrows jumped in his signature playful way and she couldn't help but laugh.

The setting sun cast a red glow on his tanned skin as she looked up at him, studying his features. "There really is no jealousy between the three of you, is there?"

Matt shook his head and reached up to wrap one of her soft curls around his finger. "Nope. Not with you." He studied her for a moment wondering how else he could explain their feelings to her. "It's not just a sexual preference, darlin'. Although, I have to say watchin' one or both of my brothers make you come 'til you're screamin' all our names is one hell of a turn on for me."

Claira blushed a beautiful rosy color and the picture of what he'd just described morphed into technicolor in his mind. Tamping down his arousal, he focused on the curled clip of hair he was fingering.

"There was a time when I thought this way of life, *our* way, was…awkward. Then one day, I noticed how many kids around us never had a homemade lunch, or parents who showed up at baseball and football games. A lot of kids only had one parent. Even those that had two were home alone more than not because their parents worked crazy hours just to pay the bills." Matt shrugged. "I mean, don't get me wrong. Bein' able to hang out at my friend's house with no parents around was awesome, sometimes, but I couldn't imagine what that would be like every day."

Matt let go of the stray curl and entwined his fingers with hers. "With the three of us, we can provide our wife and our kids with more love and support than they could ever need. With our mom and three dads, we always felt safe and loved. Some of the kids growin' up had a few snarky comments and opinions about the way we live, but most of the people around here are pretty open and accepting of it—the Grunions excluded, of course."

Claira thought about what he was saying and could find no fault in his thinking. She'd witnessed the outcome with her own eyes. Their boys were extremely well adjusted and no one man had the sole responsibility of providing for them all.

But one question kept niggling at her. "Does it ever bother you that your brothers might have…" Claira shrugged, unsure of how to word her concern. "Do you ever feel insecure, or does your male pride, or ego, or…whatever get stepped on sometimes and you fight?"

Matt chuckled. "Not really. I mean, we argue and fuss like any normal family, but not the usual macho caveman type stuff you're thinking of. We all have our own relationship with the twins." He paused and kissed the tip of her nose. "And with you, but we're also a family, with the same love and family ties that other traditional families have." He chuckled again and tipped his head. "Now that you mention it, though, I'm going to have to one up Grey on that hickey you're sportin'." He pulled at the collar of her shirt and traced the small bruise. "Jealous we're not, but competitive doesn't even begin to define us."

Claira looked down at the little, purple spot on her shoulder and her cheeks heated with embarrassment. She'd hurried through her shower so that she could help with the twins, never noticing the small bite Grey had given her that morning. She blushed at the memory and pulled her shirt over to cover it.

"Hey, don't be embarrassed." Matt tilted her face to him. "I plan to put my mark on you, too. As soon as I can gather enough energy to get you naked."

Claira laughed and gave him a dubious glance. "Remind me to hide the hammers."

Matt's brows drew together in confusion before he remembered the story he'd told her about marking his truck. He burst out laughing. The first bout of laughter morphed into a contagious belly laugh that led to them rolling on the porch floor, holding their stomachs and gasping for air. That's where Mason found them when he came out to dump the last of the bleach water he'd used to clean up the boys' bathroom.

"What the hell is going on out here?"

Matt and Claira took one look at him and lost it. Matt clutched at his stomach as he rolled on the porch, his face red from lack of oxygen.

Mason looked down at his black t-shirt and mumbled a curse. Splotched in bleach was the perfect outline of the toilet seat he'd just cleaned.

"Sonofabitch!" In his attempts to pull the shirt away from his chest he dropped the bucket of dirty bleach water, jumping back as it splashed up onto his Wranglers, some landing precariously near his crotch. "Fuck!" He toed off his boots then stripped off his pants and boxers, sprinting for the water hose at the side of the porch.

That's where their dad Jake found him when he stepped out of his truck and ambled up the porch steps.

Papa Jake took one look at Mason, naked as a jaybird with a water hose in his hand, and then swiveled around to look at Claira and Matt on their sides, gasping for breath between bouts of laughter. He made the sign of the cross over his heart as he shook his head and opened the front door. "I don't even want to know."

Mason washed himself off and stumbled up the stairs, using his hat to cover his dick which seemed to have escaped any harm. "It's real funny 'till someone loses his balls." He reached down to help Claira off the floor when he heard another car door slam.

"Mason Nathaniel, since when do you prance around outside buck naked in broad daylight? I know I've taught you better than that!" Hazel climbed the front steps, her arms laden with plastic shopping bags. "Oh," She glanced down at Matt and Claira who'd stopped howling, but kept up a steady stream of chuckles as they watched Mason turn fifteen shades of red.

Hazel narrowed her eyes at Matt, and then looked back at Mason, then back down at Matt again. "Are you boys using condoms?"

Matt and Claira glanced at each other before they burst out laughing again. Mason swore under his breath. "For Christ sake, Ma. It's not what you think, and turn around!" Mason cupped his dick and balls and moved his hat to cover his ass.

Hazel looked back down at Matt then followed Mason into the house, shouting after him. "Well, why not? You know she's perfect for you boys. What the heck is taking you so long?"

Matt sat up and helped Claira do the same. Both breathless, he reached for her face and drew her into a sweet, lingering kiss. "She's right, you know. You are perfect. For all of us." Claira smiled shyly but didn't respond. "I love you," he breathed as he licked her taste from his lips. "You don't have to say it back, but I want you to know."

"I love you, too." The words came with no regret or second thoughts. She loved them all. Now she just had to hope and pray it would be enough.

Chapter Twenty-Seven

Hazel and her husbands had been a godsend over the last couple of days. Claira helped Hazel make her coveted homemade chicken and slippery noodle soup for the twins, writing down every single step so that she'd be able to make it for them next time. Not that she expected it to be near as good. The woman could cook her under the table any day of the week and twice on Sundays.

Jake, Joe and Nate had filled in for Matt, Mason or Grey's shifts with the boys when they needed to tend to any of the ranch business. After two days of vomit duty rotation and two full days of rest, both Con and Car were back to their rambunctious selves and the elder McLendon's had vacated the premises.

Claira watched from the kitchen window as the boys played outside with a toy airplane their grandparents had brought them. Matt and Mason were somewhere close by; most likely in the barn. Grey had hidden himself away in his office to catch up on the paperwork he'd let slide while tending to the boys.

With all the commotion and family members coming and going, Claira hadn't yet told the men about her past. She'd tried once, but Hazel had called just as she'd gotten them all gathered at the kitchen table and said that Josiah was on his way over with new bed linens she'd bought for the boys' beds. She decided then to wait until this current crisis was over before she started a new one.

At the moment her thoughts were consumed with the dirty words Grey had whispered in her ear after breakfast. The boys were going to stay the night at their Uncle Cade's house while they planned to corrupt her with all sorts of blissful debauchery, which, she'd been told, included Grey *taking her ass with his mammoth cock*. A shiver shuddered along her spine and she braced herself against the kitchen sink.

When she raised her head and glanced out the window, the twins were nowhere in sight. She grabbed a dish towel to dry her hands then walked to the back door to see where they'd gone. Her heart plummeted to her toes when she spotted Con climbing after Car up the old, dead tree beside the half-finished feed shed.

Her feet flew over the uneven ground, her singular purpose to get to the boys. "Carson! Connor! Get down from there right now!"

Claira reached the base of the tree and was half way up when Con slipped from the branch just above her. She screamed as she reached out to grab ahold of anything she could wrap her fingers around. Thankfully he stopped in mid-air, but was still out of reach, the back of his shirt snagged on the branch above his head.

"Con, don't move," she whispered, afraid even the slightest wisp of her breath would send him crashing the fifteen or twenty feet to the ground. She looked down and her head spun. She didn't know how far it was, but it would hurt if he fell.

She glanced over to Carson perched on a nearby limb, and then back down to Con.

"Both of you, don't move." She gathered her skirt around her knees and looked around at the other branches. She needed to get a better grip on the branch above her to be able to reach out for Con and not drop him. Twisting around onto her other foot, she glanced out toward the barn to see if the guys were coming to help.

At first she didn't see him, only the outline of a long rifle perched on the roof of the feed shed. She followed the long, dark extension to the man's outstretched arm to see Mr. Kendal, staring down the barrel at her.

~*~*~*~*~

Mason heard Claira's shouts from the training corral behind the barn and ran around to see what all the fuss was about. When he saw Claira teetering on a limb, twenty feet in the air as she reached for Con, he took off at a dead run. "Matt!" He cleared the first fence and sprinted for the second that stood between him and his boys. "Claira, don't move!"

Everything else from that moment on seemed to happen in excruciatingly slow motion. Con had stopped climbing about midway up and slipped, his shirt catching on a gnarled knot on the side of one of the smaller dead branches. Claira climbed up after him, her long, red skirt trailing behind her. She'd settled into the crook of the two main branches and was reaching out to grab him when a loud *crack* filled the air around them and she crashed to the ground below.

Mason wasn't sure where he'd come from, but Matt reached the base of the tree the same time he had. While Matt stopped to help Claira, Mason bolted up the tree trunk toward his sons. As he reached for Connor another *crack* sounded a few hundred yards away and chunks of tree bark exploded around his head. *What the fuck!* Someone was shooting at them!

Without thinking, he grabbed a hold of Carson's pant leg, yanking him down into his arms then lunged for Connor, grasping him around his waist as he leapt from the tree, landing in a tangle of arms and legs.

"Ow! My arm!" Con screamed when Mason moved to cover him.

Two more shots cracked around them, only these were louder and much closer than before. Mason gathered his boys beneath him and covered them the best he could as he looked up to see Matt holding Claira to his chest, covering her lifeless body with his own. *God no!*

Mason looked to his left to see Grant rushing toward them, a black gun in his hand and a rifle swung over his shoulder. "Stay put and call an ambulance!" he ordered as he tossed his cellphone to him and jogged off toward the south pasture from where some of the shots had come.

Mason scrambled to his knees, but kept hunched protectively over his boys, Connor still screaming and holding his arm. "Shh, Con, it'll be okay. Daddy's got ya and we're going to get you to the hospital, buddy."

He looked over to Car as he dialed 9-1-1. Other than a few scratches and his wide eyes filled with shock, he seemed to be ok. "You ok, Car? Are you hurt anywhere? Talk to me!"

Lying on the ground next to Con, Car held perfectly still as he stared at his twin. "I'm ok, daddy," he whispered.

Mason gave a brief rundown to the emergency operator before he dropped the phone and reached for Connor, pulling him into his arms. He heard Matt and Grey's voices somewhere in the distance, but nothing seemed to be making sense except the sound of his son's cries.

He laid Con back onto the ground and tore his shirt open, running his hands over every bit of skin he could touch. No blood, no holes. He checked his scalp and then his legs. When he got to his arm, he groaned in both relief and sorrow. There was no blood, but he could see the odd angle of the bones below his elbow and a swollen lump beginning to form. His tiny limb was definitely broken.

What seemed like an eternity passed before they heard the emergency sirens. Grey ducked and ran toward the house to meet them. He'd never felt so helpless in his whole damn life. He didn't know what to do. Did he gather his boys and run? Grant had said to stay put, but he was gone. He didn't know who the hell was shooting at them or if they were still out there.

He held Con to his chest and pulled Car closer. Taking a chance, he slowly raised his head and saw Matt bent over Claira, doing something he couldn't see through the tall grass that surrounded them. Had she been shot? He couldn't see, damn it! She needed help! Con needed help! How the hell would the EMTs make it out this far if someone was shooting at them?

~*~*~*~*~

Grant dropped back a step and stopped, closing his eyes to heighten his other senses to the woods surrounding him. *One o'clock.* He held his .45 close to his chest and crept silently toward his prey. This was easier than hunting deer with a spotlight. His gut told him that this wasn't the threat he was sent to neutralize, but it was a threat all the same.

Stupid fucker. Not many people had the balls to pull the trigger on another human being. He could say he was slightly impressed, but this had crazy written all over it. Crazy led to stupid.

A round, balding head came into view as he crept up to an outcropping of rocks just inside the tree line. On the other side of the largest boulder, a middle-aged man paced back and forth, only his bobbing head visible.

Grant held back a chuckle as a mental picture of a carnival game came to mind. *Ducks.* He laughed to himself. It was like playing 'Duck Shot'. Little yellow ducks with bullseyes painted in the middle, traveling in a row across a big target board. *Three shots in a row wins a prize*! Grant closed his eyes and gave himself a mental shake. He needed to get this job done and get the fuck away from humanity.

He studied his target a moment longer. The guy was nervous, talking to himself. This fucker was coo-coo for coco puffs, alright. He could take him out from here, but he might be useful alive, if nothing else but to confirm his target. It wouldn't matter in the long run if things went to shit. His cover was blown to hell.

Taking a deep breath, he tucked his pistol into the waistband at his back and sauntered out calmly from his hiding place.

"Hey! What-cha huntin'?"

Stupid Fucker stopped in his tracks. Judging by the crazed look on the man's face, he wouldn't have been surprised to see a stain of piss bloom down his pant leg. He didn't appear to have any injuries, which pissed him the hell off. He'd been sure he'd gotten in at least one good flesh wound.

A .38 revolver shook in the man's right hand, his finger off the trigger. Beads of sweat dripped from the fucker's face as he glanced to his right at the rifle leaning up against one of the rocks…four feet away from him.

He didn't answer Grant's question, so he took another cautious step toward him and gestured to the woods behind them. "Great place to catch a buck. Saw some pretty deep tracks about thirty yards in. Thought that may be what you were shootin' at."

Stupid Fucker stared blankly at him for a moment, then drew his arm up and aimed the revolver at his own bald head.

"Don't come any closer. I'll pull the trigger!" Stupid Fucker shouted. This is where stupid turned to crazy. He didn't know *jack* about this guy, yet he was supposed to care if he pulled the trigger? Normally Grant would help him out with a bullet, but easy didn't seem to be on the agenda.

Whatever. He didn't have time for these kinds of games.

Grant pulled his pistol around and raised it to Stupid Fucker's face. The man's beady eyes widened. He was shaking now, violently, but still didn't have his finger on the trigger. What was left of his pasty-white coloring suddenly turned to putrid green.

Yeah, you really shouldn't play with guns.

"You've got until I finish this sentence to either pull that trigger or drop the gun, or I'll blow your head off for you."

A second of silence passed. Grant pulled the trigger. Stupid Fucker hit the dirt, screaming like a goddamn girl. "You shot my hand off!"

Grant shrugged. "Sorry. I'll aim better next time." It was a gamble, he knew. Fifty-fifty chance he was right and the guy didn't have the balls to pull the trigger. Not his life. Not his hand. Not his problem.

Grant cursed as he secured the man's guns and gathered his legs together. Pulling him to a sitting position, he yanked Stupid Fucker's belt from his waist and tied off his bleeding stump.

This was why it was easier to just kill the bastard. Now he either had to knock his sorry ass out and carry him back to the ranch, or listen to him scream and whimper like a sniveling bitch the whole way back. He'd probably puke once or twice on the way, too.

Before tucking his gun back into his waistband, Grant stepped back and studied the little shit, his screeching voice gaining an octave with every cry. *To hell with this.* Twenty seconds later he had the unconscious—and blissfully silent—overweight bastard flung over his shoulder as he headed back the way he came.

Chapter Twenty-Eight

Five days! Grey paced the sterile, horse-stall-sized waiting room the hospital called a family lounge. Five days and six fucking nights since he'd allowed himself to feel something, *anything*, and now his entire world was crashing in around him. This is what he'd been shutting out; this searing, gaping hole in his chest that grew bigger and deeper as the minutes ticked by with no news.

He'd thought time had slowed down when he looked out his office window and saw Claira fall from that dead bitch of a tree. Then gunfire erupted and World War III broke out on his ranch. That was nothing compared to this. Time stopped all together now. Every time he looked at the clock on the waiting room wall, what seemed like hours had been mere minutes.

"What's taking them so long?" Grey turned, focusing on the green linoleum as it passed under his feet. He reached the end of another pace across the room and turned, stopping to look at the clock again. He couldn't do this anymore. "I'm going in there."

"Greyson, don't." Hazel pulled him back from the door and stepped in front of him. "They are doing everything they can. You know it won't help."

Grey dug the heels of his hands into his tired eyes and growled. "It's been over an hour since she came out of surgery. Why can't we see her?"

"Son." Josiah approached his eldest son and clapped his big hands on his shoulders. "Let's go outside and get some fresh air. I'm sure they'll have her ready for visitors when we get back."

"I'm not leaving her, dad." Grey shrugged off his dad's hand and began pacing again. Pictures of Claira's lifeless body flooded his thoughts. Lying on the ground, her face was white and dotted with drops of her blood. "They said the bullet passed right through her shoulder. Why would they be taking so goddamn long if nothing else is wrong?"

Hazel patted his arm and turned him toward the row of chairs that lined the back wall. "Honey, they also said she has a severe concussion from the fall. Give them time. Give her time. She's been through a lot and her body needs to rest so she can heal."

The waiting room door swished open. Grey jumped from the seat he'd just taken when Matt walked in carrying Connor, Mason right behind him with Car in his arms.

"Daddy Grey?" Con whimpered and reached toward him with his uninjured arm. Grey reached out, took him from Matt and cradled him to his chest. "It hurts, daddy," Con sobbed.

Another piece of Grey's heart broke away as he tucked Con's head under his chin and held his youngest son, hoping to never feel that all-consuming fear of losing him again.

"I know, buddy. It will be better soon, I promise." Grey stepped over to Mason and reached for Car. "Come here, little man."

Car hesitated at first, but latched onto Grey's neck and pulled himself into Grey's arms. "I'm sorry, daddy. It was my fault. I told Con it would be a good idea to fly the airplane from the top of the tree."

"But I wanted to do it!" Con protested through his hiccupping cries. "Please don—don't be mad—mad at him, Daddy. It—it—was—my—fault—too."

Grey's knees buckled and he sank back down into one of the lounge chairs, hugging both his boys as tight as he could. "I'm not mad." He was sure he'd be mad later, but now? Right now he was grateful, and scared shitless.

Jake and Josiah huddled together in a whispered conversation before Jake stepped over to Grey, knelt on his haunches in front of him and cupped his grandsons' little faces. "Your Mom and I are going to take them home with us. The police are still out at the ranch with Nate and Uncle Cade, working things out. When they're done we'll go over and gather some of their things. Joe will stay here with you until one of us comes back with a fresh change of clothes for all of you."

Grey tensed when Jake reached for his boys, unwilling yet to lose the feel of them, alive, and safe in his arms. His mom stepped over and placed a kiss on the top of his head "We'll take good care of our grandbabies."

Moments later the room exploded in a cacophony of loud curses as the McLendon men began to vent some of the anger they'd subdued in front of their mother and the twins. A loud thump broke through the chaos and Grey turned to see what was left of one of the chintzy coffee tables Mason had thrown against the wall.

"If that sonofabitch ever steps one foot outside of a jail cell I'll rip his throat out with my bare hands and feed what's left of his sorry, goddamn carcass to the coyotes."

Joe, Matt and Grey stared slack-jawed at Mason. Ever the silent presence of calm and the self-appointed peace keeper of the entire McLendon family, the normally cool and collected Mason had come completely unglued.

"I want every goddamn faculty member on that fucking schoolboard fired! No, not fired. Gone! I'll burn down every one of their goddamn houses and see to it *personally* that none of them ever step foot in this town again! And so help me *God*, if I *ever* hear that prick's name uttered anywhere other than an obituary I'll kill the sorry sonofabitch that dared to say it out loud!"

Matt was so entirely awestruck at his twin that he jumped when the waiting room door swung open. Two official-looking men in suits strolled in as Mason kicked another chair across the room. The men stopped in mid-stride and everyone in the room paused to glance back at Mason. He ran his hands through his hair and turned away from them with a frustrated snarl.

The older of the two men cleared his throat and offered his hand to Grey. "I'm detective Handleman. This is my partner, Detective Simms. We're from the Boswick County Sheriff's Department. Sherriff Long called us in to assist him on this case."

Grey shook the man's hand. Matt and Josiah followed suit. They looked over at Mason but didn't make an attempt to greet him. "We have Preston Dawes in custody—"

Mason's growl was more animalistic than human as he lunged at the Detective. Grey and Joe stepped up to block his path and hold him back. Mason fought against their hold, reaching out to grab whatever handful of flesh he could get his hands on as both the Detectives took a step back from the shocking scene.

"Uh, this isn't such a good time." Matt felt a strange but welcome sense of calm as he opened the door to usher them from the room. Mason had lost his damn mind and, for the first time in his life, he was the rational twin. He almost laughed at the odd thought. It made his skin itch a little, but he kind of liked the unexpected switch. "Give us some time to process this," Matt requested once they were out of the room. "We'll all still be here, and hopefully a little more cooperative tomorrow. Can you come back in the mornin'?"

"Mr. McLendon," the younger Detective said. "I'm sure you understand that it's best if we get the details down while they're still fresh."

Matt urged him down the hall toward his partner. "And I'm sure *you* understand that, if you go back into that room, my brother will rip off your head and shove it up your ass, and I'll be hell-bent to help him." *So much for calm and collected.* He shrugged and turned back toward the waiting room from hell. *It was nice while it lasted.*

Three more agonizing hours passed before they allowed anyone into Claira's room. Even then it was only one at a time. Grey and Matt held back and let Mason go first, with the hope that seeing her would help him climb back into his own skin. When he returned a short while later, he was little more than a broken shell.

The aching twist in Grey's gut grew tighter as he slid into the seat beside to Claira's bed. She looked so fragile, more than usual. He couldn't help but stare in awe as he wondered how such a tiny person wouldn't just crumble into a million unrecognizable pieces after taking a bullet like that. Thank God it hadn't hit anything vital. The thought that it could have been one of his boys lying in that bed... He closed his eyes and drew in a deep breath. It was unthinkable. She'd saved their lives. All of them.

That sick fuck, Dawes, puked up a full confession, still spouting off at the mouth as Grant carried him up to the house and dumped his sorry, bleeding ass on the ground in front of one of the ambulances. He had a debt to pay to Grant, too.

Apparently, somewhere in Preston Dawes's twisted mind, he believed they had somehow stolen Sarah from him. *"It's your wicked and corrupt witchcraft that made her stay with you! You filled her with your demon spawn and they killed her!"* he'd shouted as they lifted him onto a gurney. *"I'll not let you corrupt another innocent woman."* Dawes had twisted and flopped on the gurney, glaring at Grey as they wheeled him to the ambulance. *"I'll not let you! She's mine!"*

Grey felt like vomiting, again as he heard Dawes' whiny voice in his head repeat on a constant loop. He still couldn't believe how much he'd underestimated the crazy fucker. He knew the man was prejudiced—all of the Dawes' and Grunions were—but he'd never once imagined one of them would stake out their home and start shooting at them.

Grant had spotted Dawes slithering across the pasture. He'd retrieved his rifle and climbed to the roof of the feed barn to scope him out, thinking he'd caught a hunter poaching on their land.

When he'd watched him set up at the edge of the property and scope out their home, Grant knew they were in trouble. Before he could climb down to warn anyone, the twins had begun to scurry up the tree that stood between them, and then all hell had broken loose. He couldn't get a clear shot until Con had slipped down to the lower branch and by then it was too late. Claira took the bullet that Dawes had intended for his son.

Now, she was lying there, unconscious, tubes and wires snaking their way around her every limb. The doctor's said her head injury caused her brain to swell and they were keeping her in a coma with medicine until the swelling subsided.

They were saying there was a chance, a small chance, she might not remember them or what had happened when she woke. She could even have brain damage.

Grey got up and paced to the other side of the room. He wouldn't let himself even think it. No one knew what she was going through, locked away behind all those medications that made her sleep. She would be fine. And if she wasn't, then they would take care of her and help her until she *was* fine. She was their heart. She was the heart of Falcon Ridge; their gift from heaven and he wasn't giving her back!

Two days passed and the swelling had stopped. She was breathing on her own and they had removed a few of the more intimidating machines from her room. The men came and went on a constant rotation. One or more of their dads was always there for support. Josiah had gone in to sit with her a bit that first night. He was wiped when he came back into the waiting room and no one acknowledged the red rims around his watery eyes. Nate and Jake hung back with the rest of the family whenever they were there, always offering a strong shoulder if the men needed it. No one cried in front of the family, but they had all shed a million tears between them when they were alone.

The constant drone of the machines beeping and whirring had lulled Mason into a dark and fitful sleep. Sitting on the rigid edge of the only chair in the room, his upper body slumped over the edge of Claira's bed, her hand in his. Her tiny fingers twitched against his palm. At first he'd thought it had been a dream. He opened his eyes, wiping away the crusty haze only a mixture of tears and exhaustion can cause. He held his breath in a motionless trance, waiting to feel the movement again, praying that it wasn't a dream.

Another twitch followed by a wispy moan jerked Mason into the realm of the conscious. The numbness in his legs and feet had him scrambling for purchase when he stood. He ignored the pain as the sudden rapid beat of his heart pumped a rush of blood to his legs.

With a touch as soft as a feather, he caressed her pale cheek and brushed his lips against her temple. In a whisper he repeated the request that had been his silent plea to her for the last two days. "Hey, Sweetheart. Please wake up for me."

Chapter Twenty-Nine

A small, shiny dot appeared in the middle of the most complete darkness Claira had ever known. It was as if the sky had turned to black and the sun had shrunk to the size of a distant star. When she tried to focus on the dim light, a spike of pain pierced her skull. A haze of reds and oranges floated in her peripheral vision and set her chest on fire.

She heard a faint groan in the distance. It grew closer as the light grew brighter and her chest burned hotter. Then she was falling. She grasped frantically at the dark nothingness that was swallowing her whole, but found only more darkness and pain. She heard voices and shouts and piercing sirens of noise. In a snap everything fell silent. A warm numbness enveloped her. She welcomed the darkness as she faded away into its depths.

Mason scrambled toward Claira's bed as the nurses pushed him back. "What's wrong with her?" He shouted over her screams and the alarms and the doctors barking orders. Claira's body convulsed wildly. Whimpering incoherently, she grasped blindly at anything within reach. One of the nurses pushed him toward the door. He slumped against the wall in a boneless heap as whatever medicine they'd injected into her IV took over and she relaxed back into her bed.

"This is expected, Mr. McLendon." The attending physician extended his hand and helped Mason to his feet. He'd long ago given up trying to remember any of the nurses or doctors' names. "She's coming around, slowly, but with everything her body has been through things can be a bit...confusing for her. This is a good sign, trust me. She's fighting her way back."

Mason trembled as he nodded at the doctor. He glanced over at Claira's now sleeping form. "So this..." He swallowed against the dryness in his throat and scrubbed a hand over his face. "This means she *is* going to wake up? She's going to be ok?"

The doctor gave him a sympathetic look then turned to look back at Claira. "I can't make that promise, Mr. McLendon. But I *can* say that she seems to be a fighter. The swelling went down quickly and she's responding to more stimuli each day. There's only so much we can do. She has to do the rest." Mason nodded but couldn't say anything through the lump in his throat.

"It's only been forty-eight hours. Give it time." The doctor opened the door and ushered him from the room, away from Claira. He glanced back over his shoulder at her frail form as the door closed behind them.

"Go for a walk, Mason." The doctor said. "Let one of your brothers take a shift. If you don't mind me saying so, at the risk of losing my head, you look like shit. You're no good to her or your family like this."

Mason began to argue, but the doctor held up a staying hand and blocked his attempt to go back to her room. "That wasn't a request, Mason. It's not good for you or her."

Two days following the nightmare episode Mason had witnessed, Grey sat slouched in the chair next to Claira's bed, fingering the ring they'd bought her the night before. Being able to focus on something besides the wreck their lives had become had given him back a little strength. But, buying that ring on faith that she'd be ok, and would accept their proposal, had set him back more than a bit in confidence. Different scenarios played in his mind, too many of them without a happy ending. *How could she still want us after this?*

Over the last two days Claira had several more episodes like the one she'd had with Mason. Now she rested comfortably, muttering words and phrases that made no sense but gave him more hope than he'd had the day before. He sat listening to waves of silence intermingled with quiet mumbling, her voice like a lullaby rocking him to sleep. He was so immersed in the sounds that he didn't answer when she first whispered his name.

"Grey?"

Grey's eyes opened and a wave of adrenaline washed over his skin.

"Grey?" Claira whispered again and he turned to see her big doe eyes staring back at him.

"Claira?" *Oh thank you God!* "I'm right here, baby bird." Grey rushed to her side and cradled her delicate face in his hands. "You remember me," he said in an excited whisper. "You're really awake and you're going to be ok. And you remember me!"

"Of course I remember you." Claira half smiled, but then closed her eyes on a painful moan. "Where am I?" Her mouth was as dry as a desert and her throat burned.

"You're in the hospital, baby. Let me get the nurses and I'll be right back." Grey didn't want to leave her, but he had to get a nurse or someone to make sure she was ok.

Hospital? What was she doing in the hospital? "Wait, Grey?" She tried to sit up, but something skewered her to the bed like a white-hot poker through her chest. "Ow!" She looked down at the bandages over her chest that extended to her shoulder and adrenaline rushed through her veins as the memories flooded back.

"Grey!"

Grey jumped when he heard a fear laden scream from Claira's room. He dashed back in to see her trying to rip the IV from her arm. "Claira! Baby, don't do that! What's wrong?"

"Grant! Grey, you have to get away. Grant tried to kill me and he'll kill you too! He'll kill all of you!" She wrestled with the nurse and the tangles of wires and tubes as she choked on a sob.

"Claira, baby, Grant saved you. It was Preston Dawes that shot you."

"Grey, he won't stop. Lucien found me. He won't stop until everyone is dead!" The nurse wrestled her arm down to the cuffed restraints and buckled it in. "Please don't! Please let me go!" she sobbed. Grey watched in confused horror as the nurse pumped something into her IV port. "Grey, please! Please believe me. Lucien doesn't care about the babies. He'll kill the babies! Please!"

The room spun. Grey stumbled back as he watched his baby bird sink back into the bed, quiet sobs wracking her tiny frame as the sedative worked its way through her system. He felt someone holding him up and dragging him away but couldn't seem to stop the room from spinning.

"Grey, what is she talking about?"

Matt. Focus on Matt's voice. Grey shook his head and everything popped into focus as he found his footing. Pushing against Matt, Grey made for her room and ran to her bedside, but it was too late. Whatever drug they'd given her had taken full effect. Her chest rose and fell in an even rhythm as she slept, trails of tears streaking down her tender cheeks.

"Grey?" Ignoring the single family member rule Matt stepped into the room and pushed his way between Grey and the nurses to get a glimpse of Claira. "Grey, what was that about killing babies and Grant Kendal?"

Seething with a white-hot fury he knew would never die until someone had paid for what they'd done to her, Grey turned for the door. "I don't know, but I'm damn well going to get some answers."

Thirty minutes later, seven pairs of eyes turned toward them as Grey, Matt and Mason stormed into their family room. "Where are the twins?" Matt roared as Grey swept past him and his family, not noticing the stranger among them, and plowed into Grant Kendal with a feral growl, grasping his shirt and slamming him against the nearest wall.

"If you've so much as touched them I'll kill you!" Grey spat the promise through his clenched teeth. Panic-laced fear had consumed the brothers as they raced home with the Sheriff to find Grant and get some answers.

"Let him go," their Uncle Cade ordered, ignoring the Sheriff who had followed them.

Matt twisted away from the Sheriff's hold and clawed his way toward Grant before another set of arms wrapped around his shoulders like a vice. "It's not what you think, son." Jake tightened his grip and held him back.

"Not what we think?" Grey clung to Grant's shirt, ripping it at the seams as one of his dads pulled him away. "You fucking bastard! You shot her, didn't you?"

Grant neither confirmed nor denied it. He stood stoically against the wall, straightening his torn shirt. Grey lunged at him again, but was no match for whatever army had him in their grasp. "I'm going to rip you're goddamn dick off and shove it down your throat!"

"Greyson!" Hazel screamed, tears swelling in her eyes as she ran to her son, braving his wrath and stepping in front of him. "Greyson, please. Calm down. Look at me!" She cupped his flaming cheeks in her hands and forced him to see her. "Look at me. That's it. Breathe." He was turning purple before her very eyes.

Grey felt the world fall out from beneath his feet as the red faded from his vision enough to see the tormented look in his mother's eyes. She was scared, and crying. "Mom?"

"Yeah, honey. It's me. The boys are fine. They're at my cousin Hanna's. I promise. I need you to calm down and listen to us."

Grey blinked and shook his head. His boys were fine. They were okay. She wouldn't lie to him. He closed his eyes and opened them again, the fear and anger induced haze subsiding enough to take in his surroundings. He was numb as he looked beyond his mom to see Uncle Cade standing by Grant, their faces a matching blank slate. He felt the grip on his arms loosen a notch.

"Someone had better start explaining." The Sheriff's loud voice filled the room. Grey twisted to see him standing next to Matt, a restraining hold on his brother's shoulder.

Grant cleared his throat and began to speak, but their Uncle Cade stepped up and cut him off. "We need to get these boys a drink, then we'll tell you everything."

"Fuck that!" Matt charged up to Grant, poking his finger into his chest. "The love of our life is lying in a goddamn hospital scared out of her mind and convinced you're the one who shot her! You'd better have a damn good explanation for that and you'd better tell us right-fucking-now!"

"The woman you know as Claira Robbins isn't who you think she is."

All three McLendon brothers turned to face the icy voice that echoed behind them. A tall, middle-aged man with a salt and pepper flattop stepped from behind the long sectional sofa that filled the far end of the family room.

"Deputy U.S. Marshal Daniel Gregory. Well, I'm retired now, officially. It's just Daniel now."

"What?" Matt and Grey asked in unison. Grey looked to their dads for an explanation. "What's he doing here and what the hell is he talking about?"

"Grant wasn't trying to kill Claira," Uncle Cade offered. "He's here to catch the man who is."

"What the hell?" Mason looked from the Marshal to Grant Kendal, then took in their Uncle Cade's stance next to the man Claira thought had tried to kill her. "You know about this." It wasn't a question. *He knew*!

Cade's head fell forward. Clapping his hand to the back of his neck, he nodded. Releasing a long, slow breath, he looked to his sister, Hazel, with pleading eyes. "They may need that drink now. I know I do."

Chapter Thirty

After knocking back his third glass of whisky, Grey paced the floor in their family room. "Let me get this straight." He turned to their Uncle Cade, barely containing the rage that clawed at his insides. "You brought a known killer's daughter into our lives as—as some kind of…what? Some sick matchmaking game? And then had Grant use her as bait to catch *another* killer?"

He couldn't believe what he was saying, what he was hearing. He turned to his dads in disbelief. "And you helped him? Do you have any idea what you've done to us, to our boys? What kind of danger you've put them in? They were shot at for Christ sake! Are you insane?"

"Dawes didn't have anything to do with this," Grant spoke up, trying to give some form of clarity to the screwed up mess they'd created.

"You shut the fuck up!" Matt sneered at Grant. "You lied to all of us. You don't get to talk."

"Don't forget that he's the one who took out Dawes." Daniel Gregory's monotone, emotionless statement cut through the air like a razor sharp knife. "If it wasn't for him you'd have lost her and your sons."

A chill ran down Mason's spine as he remembered the sounds of the bullets whizzing by and the scared look on Con's face. "Thank you," Mason said begrudgingly. No matter what kind of cluster this whole thing with Claira had become, they owed Grant at least that much.

Grant shrugged and pushed off from the wall he'd been leaning against. "Dawes is a lunatic, but he's a piss-ant compared to Lucien Moretti." Grant blushed as he glanced over to Hazel. "Sorry, ma'am."

Hazel frowned but nodded.

"We didn't know the specifics when Cade asked us to keep an eye on her," their dad Jake said with a grimace as he glanced over to his brother-in-law. "We only thought we were helping his friend, Daniel. Then we saw how you boys took to her, and well…believe me, we'd have never agreed to this had we known."

Mason sat perched on the edge of the overstuffed loveseat in the corner, his elbows braced on his knees, his head in his hands. "I don't understand," he huffed. "Why does this bastard want Claira dead? She's as innocent as they come. Did she witness something? Is that what this is? Some kind of witness protection thing?"

Cade glanced over to Daniel for permission and he nodded for him to continue.

"There are some things we can't share with you. Only Gabriella—the woman you know as Claira—can tell you about certain things, but, in general, yes," Cade nodded, brushing his hands over his face. "Daniel has spent his career putting her father in prison. She was instrumental in convicting him on multiple federal counts. In exchange for her testimony, the Feds agreed to give her a new start. When Daniel needed to put her somewhere safe, I offered to keep an eye on her here."

"Multiple counts of what? What is she involved in?" Matt asked.

"She wasn't involved in her father's business," Daniel said with a snarl. "She was nothing but victimized by that monster!"

Grey darted a glance at Daniel. It was the first sign of true emotion he'd seen from the icy statue that had claimed a position holding up the doorframe.

"Monster?" Matt's blood ran cold. "What…what kind of monster?" As if it mattered. He knew whatever had been done to Claira was bad. He'd seen the fear in her eyes.

"The worst kind, Mr. McLendon." Daniel remained motionless as he stared at Matt. "I won't betray her trust and give you all the gory details, but her father, Hector, was the head of a national human trafficking ring; modern slave trade."

Bile burned its way up Mason's throat. He thought back to the first time they'd taken her. She was as close to being a virgin as one could be without actually being one, of that he was sure, but he had to ask. "Sex slaves?" The question squeaked through his tightening esophagus. Thinking about the possibility of her being sold, or traded, or whatever this bastard did, stole his breath.

Daniel nodded and several agonized groans filled the room. Hazel sunk to the edge of the sofa, her hand covering her mouth as tears filled her eyes.

"Hector Morganti was convicted on thirty eight counts of human trafficking and kidnapping, among other things." Daniel broke away from the family and strolled to the picture window that overlooked their south pasture.

He braced his forearm above his head on the double paned glass, staring out at nothing for a while longer before he continued. "We never found his ledger of clients, but we know there were thousands more. His second in command, Lucien Moretti, stepped up to the plate after Hector's conviction and took over the trafficking ring. After a lifetime of working this case, of searching, it's as if we've accomplished nothing. Gabriella is in more danger now than she ever was."

"So, this Lucien guy. He's still working for her father?" Grey stumbled over saying her name. *Gabriella* somehow didn't fit his baby bird.

Cade blew out a sardonic sigh and stuffed his hands into the pockets of his faded and torn jeans. "No." He stepped toward Daniel but stopped, seeming to think better of it. "Hector considers him a traitor. He wants Lucien taken out as bad as we do. But Lucien?" Their Uncle leaned his shoulder against the window frame beside Daniel. "Lucien is much smarter than Hector. Kept himself as clean as a whistle while he worked for her father. He's playing with the same players now, but by a whole different set of rules."

"So why don't you just kill him?" Matt scoffed. "That's why *he's* here isn't it?" He nodded in Grant's direction. "Why not have Grant take him out where he lives instead of bringin' him here?"

"We can't. It's not that simple." Daniel didn't turn away from the window or offer any further explanation. Which wasn't going to cut it with Matt.

"Why the hell not? It's not bad enough our six-year-old sons were shot at four days ago. Claira or Gabriella or—whoever she is— is laid up in that hospital, defenseless, with a madman after her and all you can offer is *'we can't'!*"

Josiah gripped his shoulders when he jumped from the sofa toward Daniel. "If that's all you've got to offer I'll be damned if I'm gonna just sit around here and wait for more of this shit to come crashin' down on us. We'll pack her and the boys up and take her somewhere you can't even dream of, much less find."

"And you'll all be dead before you get there." Matt froze at his uncle's words. Cade didn't soften his statement with any tone of doubt. "She's protected, for now. We have a man at the hospital."

Grey rolled his eyes. "I feel *so—much—better.*"

"What are you saying?" Mason stood, ready to bolt out the door to get to Claira the moment his fears were confirmed. "This Lucien guy, he's already here, isn't he?"

Daniel turned from the window and studied the family members standing around the room. He was tired. Tired of all the games and secrecy, the chaos of it all. Tired of fighting forces they couldn't see and losing. Always losing.

He had to keep going. Retirement didn't mean he could give up. Normally he could internalize a family's grief and anger; process and either ignore it or discard it, but not with these people.

The pain of betrayal shone clear in all their eyes when they looked at their Uncle. Cade was important to him. They'd shed more than blood together. He knew these people would never forgive Cade if he didn't make them understand. He'd lose nothing of importance by giving them what he could of the truth. Cade would lose his family if he didn't.

Ignoring Mason's correct assumption, Daniel started as close to the beginning as he could. "Gabriella's father kept meticulous records, a file of all the victims he bought, sold and moved around the country. When we raided his compound in D.C. it wasn't there. It wasn't anywhere. His second in command, Lucien, has it and now he's using it to blackmail Hector's list of very powerful customers."

"But what does this have to do with our Claira?" Hazel's voice trembled, as did the rest of her. Josiah and Nate snuggled in closer to her on the loveseat.

Daniel glanced briefly at Cade before he continued, almost smirking at the grateful look on his friend's face. *Yeah, I'm getting there.*

"Lucien was—is—obsessed with Gabriella. He has been since she was a child. When she was twelve, Hector owed Lucien a debt. Gabriella doesn't know what it was, but Lucien demanded *her* as payment."

Hazel gasped and a cacophony of growls spirited around the room, but Daniel continued. "In a rare show of decency, Hector agreed to Lucien's demand, but mandated that Lucien wait until her twenty first birthday. I suspect the delay was to give Hector even greater control over Lucien. He could hold her as future leverage should he need it."

Mason's head swam with sick images of child exploitations and tidbits of conversations they'd had with Claira. Something about her birthday sounded familiar. "Her brother!"

Daniel nodded. "Hector killed Stephan when he tried to stop Lucien from taking her. A fight ensued and Gabriella was beaten unconscious. Afterward, when Gabriella recovered and refused to go along with Lucien peacefully, the cops in his payroll arrested her for Stephan's murder. None of which she can remember or prove, but it doesn't matter. Gabriella—Claira, she accepted the Fed's offer the moment Lucien posted her bail and threatened to take her from the jail."

"Again," Matt choked back another wave of rage and nodded over at Grant. "Why didn't you just kill this bastard there instead of luring him here?"

Daniel glanced at Grant. He had to tread lightly here. Grant—one of his more likable aliases—was an enigma, a far cry from the 'wet behind the ears' kid he'd taken under his wing over a dozen years ago. He hadn't lasted long with the Marshals before the CIA grabbed him up.

Now, although he was thought of as a rogue asshole by his superiors, he was still a Triple-D class agent—dangerous, dedicated and deadly—and he didn't want to cause him any more grief than necessary to get this bastard. Daniel knew he was already on thin ice asking Grant for this favor. He was more than a little shocked that he'd stuck around this long. Grant didn't usually do messy clean-ups.

"Just spit it out already," Grant barked from the open doorway. "I'm done after this is over. It doesn't matter."

Daniel huffed and shook his head, unable to picture his friend retired, stuffed into a Hawaiian shirt and flip-flops sipping a hot pink mai-tai on some exotic beach. Regardless, when it came to Grant, it was best to hold his cards close.

"When we learned that Lucien was still searching for Gabriella, dead or alive, we used Hector to recommend Grant for the job. The only stupid move Lucien has made is still trusting Hector." No matter how hard he tried, Daniel still couldn't figure that one out.

"We'd planned on using the down payment as evidence and busting him then, but after the drop, the op got snared in bureaucratic red tape. Lucien was either tipped off or got impatient. He disappeared before the new warrants cleared and we could take him into custody.

"Knowing that he was still looking for Gabriella, I was desperate. The Feds wouldn't authorize a protection detail, so I asked Grant to come here to watch over her, knowing that it was only a matter of time. When Lucien started pinging flight reservations to Montana using one of his lesser known aliases, we knew he was close. Grant needed to be able to keep a closer eye on her and, with her involvement with the three of you, having her here at the ranch made it easier to keep an eye on everyone."

"So you pushed her toward us with hang up calls and flat tires!" Matt scowled as the scenario played out in his memories. The fucker had tormented her for days!

"The fire." Grey sighed, not believing what he was hearing.

"I told you it wasn't the water heater we installed!"

Grey didn't respond to Mason's defensive outburst. The bullshit and torture he'd put himself through…They'd all been manipulated into this. Had any of it been real? Would she have told them any of this? *She said she was ready to tell us something.* This wasn't just *something.* This was deal-breaking huge. *Nothing about her is real.* How could she keep something like this from them after knowing what Sarah had done to them? *She's not Sarah. This isn't the same.* Their entire lives had been upended over this woman. *None of this is her fault.*

"I had nothing to do with the dead cow, the pictures and the phone calls," Grant said. "Dawes had cornered the market on those."

He looked at Grey. "The tires and the fire were an unfortunate necessity to get her here." He ignored the menacing sneer on Grey's face. None of that mattered now. "Lucien is here and he will *not* stop until he rapes Gabriella and-or kills her," Grant said. "And trust me. I don't think it matters to him in which order that happens."

"So Gabri..." Hazel choked off her question. She lowered her head and massaged her brows with the tips of her fingers.

Running his hand in comforting circles on her back, Nate leaned forward and tipped her chin toward him. "Haze, can I get you some water, babe."

She nodded and rubbed absently at a spot on her chest. "Thank you. I could use an aspirin too." Nate gave her a peck on her cheek and left to tend to his wife's needs.

"So," Jake said, taking Nate's place next to their wife and continuing to comfort her as he spoke to Cade. "What's the game you're playing with this Lucien bastard? If you can't just kill him, what does he have that's worth risking our family's live for?"

Josiah narrowed his eyes at Hazel's brother, waiting on his reply. He was going to enjoy joining his brothers in beating the hell out of Cade when this was over. He looked up at his brother-in-law and caught the pleading glance he was casting Daniel. "What are you not telling us, Cade? Or should I ask what *else*?"

Cade shook his head and gave one last pleading glance to his friend. He hated asking this of Daniel, but it was the only way his family would understand why he'd had to do this. Even then, after what those boys had been through, it might not be enough to keep from dying at the hands of his own family, not that he didn't deserve it.

Daniel cleared his throat and leaned back against the window sill. "I came to care for Gabriella very much during the time I spent with her." No longer noticing any of the people in the room, he retreated into his own private hell, pulling a worn, blue length of ribbon from his pocket, rubbing it between his fingers as he relived the nightmare that had started it all.

"She's like a daughter to me." After a long silent moment, Daniel forced himself to continue. "She's one of the kindest, strongest women I've ever known, but she's not the only reason I will hunt

Lucien to his grave." He fingered the ribbon, braiding it through his fingers then pulling it free. He schooled his features, tucked the frayed length of ribbon back into his pocket and pegged Grey with another icy stare. "Gabriella's father took my daughter."

Grey visibly blanched at the pure hatred that spilled from the retired Marshal's eyes. He swallowed against the knot in his own throat as he and Daniel came to a complete and total understanding. At least he thought he understood the man, until Gregory continued. He soon learned there were some furies in life he hoped he'd never experience or understand.

"She was sixteen." Daniel paused, looking for a moment as though he would puke, but the moment passed and he re-schooled his expression. "He took her and sold her to the highest bidder. I need Hector's records from Lucien so I can track down every piece of scum that ever laid a hand on her, rip the skin from their bodies, piece by piece, then feed it to them before I tear out their hearts with my bare hands and send their souls back to the pits of whatever hell spawned them."

Chapter Thirty-One

"Dad...I...this..."

"I know this is hard, Grey." Josiah placed his hand on his oldest son's arm, stopping him before he could open the driver's door to his truck. "The boys will be fine. Me and your fathers will take Cade and go get them. Take your brothers to see Claira."

Grey's head snapped up and an unfamiliar anger filled his veins. He hadn't forgotten the part his dads had played in this. "Don't you mean *Gabriella?*" They knew about this, and he'd be damned if he was going to be further manipulated into caring about her. "I think your matchmaking days are over, old man."

Grey reached for the door handle again but Josiah grabbed his shoulder and spun him around. "You listen here, boy. I may have screwed up by not getting more details from Cade before I agreed to this—God forbid we help one of our own around here—but I'll be long dead and in the grave before you get by with disrespecting me."

It only took one glance at his dad to recognize the error of his ways. Grey released his death grip on the door handle. He might be getting up in age, but no doubt his dad could and *would* still kick his ass. "Yes, sir." He scrubbed his hands over his face and leaned against the door. "Sorry."

"Listen, son." The anger in voice gone, Joe cuffed Grey's arm and pulled him to lean against the truck bed. "I know what you went through with Sarah. I never told this to anyone but, I was there that morning she died."

Grey looked over and noticed a slight tremble in his dad's hands. "What do you mean?"

His arms stretched out over the bedrail, Joe bowed his head and looked at the ground, giving the back tire a frustrated kick. "I drove over early that morning to help your brothers weld up one of the stock tanks that had sprung a leak. When I heard dishes crashing and you yelling at her, I froze outside the door. I didn't know what to do." Joe stood to his full height and turned to look at Grey. "But I do know what it's like to say things you don't mean and not be able to take them back, son, and it's time you let that shit go."

All the air left Grey's lungs as the memories came flooding back. He thought telling his brothers was hard. Knowing that his fathers knew what a bastard he'd been was too much.

"Hell, I let this go on long enough. Too long." Joe tipped his head and spit in the dust. "It's not your fault she died, Grey. These things happen. Shit happens, every day; to good people. Sarah lied to you, to all of us. She didn't deserve the things you said to her, but you didn't deserve to be lied to, either. It doesn't make any of it right or wrong. It just is."

He cupped the back of Grey's neck and held him at arm's length. "Things might be screwed up right now, Greyson, but the life that woman has brought to this family is worth fighting for. She's worth fighting for. Don't try to undo one mistake by making another. Take your brothers and go get this thing with her straightened out."

Grey fought for each breath as his dad's words hit him like a sledge hammer to the gut. Nothing felt worse than the guilt over what he'd said to Sarah that day, except knowing that his father had known all this time. "Why?" He shook his head as he remembered all the times since that day his dad had treated him with nothing but love and respect. He hadn't deserved either. "Why didn't you say anything? I needed my ass kicked. You raised me to be better than that."

Joe released his son and removed his hat, pushing his sweaty, graying hair back with a trembling hand. When he looked at Grey and all he'd become, his heart swelled with pride and ached with regret that he hadn't told him the truth sooner.

He could see the shame and humiliation in Grey's green eyes; eyes that reminded him so much of himself. Clearing the sob from his throat before he castrated himself and started bawling like a baby, Joe plunked his hat back onto his head and gave his son a wavering grin.

"Because you are your father's son, Grey. I knew you'd punish yourself far worse than any ass whippin' I could give you. It's my fault you're still all screwed up about it, though. I didn't realize I'd let it go on for so long."

Grey swallowed hard and forced back his own pussy tears. "Goddam, dad. You're going to make me cry if you keep that shit up." Grey took off his own hat and wiped his face and forehead with the crook of his arm. "Nothing's your fault. I screwed up. I'm dealing with it, but this thing with Claira...." Grey shook his head. Claira. Gabriella. He didn't even know what name to call her.

Fear, anger, love, lust, betrayal, all swirled together creating a confusion Grey was helpless to fight as it ate up his mind and thoughts like a cancer. "I can't think about that, about her, right now, dad. Matt and Mason can go, but I need some time. I need to see my boys; to know they're okay."

Joe didn't push him any further, but didn't give him any slack either. "I'll ride with you to Hanna's to see the twins, and then I'll drop you off at the hospital on the way back home."

Grey shook his head and started to argue, but the sound of Jake's voice yelling from inside the house had them both running from the truck and up the porch steps inside three seconds.

"What's going on?" Grey stumbled through the screen door. Joe plowed over him to get to the source of all the noise.

"Get my phone out of my pocket and speed dial number four," Nate shouted as Grey and Joe rounded the doorframe to see him holding Hazel in his arms. Their mother was as white as a sheet of ice and holding her fist against her chest. "Tell Dr. Pendercast to meet us at the hospital. Your mamma's having another heart attack."

"Another? What the hell? When was the first one?" Mason asked, grabbing the phone as Matt cleared the hallway and held the front door open for them.

Nate blew through the doorway and cleared the steps in two long strides. "Stop asking questions and make the call!"

Mason dialed frantically as their Uncle Cade, Daniel Gregory, Grant Kendal and the Sheriff preceded Grey, Joe, Matt and Jake out the front door. Sheriff Long called dispatch to notify the hospital and let them know that he was giving them an escort into town since it was quicker than waiting for an ambulance.

Four pick-up trucks, a full size blazer and a trail of dust a half-mile long followed the Sheriff's car down the long gravel driveway and onto the two-lane road that led into town.

Mason sat in the back seat of Grey's truck with his eyes closed, praying like he'd never prayed in his life for a convoy of cowboys to sprout wings and fly. No one said a word as the road passed under their tires like a treadmill going nowhere and the sounds of the distant siren from the patrol cruiser filled the cab. They couldn't lose their Ma. No matter how bad things had gotten, nothing they'd gone through in the last week could have prepared them for this.

~*~*~*~*~

Blood seeped through the cotton bandages and stained the pale-yellow hospital gown Claira held to her shoulder. Finding a pair of not-too-dingy nurse's scrubs in an abandoned waste bin had been luck. Changing into them with her arm taped to her chest had been close to impossible.

The pain was nauseating, nearing intolerable. She feared she'd pass out at any moment if she didn't find a place to hide and catch her breath. *Some escape artist you've become.* She didn't have time to lose it now. She didn't know how, but she knew Lucien was there, in the hospital. She'd awoken to find the air around her had taken on a sudden, slimy chill she'd long ago associated with him.

After the last nurse had come to check on her, she'd yanked out her IV—which hurt like crazy and was so much messier than they showed in the movies—then she'd spied her cellphone lying on the table by her bed. Thank God for small miracles. She didn't waste any time snatching it up and darting out of her room and down the hall, her head hung low to shield her face.

Turn after turn she found herself lost in a maze of double doors and identical rooms with an elevator nowhere in sight. Glancing over her shoulder as her legs carried her further into a maze of confusion, pain sliced through her shoulder as she was struck by what she could only guess was a Mack truck.

She heard someone mumble *'sorry'* as she spun off an empty gurney and stumbled a few feet further down the hall. Black edges crept into her field of vision. Her legs were numb, but she could tell by the way the lights above her moved within her slowly fading field of vision that she was still moving.

Have..to..hide. Keep moving. Running through what felt like molasses, her eyes darted from side to side. Every metal object took on a shiny halo as her vision blurred further. Desperate not to pass out, she grabbed onto the only object that made its way into the gathering darkness that surrounded her.

Relief flashed through her veins when the silver door handle turned. She fell into the darkness beyond the door and it closed behind her with a soft click. Rolling into a ball, everything but the pain disappeared as she forced air into her lungs.

Breathe damn it! She could hear Matt's voice in her head and pictured him hovering above her, showing her what she needed to do. After what she was sure was only minutes, but could have been hours, she began to notice small slivers of soft light surrounding her. A chill from the cold tile floor seeped into her bones. Sweat coated her skin and the pain in her chest and shoulder had lessened from searing to a burning ache.

Unable to move more than her head, she glanced around the unlit room and noticed a metal desk and chair, a thin bookcase full of books hugging one wall. A few frames hung on the other wall, but she couldn't make out what, if anything, they displayed.

She was in someone's office. Claira ignored the ache in her joints as she reached into the front pocket of the scrubs and pulled out her cellphone. She turned on the power and waited, breathing through the pain, as her phone went through the usual startup routine. Once her contacts were displayed, she found the name of the only person she knew could help her, pressed the send button and hoped he would answer.

"Gregory." Daniel Gregory's voice barked in her ear and a sudden rush of adrenaline flooded her veins. She tried to sit up, but that only induced a loud, pain-filled groan.

"Gabriella? Gabby is that you?"

Unable to push the words past her lips, she nodded but quickly realized that wouldn't help her. "Yes," she croaked, pushing back the sob inside her that ached for release. "Daniel, he's here," she whispered. "Lucien is here."

An odd mixture of ice and lead poured over Grey as he heard Daniel shout her name. Cold fear gripped his chest. His legs felt weighted to the pavement. He forced himself to move as he followed the Marshal through the hospital parking garage, in through the emergency room doors and down the hall to a huge bank of elevators. "Is it Claira? What's going on? Is that her? Is she okay?"

"Stay here, Grey." Grant shouldered him back as one of the elevator doors opened and they stepped in. "Stay with your family and tend to your mother."

"Like hell!" Grey pushed his way back through the closing door. "What the *hell* is going on?"

Cade slipped in behind him before the doors closed. "I spot two at the main entry and one near the stairs."

"Two what?" Grey asked.

Daniel continued to speak calming words to Claira—Gabby. Ugh! Grant ignored Grey as he punched the elevator button for the second floor then turned his attention to the phone in his hands. "Keep her talking, Daniel. I've got a tracking app on her phone. We'll find her."

"Where are you?" Daniel asked as he watched Grant push another button for the third floor. "She's in an office," Daniel relayed to Grant. "She doesn't know where."

"She's on three," Grant barked at Cade as he palmed his phone and pulled his .45 from his shoulder holster. "You take the right," he told Cade. "Daniel and I'll take the left wing and we'll meet at the other end of the floor. Check every room and keep your back to the wall. Lucien won't be alone."

Grey's heart felt like it would stop at any moment. All he could see was some faceless monster dragging Claira away from him. He didn't care if she'd lied or had a different name or, hell, she could be a damn alien. He wouldn't care as long as she loved them; as long as he didn't lose her.

This was all happening so fast and he didn't have a clue how to help her. He just knew that if they didn't find her alive and in one piece, he and his brothers may not survive. They needed her. "I'll go with you." He turned to Cade. "Jesus, I don't have a gun."

"Stay here, Grey." Cade pushed past him as the doors slid open. "We'll find her before Lucien does."

Grey watched in a speechless daze as Grant and Daniel flowed out into the bright hallway to the left as they'd agreed, his Uncle Cade peeling off to the right. He stood motionless for all of ten seconds then swiveled back and forth from left to right, watching in turn as the men disappeared into the first set of rooms. "Fuck!" He ran a hand through his hair and took off in the same direction as Cade. *Family stuck together, right?*

Claira groaned as she pulled the silent phone from her ear and studied it, gritting her teeth against the pain even that small movement caused. *No! No-no-no!* The battery was dead. Dead! Dead! Dead! Just like her if they didn't find her before Lucien. She had to get up. Get moving. They were on her floor. All she had to do was get Daniel's attention.

She groaned as she pushed herself up onto her knees. A stabbing pain shot through her shoulder, but she pushed herself to ignore it and rolled to her feet. More sweat broke out across her forehead and upper lip as she breathed through the waves of pain, focusing hard to keep the room from tilting any further on its axis.

One foot in front of the other. That was all she needed to do. Just a few steps and she'd be able to lean against one of those tilting walls near the door. Hopefully, if she leaned hard enough, it would stop moving.

Three agonizing steps and Claira had a death grip on the door handle. A loud clang of metal on metal made its way through the pounding in her ears. Adrenaline laced her veins as she heard the faint timbre of Daniel's voice in the distance. *He's here. Oh thank you God, Daniel found me!*

She ignored the blackness closing in on her again and concentrated on turning the door knob. With an unfamiliar strength, she pulled the heavy door with her good arm and threw herself into the brightly lit hallway, straight into the oncoming path of her own personal demon.

In slow motion Grant's arm uncoiled and aimed a huge, black gun at her head. She turned to run, but her socked feet slipped out from under her. She tumbled backwards, her elbows cracking against the hard tile floor as a loud boom filled the hall. *It's over.*

She pulled her knees into her chest, making herself as small as possible, covering her head as she waited for the final shot that would end her life. When another shot rang out, she felt and heard the bullet hiss by as it whizzed over her head.

Confusion warred with disbelief when she opened her eyes. *He missed?* She peeled her arms from her face and caught a glimpse of Lucien as he retreated down the hall in the opposite direction Grant had come from. Grant sprinted past her and disappeared down the hall after him, Daniel right behind him.

"Claira!" Grey called out to her.

An eerie numbness flowed through her limbs, flushing all the pain from her body as a pair of big hands wrapped around her shoulders and pulled her up to lean against the wall.

"Grey?" Her brows pinched together as she studied the man in front of her. She'd heard Grey's voice, but the man in front of her was not Grey. "Who are you?" She slapped at his hands. "Grey!" She began to panic as things made less and less sense. Who was this man and why was Grey so far away?

"Sit tight, Gabriella." Cade squatted down in front of her and gently cupped her shoulders. "As soon as Daniel gives me the okay I'll get you back to your room and get you some help."

What? "You know Daniel? M....Marshal Gregory?"

"My name is Cade and yes, Daniel is my friend."

"Cade! Is she hurt?" Grey shouted from somewhere to her left. Cade turned just as she did to look for the voice that belonged to the man she loved but couldn't see.

"Grey!" Claira bolted to her feet, but her legs crumbled beneath her and she fell to her knees. "Grey! You're hurt!" Ignoring the pain in her knees and shoulder, she scrambled across the hard, cold floor toward the hunched over form in the distance.

Blood. There was so much blood. "Oh God! Grey. I'm sorry! I'm so sorry! I never meant for this to happen!" She watched as a group of nurses and doctors worked to cut Grey's jeans from his leg. One nurse pulled a gurney beside him as a rush of other nurses hurried toward her.

"It's not bad, baby bird. Are you okay? Did he hurt you?" Grey reached for her, but a man in a white coat secured his arm as they lifted him onto the gurney.

"I'm okay!" She reached for him, pulling against an army of arms and hands that grabbed at her. "Grey, please don't leave! I'm so sorry!" She sobbed as she collapsed, no longer able to fend off the forces that kept her from his side. She'd done this to him. *Please don't let him die.*

Chapter Thirty-Two

Depressive clouds filled the sky. An unusually cool breeze blew drops of rain under the porch roof, a few stray drops landing on Gabriella as she sat in one of her rickety rocking chairs and stared into the storm. "I can't believe he's dead." She turned the hot cup of tea in her hands, fiddling with the string hanging over the rim. "Everything is still so raw; so unreal."

"Give it time, Gabby." Daniel reached over and took her cold hand in his warm one. He was always warm. Her warm safe place. She nodded, forcing a smile she knew he would see straight through. It was all she was capable of.

The screen door creaked open. A shiver ran through her, something that always happened when she laid eyes on Grant Kendal. He looked so different than he did when she first met him. His hair was lighter and shorter; his brown eyes now the color of a golden god. His Midwestern accent sounded strange to her ears, a three day old scruff covering his once clean-shaven jaw. He had a dangerous look about him now, all lean muscles and hard edges he'd somehow hidden before.

His chin came up in a silent greeting as he dropped a duffle bag next to the front door and took a few cautious steps toward her. He stopped a few feet in front of her, crossing one ankle over the other as he relaxed against the porch railing behind him. The sounds of the rain and the late summer storm filled the air around them for an indeterminable amount of time before he spoke.

"The house is fixed up. I put the left over can of paint under the kitchen sink in case your landlord ever needs to do some touch-ups." He swiped a hand over his strong, stubble-covered jaw and then cupped the back of his neck, glancing over his shoulder. "I'm sorry, again, for all the trouble the fire caused."

Gabby peeked up through her lashes at the man who had replaced Lucien in her nightmares. She still couldn't look at him without seeing his gun pointed at her. She knew now that he hadn't been trying to kill her. He'd saved her life, for better or worse, but he still made her nervous. She opened her mouth to thank him again, but she couldn't get the words past her lips.

"You're going to ground." Daniel's voice pulled her from her mangled thoughts. He glanced at Grant's duffle bag.

Grant nodded and folded his arms over his chest. "It's time. I need to find a deep, dark hole to crawl into for a year or ten. Decompress for a while."

Daniel pushed to his feet and reached a hand out to his friend. "I appreciate everything you've done. I know you said we're even, but I consider myself in your debt on this one."

Grant shrugged and shook the man's hand. "Don't. That bastard deserved worse than what he got. Killing him was well overdue, but it didn't get you any closer to finding Natalie."

Daniel shook his head and glanced down at Gabby with more love than her own father had ever shown her. "She's free now. You've done more than enough. I'll find Hector's ledger and put the rest of those bastards in hell eventually."

"I'm still sorry." Grant pushed away from the railing. Taking the distance to the front door in two strides, he bent and hoisted the single strap of his bag over his shoulder then stood and faced them. "I hope you find it." Giving a quick, lazy salute, he started down the steps, but stopped when she called out to him.

"Grant, wait!" She stood on shaky legs, her healing shoulder protesting the quick movement. She cautiously approached him, hiding her trembling hands beneath the thin blanket draped over her shoulders. "Thank you," she said.

The fear she had of him was unfounded. He deserved more than she could give him. "Thank you for saving my life." She swallowed against the nervous knot in her throat. "And for killing Lucien."

A weak grin pulled at Grant's lips. He reached up to touch her angelic face, but stopped when she flinched away from his hand. "No thanks necessary, Gabby." He winked at her and jerked his chin toward his friend. "Keep him out of trouble, okay?"

She nodded and backed away from him, pulling the blanket tighter around her shoulders as she stopped next to Daniel. With one last glance at the house behind them, Grant hiked his bag higher onto his shoulder and walked through the rain to his rented sedan, slid behind the steering wheel and drove away.

"Looks like you have more goodbyes to hand out today." She followed Daniel's gaze to see a familiar silver truck turning onto her street. It passed Grant's car with a quick honk and pulled into the spot he'd just vacated. "I've got a few things I need to pick up from Cade's place before we ship out." Daniel pulled a set of keys from his pocket and left Gabriella standing alone on her porch. He waved to Matt and Mason as they slipped out of Matt's truck.

The twins' gazes followed him as he backed out of the drive. When he was gone, they turned back to face her. Gabby gripped the railing to keep from falling to her knees at the conflict she saw in their sea-blue eyes.

She wasn't surprised to see that Grey hadn't joined them. Why would he? She'd nearly gotten him killed; nearly gotten them all killed, including their precious babies. How could she have put them all in so much danger? Why were they even there?

She held herself together as the brothers, shoulder to shoulder, walked toward her and stopped at the foot of the concrete stairs. Lazy drops of rain fell into their sandy-brown hair and streaked their beautiful faces.

She hadn't seen them since the day after Lucien was killed. The day after he'd shot Grey in the leg. The wound itself had been clean, she'd heard, but the bullet had nicked his artery and he'd nearly bled to death before they fixed the tear. She ached to take it all back, to make it so he'd never know that pain.

She'd never been more scared in her entire life than she'd been that day, except for now. She was leaving tomorrow, going back to a house she knew was empty of all but the ghosts of a past she'd yet to face. Her only option was to sell everything and start over.

After today she'd be well and truly alone, and she'd stay that way. She'd never love anyone else but these men, and she knew she would never have them. Facing a lifetime of loneliness was nothing. She was used to that life. Facing life without the three men she loved? Without the twin boys she'd almost gotten killed? Without the love their family had shown her was possible? That was the fate that would break her.

Against Daniel's advice she'd ignored their calls and denied their requests to see her in the hospital. She couldn't face them. Daniel had finally contacted them the night before and told them they were leaving.

After another fitful night's sleep she'd decided she deserved to hear whatever they had to say to her, no matter how painful. They had every right to hate her. She'd lied to them. She hated herself for doing it, for letting herself get so close to them.

Matt's hand trembled as he reached up and ran his long fingers through his hair. *Don't cry. I will not cry.* Their silence was deafening. She closed her eyes against it and sucked her bottom lip between her teeth to keep it from quivering. *Please, yell at me, say something.* She could take anything but the silent censure that rolled off them in waives.

A sharp yelp in the distance caught her attention. Her lips parted with a gasp. Beyond Matt and Mason, the back door of Matt's truck opened and Grey eased out, bracing himself on the bed of the truck as he closed the truck door. The rain fell a little heavier as he turned and began a slow trek toward her, a heavy limp accenting his stride.

He looked well; magnificent even. He was perfect and she'd nearly lost him. He may hate her, but at least he was still alive and she knew she wouldn't have to live in a world where he didn't exist.

Her heart broke as she took in the somber, resolved look in his striking green eyes. She followed the line of his strong jaw to his broad shoulders, memorizing every hard line and curve. A sob bubbled out of her aching chest when she reached his arms to the wiggling black puppy with a big red bow tied around its neck. She clamped her hand over her mouth to hold in all the pain and love and heartache that clawed at her chest.

Grey stopped next to Mason. A sad smile touched his face as he looked up the stairs at her. "Con wants you to have him, to keep you safe."

Gabriella collapsed against the railing and slid to the wooden floor, a sobbing cry escaping despite her best efforts to hold it back.

"Why?" She cried into the blanket clutched in her hands. "Why would he do that?"

"Aw, sweetheart. Don't cry." Mason shot up the stairs and gathered her into his arms, cradling her into his chest as he sunk down into one of the rockers.

"But that's his favorite puppy." She said, sobbing against Mason's shirt. "He can't do that!"

"Darlin', why would you say that?" Matt stooped down and cradled her cheeks in his hands, wiping away the steady stream of tears from her eyes with his thumb.

She turned her face away from Matt's hand and buried it deeper into Mason's shirt. "I lied to you," she cried, shaking with her sobs. Mason held her as she cried, rocking her in his arms. When she was able to take a shuddering breath without the tears starting over again, he loosened his hold on her.

"Look at me, baby bird." Grey tipped her chin toward him. He leaned in and brushed his lips against hers, tasting the salt in her tears. He licked the taste from his lips and repeated the action, taking only what she would give him.

After a lingering pause, he pulled back and looked into her puffy, chocolate eyes. "You deserve to be happy. We understand why you had to lie. We also understand why you want to leave. After what happened, we can't blame you for not wanting to stay with us. No one deserves what Dawes did to you. Not everyone is homicidal over their beliefs, but there will be more people lined up behind him that won't approve. We can't ask you to go through that after what happened to you."

What? She pushed against Mason's chest and turned to look at Grey. "I don't understand." She sniffled and tried to clear her throat. "You don't want me to leave?"

Matt crouched next to Grey. He took her hand in both of his and brought it to his beautiful lips. His eyes filled with tears as he kissed the palm of her hand and held it to his cheek as if he were savoring every last touch he could get from her.

"We love you. We know it's not what you want now, but if you ever…" Matt closed his eyes and she could see the tick in his jaw as he bit back his words. He lowered her hand to her lap. His eyes danced between Mason and Grey before he stood and paced to the railing.

"I can't do this." Matt ran his fingers through his hair and paced back to stand in front of them. "I know we agreed that we should let her go, but I can't. I can't sit back and watch her walk away without a fight."

"Matt, stop."

"No, you stop, Mason. All of you. This is crazy." He slid down onto his knees in front of Gabriella and took her hands in his again. "Claira—Gabriella—I know…" He paused and shook his head. "We understand that all this is new for you, and that…that you've been through hell. Not only in your own life, but also because of who we are and how we live our lives.

"Our souls know you are the one we were meant to be with. Nothin' in your past, or ours, changes that. The chances of some other crazy loon goin' off the deep end like…like that bastard did, they're not…" He let go of her hands and cupped her neck as he struggled for the words he needed to convince her. "We won't let you go without a fight, darlin'. You belong here, with us, with our boys and our crazy family. If you want to leave…"

"I don't." Gabriella sucked in a strangled breath.

"What?" Mason and Grey asked in unison.

"I don't want to leave you." Her shoulders tightened as another sob built in her chest. "I belong to you. All of you. I love each of you with all my heart, but, how can you ever forgive me for bringing your family into this…this…nightmare? For putting you at risk like that?"

"Forgive you?" Grey drew back as if he'd been slapped. "Baby, what are you talking about?" He pushed to his feet and stood next to Matt. "We're the ones asking for forgiveness here. You were shot, for *Christ sake*! Dawes shot you, and tried to kill our sons because of the way we live. We can't ask you to forgive us for dragging you into that!" He scrubbed his free hand over his face and shook his head. "God, not after everything you've been through."

Forgive *them*? What did she have to forgive *them* for? She knew what she was getting involved in was unconventional. Most people didn't always accept what they didn't understand, but Dawes was crazy; creepy crazy.

Sure she might get a nasty look or hear a rumor or two in the future, but surely no one else in their right mind would try to kill her for it; unless it was out of jealousy. She glanced between Matt and Mason, and then up at Grey. Yeah, she'd definitely have to watch out for the occasional jealousy-induced hormonal rampage from the locals.

"Grey, you were shot, and almost died because of me!" She choked back a lingering sob, but for the first time in two weeks she could feel a glimmer of hope.

Matt chuckled when he saw the look in her eyes change from broken to breathtakingly hopeful. Going out on a limb he was sure wouldn't hold his weight, he shrugged. "So, you were shot, Grey was shot. Doesn't that make us even then?"

Grunts and giggles burst from all of them. Even Con's black puppy squealed and wiggled in Grey's arms. Claira sniffled and wiped at her tears, giving Mason a disapproving shove. "It's not funny."

"Claira?" Grey held out his hand to her as the other cradled the puppy to his chest. "Come home? Please?"

She shook her head, more tears pooled in her eyes. "There's more." Matt began to protest but she continued on before she lost her nerve. "You have to know that I..." God, could she say the words? She had to. They deserved to know. Stephan deserved her admission. "I killed my brother."

"Claira—"

"No, Mason. You have to know. I don't remember anything other than having the gun in my hand. I had to protect him from Lucien, but then I don't know what happened. They arrested me for murdering him. I could have..."

"Daniel told us what happened," Grey said, shaking his head. "You don't honestly believe you are capable of the cold blooded murder of your own brother, do you?" His tone held no doubt of her innocence. "Claira, baby, that's ridiculous. You couldn't hurt a fly if you tried."

Mason curled her into his arms as another lingering sob wracked her body. Matt cupped her cheek in his hand and wiped away the new tears. "Claira, there is no way we'll ever believe it, even if you signed a full confession, darlin'. We love you. All of you." He turned her face to look at him. "Come home with us, where you belong."

Gabriella took Grey's outstretched hand but didn't stand. She remained in Mason's lap and cradled her face in Grey's large, calloused palm. How had she gotten so blessed? How could she ever deny these men anything?

She should have argued with them, tried to convince them they were making a mistake, but she didn't want to. She wanted them to love her. She needed them. Unable to contain the happiness and hope that filled her to near bursting, a small hiccup of laughter bubbled up and she blurted out the next thought that popped into her head. "Can you call me Gabby?" She said with a sob, happier tears clouding her eyes. "I miss my name."

Matt plunged forward and claimed her mouth with his kiss. His hot tongue skimmed her lips then wrapped around hers. When she tasted the salty tang of tears she knew they were not only hers. Her heart sang with happiness and joy that these men loved her enough to help her overcome her demons and haunted past. She tasted true freedom and love for the first time in her life and she was never going to leave it behind. She was home.

Chapter Thirty-Three

Three Weeks Later

"Eh-ehm!" Nathan McLendon cleared his throat as Hazel reached for the salt shaker. She froze and scowled at her beloved Josiah as his hand shot out and seized it from her reach, passing it to Jake, who deposited it at the far end of the table in front of Grey.

Gabby frowned, her shoulders slumping in disappointment. "I'm sorry, Hazel. I followed your recipe exactly." Her fork fell to her plate and she dabbed at the corner of her mouth with her napkin, her appetite dwindling as she tasted the blandness of the cornbread stuffing she'd thought she'd perfected. "At least, I thought I did. I must have missed something."

"Nonsense, darlin'." Hazel narrowed her eyes at Nathan and reached for the pepper instead. "It's perfect. My taste buds haven't been up to snuff since I got this darned summer cold. A little salt never hurt anything."

"Don't even think about it," Joe barked as she reached for the butter.

Grey, Mason and Matt laughed in unison as they watched their formidable mother being railroaded by her three loving and understandably overbearing husbands.

Hazel stood abruptly from her seat and all laughter ceased. She pointed at her husbands, shaking her finger as she spoke. "How many times does the doctor have to tell you? I did *not* have another episode. It was indigestion. Not a heart attack, for goodness sake."

With her head held high, she walked to the end of the table and snatched up the salt shaker, ignoring the protesting grunts and waving off the hands that reached to take it away from her. "And I'll do you one better," she said as she sat back down and dashed a few light shakes over her potato. "This keeps up and I'm telling Dr. Sands about your increasing trips to the john every night, *Nathan*." She wrinkled her nose and pointed her fork at Nate. "See how you feel after the examination he gives you for *that!*"

Mason choked on his gulp of tea and covered his mouth, nearly spewing it through his nose.

"You don't play fair, Hazel," Daniel chuckled from his seat beside Matt

Hazel took a bite of her butter-less potato and scowled up at Joe, making a dramatic scene as she swallowed the bland mouthful. Gabby couldn't help but laugh as Joe reached over and cut a small strip of butter from the stick and brought it to her plate. Hazel smiled and patted his cheek, Jake grumbling beside him.

"What? You think I'm stupid?" Joe said after he gave Hazel a quick peck on her cheek. "Don't think she won't add your name to that little chat with Dr. Sands. You're crazy if you think I'm going through that over a pat of butter or a dash of salt."

Grey laughed as he watched his dads fuss over their mom. He leaned closer to Gabby and whispered in her ear. "I like your stuffing, baby." She slapped his arm with her napkin at the naughty look he gave her. It didn't deter him for a second. He leaned in closer this time, his lips grazing her earlobe, his warm breath caressing her neck as he spoke low enough that only she could hear him. "I like stuffing *you* full of my cock better, though."

Heat flushed through her veins. She was sure the entire table had heard him because, suddenly, all the chatter ended and every eye at the table was focused in her direction.

Oh God. Did they hear that?

She could have choked Grey at that very moment, but her plans went up in smoke as both Matt and Mason stood and walked to stand behind Grey. He turned his chair to face her and reached for her hands. *What's happening?*

"Grey?" She couldn't make sense of his smirk or the worried looks on Matt and Mason's faces as they watched something over her shoulder. She flinched when the front door slammed. Glancing over her shoulder, she saw Con and Car running into the room chasing Con's black puppy, who he'd aptly named *Trouble.*

The rapidly growing puppy ran between Hazel and Josiah, underneath the table and jumped straight into Grey's lap, diving for the leftover scraps on his plate. Thankfully, Grey grabbed him up before he'd snagged any treats for himself, then settled Car on his left knee with the puppy on his right.

Mason sighed in relief. He reached down and adjusted Trouble's collar so the small box attached to it, nestled between two red ribbons, was sitting in front for her to see. He gave Car a wink and lifted Con into his arms.

Grey smiled when she glanced repeatedly between the box and him, and then up to Matt and Mason. "We thought about doing this in a more private, romantic setting, but no matter what we came up with we couldn't find a better way to express what you mean to us; what we want to give you."

Mason stroked her hair. "We want to give you the world, sweetheart. Our world." He stooped down onto one knee in front of her and took her other hand in his, careful of her still healing shoulder. "Our name, our family, our love. We want you to be a mother to our children and the love of our lives. Our wife and lover and friend, forever."

Tears pooled in her eyes as she glanced up at Matt, seeing both trepidation and excitement flickering in his usually more playful expression. "What he said." Matt pointed at Mason, his cheeks reddening as his expression turned to pleading. "You know me, darlin'. I get all tongue tied when I'm with you like this. I say the first thing that pops into my head." His eyes darted between Con and Car, then to his parents and Daniel. "And I'm confident that some of those things aren't 'G' rated. So, the less I talk right now the better."

Nathan chuckled behind them. The sound of Hazel's light slap followed.

Can this be real? Could she be so lucky?

"Will you marry us?" Con asked as Car opened the lid on the tiny box that Trouble wore. Car squinted and squirmed away as Trouble snuck in a slobbery kiss for his efforts.

Gabby swiped at the first tear that ran down her cheek. She tried to focus on the ring, but she couldn't stop the flood that poured from her eyes. She didn't need to see it to know that it was beautiful, like the family they were giving her.

Her head bobbed as she struggled to get the only word that existed in her vocabulary in that moment past her lips. "Yes." Yes to everything.

"Yes!" Matt rushed between her and Grey and plucked her from her chair. "Oh, darlin, I'm sorry." He eased her down when she winced a little at the pressure on her shoulder. "I just can't *not* touch you right now. I love you so much."

Mason and Grey leaned in, both claiming a corner of her mouth in a chaste kiss, but Grey lingered and whispered in her ear. "I can't wait to get you beneath me."

She barely contained a squeal when Grey slipped the ring onto her finger. He clapped his brothers on the shoulder before pulling them into a congratulatory man-hug. Wiping away more stray tears, she focused on the three sparkling diamonds in her ring, representing the three loves of her life.

She'd barely had time to appreciate it before she was pulled into a series of hugs and kisses from Daniel and Joe, Nate and Jake. Gabby squealed when Hazel pulled her into her arms, her own tears of joy falling down her plump cheeks.

"Welcome to our family, Gabby." Hazel hugged her a little tighter before standing back and pinning her with a stern look. "If you ever need help with these hellions, or ever just feel the need to escape the testosterone for a while, you let me know. I've had to come up with all kinds of ways to keep my sanity over the years. I'll gladly share my experience and wisdom with you."

Gabby laughed and nodded, but was saved from responding by a gentle tug on her hand. She looked down and saw Car and Con peering up at her. "Can we call you momma now, instead of Miss Claira?" Con asked, his brows creasing in concentration.

"It's Gabby," Car whispered to Con with his hand cupped around his twin's ear.

"Miss Gabby, sorry. Ow!" He hissed as Car nudged him with his shoulder. "I was trying to remember."

Gabby froze and looked to Grey. He mouthed the words *I love you* from across the room. That was the only answer she needed. She nodded at Con and pulled both boys into a hug. "You can if that's what you want. I'd love to be your mom."

"Yes!" Car shouted and pumped his little fist into the air. "Daddy Grey! She said we could!" Gabby's heart squeezed in her chest a little. The relationship between Car and Grey had improved over the last few weeks. She'd taken a chance and talked to them about the differences she'd noticed in the way they treated Con, and how it was affecting Car. They'd listened to her. Really listened.

The boys ran back to their dads and Con grabbed Trouble from Grey's arms. "I have to take him out for his treats now. Daddy Mason said it's important to give him his reward right after he did a good job." He ruffled Trouble's head. "And he done it just like we practiced didn't he, Daddy Mason?"

Gabby gasped. "So that explains where the dining room chairs disappeared to this week and why you and Grey kept sneaking off into the barn. And all the red ribbon I found in the bottom drawer when I went to grab a pair of your sweats the other day."

Mason flushed and pulled her into his arms. "Well, yes, but actually, the ribbons were for later," he smirked. She read the flash of lust in his blue eyes.

"Oh," she said, heat pooling in her belly and sinking all the way to her toes.

"And that's our cue," Jake laughed and turned toward the door. "Car, Con, come on boys. You're staying with us tonight."

Gabby blushed as the twins ran past her and followed Jake to the front door. "No, you don't have to do that. We're not..."

Hazel giggled and took her hand, patting it affectionately as she looked beyond her to her sons. "Believe me. You'll have your hands full tonight."

"But..." Gabby looked past her to see Joe and Nate waiting behind her, too embarrassed to look them in the eyes.

"Daniel, you're welcome to join us for a beer," Joe offered. "There's a good football game on tonight."

"Thanks," Daniel said, stopping to give Gabby a kiss on her cheek. "But I still have one more load of my things to move in to Cade's place tonight. Maybe next time."

"I'm glad you decided to stay," Gabby said, giving Daniel's arm a tender squeeze. "It was nice of Cade to offer you a room. You'll be so close."

"Me too," he said and gave her a quick hug. "Congratulations, by the way. Happy looks good on you."

"Thank you."

"Say hello to Cade for me when he gets back from Butte," Hazel told Daniel.

"I will. And we'll be over for Sunday dinner." Daniel gathered his jacket and followed Joe to the front door.

Hazel turned back to Gabby and her smile fell as she glanced over Gabby's shoulder. Her eyebrow arched as her gaze traveled back to Gabby. The seriousness in her expression had Gabby's immediate attention. "Darlin', you'd better run."

Gabriella looked over her shoulder to see her three men closing in on her, their primal lust evident in their expression. Excitement flashed like lightning through her veins and her head snapped back to Hazel. What was she supposed to do?

The corner of Hazel's mouth quirked up into a crooked grin and she nodded. "Run."

A cacophony of laughs and shuffling chairs followed Gabby as she fled down the long hall and bolted up the stairs, unsure of where she was going or why she was running. She wanted them to catch her.

She giggled as she ran through the open doorway of Grey's bedroom, now the bedroom they all shared. She darted toward the closet, but changed her mind at the last second opting for the far side of the bed instead. That last minute change cost her. She squealed as a pair of strong, tanned arms locked around her waist and dragged her back toward the foot of the king-sized bed.

"I've got you now, darlin'."

Matt. She loved his playfulness and the way he made everything he did mean more with his devious, playful smile. She squealed again as she bounced on the bed. Several pairs of hands descended on her, removing every stitch of her clothing within mere seconds.

Grey released a growl as he cupped the back of her knees, dragging her to the edge of the bed, his naked and stiff cock already probing her wet, throbbing entrance. The image of his ruggedly handsome face was replaced by the boyish grin on Mason's mouth as he bent over her and took her lips in a primal kiss that made every other thought fly right out of her head. She cried out into Mason's mouth as Grey's cock slipped inside her to the hilt, filling her to the brim with blinding desire.

Gabby gasped for breath when a sharp, white pain sliced through her nipple then warmed when Matt lapped at his bite with his tongue.

"Uhhh," Grey filled her over and over, nudging her womb with each thrust, and then he was gone. She moaned as her channel clenched at the emptiness.

"Don't you worry, sweetheart. I need these beautiful legs wrapped around me for a minute. Ahhh…" Mason sighed as he took Grey's place and filled her. "*Sweet Jesus*, forever wouldn't be long enough to get my fill of you." His hands clenched her thighs and traveled up to her hips. Grasping her bottom, he lifted her hips off the bed and pushed deeper inside.

A familiar current prickled at the base of his spine and knew he wouldn't last another two seconds. He closed his eyes and tried to think of mix ratios for bovine vaccinations. Anything that would stop his balls from drawing up any further, but it didn't help. He couldn't lose it this soon. They had other plans for their lover tonight.

Matt released her nipple and licked a salty path to her bellybutton. Mason pulled out and grabbed the base of his cock, holding himself back.

"Are you ready, darlin?" Matt peered up into her chocolate eyes and fell right off the cliff. He didn't think he could fall any further in love with this woman, but he'd just proven himself stupid. He had a feeling he would be in a freefall for the rest of his natural life and that was fine by him. "Are you ready to take us all?"

"She's ready," Grey answered for her. He crawled onto the opposite side of the bed and tossed a bottle of lube up toward the headboard.

"I don't know," Matt said as he inched lower, his tongue twirling a playful path down the crease in her thigh next to her pussy. "I better take a taste test to make sure. *Oh yeah…*" he breathed her in, his nostrils flaring wide. "Now *this* is heaven, darlin'."

She arched against the bed as Matt stroked her slit from end to end and then settled around her clit, his tongue twirling circle after circle with the right pressure. "Matt!" Her hands reached for something, anything. Her fingers threaded into his hair, pushing and pulling him, wanting more but not sure if she could handle more. She needed to come, but she wanted them inside her. All of them. Soon. *Now*. "Matt, please."

"Enough." Matt ignored Grey's husky command. His tongue slowed to a torturous crawl, lapping her with feather-light strokes and then blew a warm stream of air over her sensitive skin.

When Matt finally released her, Grey's solid arms lifted her from the side of the bed and slide her toward the headboard. "Careful, baby. I don't want you to hurt your shoulder."

She wasn't worried about her shoulder. If he hadn't mentioned it she wouldn't have given it a single thought. The pillows were soft behind her, but she wasn't allowed to lie there long enough to sink into them.

Matt moved to the head of the bed and propped against the headboard next to her. She reached for him as he helped her straddle his hips and settled her onto his lap, the ruddy head of his hardened cock touching his bellybutton in front of her.

"Ride me, darlin', while Grey gets you ready for him." Matt fisted his cock, drawing his palm up and over the head, the blue in his eyes deepening to midnight swirls. She lifted up onto her knees and watched as he guided himself to her opening.

The walls of her pussy clamped around his thick shaft, drawing out a long, deep groan from both of them. Her sensitive breasts ached for his touch. As if Matt had heard her wish, he covered them with his palms and teased her nipples with his thumbs.

He curled up to meet her, seizing her lips, pushing his cock even deeper before he dipped his head and wrapped his tongue around one stiff nipple. He grazed the tip with his teeth, sending a flood of warmth through her core, further easing his entry.

"That's it, baby. Let him love you." Grey pumped his own cock as he nuzzled her neck, licking and feeding from the creamy skin beneath her ear. "Lean forward so I can get you ready. Just like we did before."

With a hand on her shoulder, he gentled her back down onto Matt's chest, trailing his fingers down her spine to her luscious ass. Over the last few weeks, as they both healed from their wounds, they'd begun to play with different size plugs, gradually preparing her to take his cock. The time was finally here. He could almost feel her tight heat sucking him inside.

With a lubed finger, he swirled and probed her ass, the sound of the air hissing between her teeth sending him to the edge of his sanity. "I think Mason needs a little attention, baby," he said to distract himself as much as her.

Her fingers splayed on Matt's chest, a slick sheen of sweat erupting beneath her palms. She pushed up a little and turned into the palm Mason held to her cheek. "Mmm, I want to taste you."

She licked her lips as Mason guided his heavy cock to her mouth, a pearly drop leaking from the tip she couldn't wait to taste. "Oh," she said around the head of Mason's shaft as Matt's cock jerked inside her. She took Mason deeper into her mouth, sending a pulsing throb through her that made her clench around Grey's probing finger.

"That's it, darlin'. Suck him hard." Matt clenched his teeth against the pressure building in his balls. They were drawn up so tight it hurt, but he wasn't about to complain. Seeing her swollen lips wrapped around Mason made every nerve from his head to his toes reroute to his dick. "How we doin', Grey? She feels so goddamn good I don't think I'm gonna last much longer."

"Almost there, brother." Grey slowly slid his fingers from her ass and positioned the head of his cock to her well lubed and stretched star. "Relax, baby, and push back against me."

Gabby relaxed at first, but then drew in a sharp breath as Grey began to breach the tight ring of flesh. She flinched and tightened, making the slight sting turn into fire.

"Breathe, sweetheart." Mason withdrew from her mouth and held her face in his hands, peppering her with slow sensual kisses until she released a long, low groan. "That's it, honey. Relax and let him inside. The sting will disappear in a minute and you'll feel nothing but good." He rubbed small circles on her back and glanced up at Grey, worried that his brother was pushing her too fast.

A zing of pure electricity shot through Grey's spine when he pushed past her tight as hell ring and her body sucked his cock inside to the root. "Oh, *fuck* that feels incredible!" He stopped as soon as he was inside, both afraid to move for losing control and to give her time to adjust to his invasion. "Oh—fuck," he panted through the urge to slam into her. "Christ, baby. Are you okay?"

Gabby groaned against Matt's chest, her sweat-slickened hair sticking to her face. How could he expect her to talk? "Ahhh...." The flame of heat from the burning sting rolled into a raging inferno of molten lava that warmed every cell in her body, creating an immediate need to push back for more. "Move," she panted and dug her fingernails into Matt's chest. "Ohhh!" She cried out again as Grey gripped her hips and pulled her tighter against him, his hips slapping into hers. "Oh God!"

Matt bit his bottom lip and began to move with his brother, pulling out as he pushed in slowly; too slow. "So...tight...darlin'." When she pushed back again a white flash of light exploded behind his eyelids and her pussy clamped down on him like a vise.

"Mason?" She panted for him, one hand anchored next to Matt's chest, the other blindly searching. She was beyond thought, but she could feel his absence. She needed him with her.

"I'm right here, Sweetheart." He cupped his hand around the back of her head and guided his shaft back to her lips, gritting his teeth when her groan erupted around him.

"That's it baby. Feel us." Grey was buried so deep inside her ass he swore he felt the pull of her lips on his own cock. The hair on the back of his arms prickled against his skin and gooseflesh broke out under the sweat that coated his chest. He folded himself around their woman and sunk his teeth into her shoulder, drawing out a satisfying groan.

"Fuck, yeah. That's it darlin'. Squeeze me. Oh, Jesus." Matt pushed up into her, him and Grey now thrusting together. She was close and goddamn he needed to feel her come around him.

"Ahh! I'm coming, sweetheart," Mason groaned. "I'm...Oh, angel. That's it. Right there. So...ahh!" Mason pushed to the back of her throat as wave after wave of excruciating pleasure melted his bones. He watched as she swallowed every drop of his seed. "Beautiful," he whispered, cupping her jaw as he pulled out of her mouth.

The sheer ecstasy and love in Mason's expression made her chest ache with happiness and set off a series of explosions inside her. "I'm almost there. Don't...ah...stop!"

Beyond words, Grey closed his eyes, the grip on Gabby's hips tightening as his balls drew up into his body and the last thread of his control snapped. One hard thrust, then another and lightning struck his spine as hot seed flowed through his cock and filled her in wave after wave of pure, fucking heaven.

Matt cried out at the same time Grey pulsed next to him inside her tight channel, Gabby's mewling cries sending him into an orbit he wasn't sure he'd ever want to leave. His dick throbbed, his seed shooting so deep inside her he thought for sure he'd taste it on her tongue if he had the strength to lean up and kiss her. He didn't, so he pulled her down to him and took her lips like the starving animal he was. He would never get enough of this woman.

Unable to move a single muscle in her entire body, Gabby moaned when she felt Grey slip from inside her. The warmth of Matt's arms felt better than any blanket as he wrapped himself around her and rolled to his side, laying her on the cool sheet beside him. After he slipped from her wet channel, she felt a cool cloth between her legs.

More than a little embarrassed, she groaned in protest, but Grey ignored her. "Let me take care of you." She gave up her half-hearted protest and relaxed against Matt, feeling Mason slide into the empty space behind her. Slowly falling back to earth, she looked over her shoulder at Mason. "I love you," she breathed and nuzzled her nose against his, tracing her tongue along the edge of his bottom lip.

Mason grinned and slid his tongue out to meet hers, tangling them together in a slow, lazy kiss. "Mmm, you keep that up and I promise you won't sleep for a week."

Gabby closed her eyes. Her fingers trailed down Matt's arm as he sat up and threw his legs over the side of the bed. He leaned back and placed a kiss on the tip of her nose. "I'll be right back, darlin."

Grey slipped into his vacated spot and pulled the sheet up over the three of them, wrapping her into his safe embrace, a satisfying rumble echoing deep in his chest. His hand cupped her cheek and tilted her head back to look at him. "I love you so completely I can't imagine any future that didn't have you in it, baby bird."

"Mmmm, me too," she sighed. "I love you so, so much." Her hand traveled down to his naked hip, then skimmed her own thigh as she reached back and grabbed Mason's, pulling him against her. "All of you. I can't believe you're all mine."

"Oh, believe it, darlin'," Matt chuckled as he walked back into the room. Okay, he more or less strutted, his still half-hard cock swaying with every step toward the bed, three bottles of water in his hands.

Gabby giggled and reached for the bottle in Matt's outstretched hand. He could be cocky all he wanted if he kept looking at her with that mischievous smirk of his.

Grey and Mason took several long swigs from their bottles and handed them back to Matt. After making sure she'd sipped enough from hers, Matt took it and set it next to the others on the night stand next to the bed. He slipped into the bed next to Grey, pulling the covers up to his hips.

Propped on his elbow, he reached over and skimmed his knuckles against her cheek and then carded his fingers through her sweat dampened curls. "I'm so glad we found you, Gabriella. I can't believe you're going to be our wife."

Mason's arm tightened around her waist as he snuggled his chin into the crook of her neck. "Mmm, I can't wait."

Alarm skittered through him as Grey noticed her gaze drop to the sheet in her hand. He brought his thumb to her chin, tipping her head back to look at him again. "What's that look for, baby bird?"

Gabby shrugged and a small, sad smile tugged at the corner of her mouth. "I know how this works. I'm only going to be able to legally marry one of you." She tugged at her bottom lip with her teeth, and damn if Grey didn't want to do that for her. "How am I supposed to choose?"

Mason sat up beside her. His hands found one of hers, his fingers playing over the shiny band that now bound them together. "We don't want you to have to choose, sweetheart."

Grey pushed up onto his elbows, taking her other hand in his. Matt scooted closer, his fingers drawing comforting circles on her thigh. "We talked about it." Grey swallowed and glanced at Matt before he continued. "No matter whose name goes on that piece of paper, you'll be a McLendon. We'll all be there standing next to you at the official ceremony. Afterward, we'll have a private commitment ceremony where we'll all be able to make our promise to you. But, after talking about how we met you, after everything we've been through, we thought it was only fair that Matt be the one to marry you, officially."

Gabby's eyes lifted to Matt. Her heart swelled with so many emotions she could scarcely breathe.

Mason kissed her fingers, his other hand caressing her bare back. "Not that he needs to hear it, but he was right."

"Damn straight I was." Matt scoffed, and winked at her.

Grey shook his head, an incredulous smile on his lips. "When he met you he knew. Although we knew it, too, the moment we met you, he still had to push us. He fought for you, for us." Grey cupped his hand to her cheek and studied her for a quiet moment before he leaned in and pressed his lips to hers. "He fought for this." Grey grinned against her lips as he looked into her eyes. "He never doubted for one moment that we belonged to you, and he was right."

A lone tear ran down her cheek and Gabby hurriedly wiped it away. She folded her feet beneath her, sat up on her knees, reaching for Matt. She pulled him into her arms and kissed his lips, then his nose. She pressed her forehead to his, his body trembling beneath her hands.

"I'm so glad you did." She kissed him again and then reached down behind her, pulling his brothers up to join them. "So eternally, forever, completely—in—love—with—all—of—you glad that you never gave up and gave me the chance to belong to you."

241

A True Love Story Never Ends

Now Available

A McLendon Christmas

Join Gabby and her three favorite cowboys at Falcon Ridge for a special Christmas holiday. Meet the newest tiny members of the McLendon family, catch up with all your favorite characters from DL's *'McLendon Family Saga'* and get a sneak peek at all the fun and excitement in store for their future.

HEAT WARNING: Contains three sexy cowboys who are still very much in love with their wife, love making love with her—together—and spare no details when doing so...every chance they get. Grey still has a dirty mouth, but thanks to Gabby's efforts, tries to keep it clean in front of the children. It doesn't always happen. Recommended for adult readers only.

Don't miss Connor and Carson's story in:
Rock Star Cowboys

The McLendon Family Saga Reading Order
The Heart of Falcon Ridge
A McLendon Christmas
Rock Star Cowboys
Rock Star Honeymoon

Never miss a new release!

Direct from my insider's Writer's Cave Club, read exclusive excerpts, exciting character updates, behind the scenes editorials and more when you sign-up for my no-spam newsletter at www.dlroan.com.

Also Available

Grant Kendal's heart-stopping Romantic Thriller,

Surviving Redemption
(Survivors' Justice Book 1)

The only mission Grant Kendal has ever blown was the one that mattered most. Haunted by his violent past, his bloodlust for justice cost his mentor and friend their only chance to find his abducted daughter. When Thalia Brezlin washes ashore his island of self-imposed exile, beaten, broken and hell-bent on revenge, Grant is tempted back into the world he left behind by more than her sharp tongue and long, sexy legs.

The men she's running from could bring him one step closer to righting his wrongs. Plunged once again into the underworld of human trafficking, a place where evil thrives on stolen innocence and nothing escapes alive, he sees one final chance at redemption. When Thalia's secrets are revealed, he'll do anything to protect her…including letting go of the past once and for all.

Enjoy this exclusive excerpt from Surviving Redemption

"Son of a dickless monkey!" Grant Kendal shook out his throbbing hand. He was going to hunt down the bastard who'd sold him these cheap as shit nails and take his money back in slow, even installments of pain; one rusty nail at a time.

"Don't get your tail in a wad, Winston. I wasn't talking about you." Winston lowered his hand from his face and turned his back to Grant, arms folded over his knobby knees. Crouched on his hands and knees on top of the thatched roof, Grant hung his head and let out a frustrated growl. He knew better than to feed the damn thing. "One piece of sugar cane and I'm married to a goddamn monkey!" He pounded his fist on the bare rafter he was trying desperately to cover before the afternoon storms blew in.

He'd managed to live thirty-four years—no small feat considering his chosen profession—without falling prey to a single woman's charms. He'd never considered himself much of a ladies man. Spending most of his adult life in the shadows, hunting down the cockroaches of the human species, he hadn't had much use for the social niceties women usually expected from a relationship. Procuring a warm, willing body for a night to fulfill his baser needs didn't require a lifetime commitment of manipulation and crazy mood swings. Apparently befriending a Macaque monkey did. *Retired less than a year and I'm attached at the hip to an emotionally challenged primate with a penis!*

Twisting and shuffling his way across each beam, Grant made it to the western edge of the roof. Wiping the sweat from his eyes, he stepped down onto the top rung of the ladder. "Come down, you moody bastard. I'll fix us a drink."

Winston looked over his furry shoulder, displaying his pouty bottom lip before turning away again. "Goddamn it! I'm not apologizing! I wasn't even talking to you!" Grant moved down the ladder, but stopped only a few steps down, shaking his head. When had he become such a pussy? Solitude meant being alone, right? Not having to listen to meaningless chatter or put up with a society that had disintegrated into chaos. Or having to placate the *feelings* of a damn monkey. He would have been better off if he'd painted a face on a hand grenade and called it a day.

Nearly a year ago he'd taken a job as a favor to his mentor and friend, Daniel Gregory. For some reason it had left him feeling dead inside. Daniel's daughter Natalie had been taken and sold into the sex slave industry, and Daniel had spent the last twelve years searching for her. The cockroach who ran the U.S. side of the human trafficking ring, Hector Morganti, was now behind bars thanks to Daniel's relentless pursuit and to the testimony of Hector's daughter, Gabby. Daniel, however, never found Hector's diary of transactions he hoped would lead him to the monsters that bought his daughter. When Hector was put away, his second in command, Lucien Moretti, took over the business without a hitch, apparently using the ledger of sales as blackmail and to continue the steady supply of child slaves.

Grant and Daniel had used Lucien's obsession with Gabby to lure him into a trap, hoping to find the ledger and put him away with Hector. Their plan had had failed when Lucien slipped through his fingers and he was forced to kill him before he'd killed Gabby. Putting a bullet between Lucien's eyes had felt good, even if he'd deserved a far more painful death. However much he deserved it, killing Lucien had destroyed Daniel's chances of finding his daughter. They never found the ledger. The sophisticated slave ring fell apart after Lucien's demise. It may have bought some time before some other piece of shit stepped in to fill the supply gap, but thanks to Grant, his friend may never find his daughter.

Living with that shouldn't have been a problem for Grant. Bad people did bad things to good people all the time. He was called to take out the trash and move on to the next job. No questions. No regrets. He didn't regret a single kill he'd made, but seeing the hopelessness in Daniels eyes and sweet Gabby's reaction to the monster inside him had left him feeling cold. That's when he knew he was done. For the first time in his life he hadn't liked the emotionless tool he'd become.

Setting himself up on a deserted scrub island in the middle of the Indian Ocean was supposed to give him some clarity; time to cleanse himself of the beast within and consider his next step. Ten months later, and the only thing he was sure of was that he wasn't built to mingle with the human race.

Grant banged his head against the ladder rung in front of him a few times before cursing his way back to the top. Apparently he wasn't fit to cohabitate with monkeys either. "Fine. I'm sorry. Better?" he said through his clenched teeth.

Before he could see if his half-assed attempt at placating the bratty imp had worked, the singing sound of fishing line being ripped from his reel caught his attention. Grant turned just in time to see his fishing pole fly out of the holder onto the sand and inch its way toward the water. "*Son* of a...." Winston's scolding screech had him choking back the curse as he slid down the ladder, skipping the last four rungs, and sprinting past his fire pit toward the surf. "Fish on, Winston! Fish on!"

Two days earlier he'd seen a nice sized sailfish stalking his bait from the deep channel that ran west of the island. Deciding to take up the challenge, he'd changed out his gear and reset his bait. Two whole days and not so much as a nibble. He'd obviously lost his touch if a fish could wait him out. Thanks to his newfound complacency, he was about to lose a thousand bucks worth of tackle *and* the damn fish!

Waves splashed at his feet as he made one final push off the sand before diving into the surf. His palm wrapped around the familiar corked end of his pole before another wave washed over his face, the cold salty spray stinging his eyes. Fuck all if he was going to lose this fish. Pulling the pole into his chest, his knees dug into the sand as the drag of the fish pulled him towards the deep. Digging in his heels, he set the hook, shaking the salty foam from his hair.

Snap! "Fuck!" Grant fell back into the surf, what was left of the line flapping in the wind at the tip of his pole. "Fuck, fucking godda—" The rest of his rant was cut off at the sight of the sailfish as it flew through the air with his float hanging from its bill, landing with a splash Grant could only see as a taunt. His fist pounded through the surf as he glared out at the deep, green waters. *Fucking war is what this is.*

Cold water sluiced down his face as he threaded a wet hand through his hair then pushed to his feet. He stomped through the surf toward the sandy beach, ignoring Winston's screeching cackles echoing from further down the shoreline. The damn monkey was crazy if he thought he was going to sleep inside the cabin tonight. It was supposed to rain a foot before morning. *We'll see whose laughing later, you imprudent ape!*

Grant bent and scooped up the rod holder, determined to re-rig his pole and get it back into the water. Winston's incessant screeching moved closer, and Grant looked over his shoulder to see the monkey loping towards him. When Winston saw that he'd gotten Grant's attention, he immediately switched directions, hurrying back down the beach, calling for Grant to follow him.

Waving him off, he shook his head and headed toward the pole-barn styled cabin he'd built just outside the tree line. It was only one room, but it had four walls, a roof, and a covered porch. With an added outdoor shower he'd rigged to the back, which was fed fresh, cold water by an old artesian well, it was all he needed.

Ignoring Winston's incessant protests, he leaned his pole against one of the front porch support beams and reached for his tackle box. He didn't have time for monkey business if he was going to get his bait rigged and get his roof shored up before nightfall.

A fresh spool of fishing line in hand, he turned back toward his pole and caught a glimpse of Winston from the corner of his eye. Grant paused as he watched his reluctant pet, jumping up and down and slapping at the surf as it rolled gently onshore. Shielding his eyes against the glare of the sun, he squinted toward the far end of the beach to see what had captured Winston's attention. His tackle forgotten, his feet moved with increasing speed as the object came into focus and took on an ominous form.

Grant's pulse picked up as he sprinted closer. *What the hell?* A familiar, cold calm rushed over his skin as he pushed Winston back from the pale, limp body lying face down, still half in the water. A thick curtain of black hair covered the woman's face, shielding all but a swatch of pale dead skin from his view.

It wasn't the first time he'd seen a dead body. It surely wouldn't be his last, but damn if he'd ever expected to see one here. Swiftly, Grant mentally inventoried his surroundings. He'd seen no boats milling around the island or the nearby cove lately. No one was on the island but he and Winston and a few stray vermin. Of that he was certain. Without his binoculars, he couldn't see the other nearby scrub islands well enough to scout anything out. By the waterlogged skin, he judged the body must have washed up sometime overnight. Any threat would be long gone by now. *If they had half a brain.* Of course, there could have been some sort of boating accident.

Gently he gathered the long strands of ebony hair, revealing the feminine outline of the woman's face. Preparing himself for the stench that usually came from rotting flesh, and the gore he might see from the meal the ocean's parasites had probably made of her slender form, he gingerly rolled the woman over in the sand. Letting out a sigh when the body appeared to be intact, Grant took in a cautious breath. He was relieved again to only smell the earthy scents of sea water and sand. Knowing it was futile, he placed his finger over the vein in her neck. *D.O.A. and definitely not a boating accident.*

Crouched on one knee, Grant rested his forearm across his other knee as he ran through his options. He could dig a grave and call it a day. He studied the lifeless woman before him. *Mid to late twenties.* It was difficult to tell with the swollen skin around her injuries. Her tattered shirt did nothing to hide the one inch stab wound below her left breast, or the modeled black and blue skin across her firm torso. He also recognized the bloodstains on her cargo pants as they clung to her thighs like a second skin. Someone had done a real number on her.

She had strong bone lines and manicured nails at the tips of her long, slender fingers. He gently maneuvered her arms from her sides and inspected the thin, pale skin. *No track marks.* She wore no rings or other notable jewelry. He fingered the single shock of neon blue that ran through her otherwise jet black hair as he studied her complexion. Other than the bruising and the stab wounds, she seemed too well cared for to be a homeless junkie. *Fuck!*

He'd have to call it in. Surely someone was looking for her. He had a satellite phone, but he sure as hell didn't want his tiny island crawling with local law enforcement idiots. He'd have to load her up in his boat and take her to the mainland. Tell them he fished her out of the water twenty miles or so east of his island. But not today. There was no time to secure his place and make the trip before the storms rolled in.

Resigned, Grant stood to his feet. Focused on his next task, he reached for the woman's wrist, ready to haul her over his shoulder, when he found himself staring into the ice-blue eyes of a ghost.

29935572R00158

Made in the USA
San Bernardino, CA
02 February 2016